I0548386

THE HUNG JURY

TOM BREWSTER

World Castle Publishing, LLC
Pensacola, Florida
Copyright © Tom Brewster 2016
Paperback ISBN: 9781629895291
eBook ISBN: 9781629895307
First Edition World Castle Publishing, LLC, September 12, 2016
http://www.worldcastlepublishing.com

Licensing Notes

Cover: Karen Fuller
Editor: Lisa Petrocelli

CHAPTER ONE

Sunshine illuminated the living room and swept across the TV, glaring over the image of Jennifer Lopez who was making a special performance on *Dancing with the Stars*. It was the beginning of the final four selection process. Morgan Cooper watched, not caring that the picture was distorted by the light. He wasn't a fan, not even a casual watcher. He hated TV. It was only seven p.m., but he had already stripped down to his boxers and a T-shirt. A glass of pinot noir teetered on the leather ottoman where he placed it off balance as if to test the forces of gravity, knowing that it would eventually fall if not attended to. He watched and waited, hoping he would be able to intercede once it headed for the floor.

Special Forces sent Osama Bin Laden's soul tumbling into the hereafter on Sunday night. Morgan was glad he was dead, but the news coverage was becoming annoying. Talking heads rambled on endlessly putting their own spin on it, heaping praise upon President Obama without revealing that it was the very policies he objected to in his campaign that had brought Bin Laden to justice.

Either way, Bin Laden was dead, and it was a triumph for the country. Morgan didn't believe in the afterlife, so eternal peace didn't seem at all appropriate for a man who had killed several

3

thousand innocent people and sent the world into an extended state of anxiety. For Bin Laden's sake, Morgan was willing to believe for a moment in divine castigation, if only hypothetically, in order to pour a hefty portion of hellfire and brimstone onto his head. To see him as an earthworm squirming around in a bed of embers in everlasting torment seemed a more suitable finale.

Morgan was bored. Molly was in Wisconsin with their son, Ryan, where she had been staying for the past two weeks. When she was home they were both bored, but somehow monotony was more tolerable when she was there. Molly was filling in for Ryan's babysitter who had quit, leaving him scrambling for a new one. Molly went to the rescue, subbing until a replacement could be found. Molly's purpose in life was family, so the detail was a blessing.

Everybody has a purpose in life. Morgan couldn't believe it was his purpose to sit on the couch and sigh in exasperation for lack of anything better to do. At sixty-three, he had been a police officer for the greater part of his life in Willoughby Hills, Illinois, a small town in the middle of the state. He had retired when he was eligible at fifty-five, and then worked for two years as an investigator for the state's attorney's office. When that job turned into a paper-pushing nightmare, he took the Illinois Private Detective test. He acquired a license, established a clientele, and worked until his mustache and hair turned gray. The greater part of his business was mostly contractual work for the two larger cities that bordered Willoughby Hills. He and his three employees were responsible for serving process for municipal code violations and other insignificant details. Occasionally they were directed to help the uniformed officers serve search warrants and stand by while arrestees were "perp-walked" to the hoosegow, which was as eventful as watching grass grow.

Morgan had written and published two novels. Neither of them had garnered fame and fortune, but he had acquired local notoriety and padded his savings account a little. Now as he sat on the couch contemplating death and the afterlife, the notion of writing another novel was creeping into his head. He might write it if for nothing more than to occupy his time.

There was a story that had bounced around in his mind for over thirty years. It was suitable for a novel, but there were so many unsolved details that he wouldn't dare write it for fear that he would have to write "The End" in the middle of the book without ever having tied up all the loose ends. It was a tale about treachery and murder at a time when murder and treachery were less common than in 2011. It would be based on a true story — an event that Morgan experienced firsthand, a tale of suspense and danger.

At the time Morgan was twenty-six years old and had been at the Willoughby Hills Police Department for five years. A local college student by the name of Roderick Constance was convicted of killing a young grocery clerk, his wife, and their unborn child in a shoplifting case. Morgan was the arresting officer. The victim had the misfortune of seeing the theft and took the appropriate action of chasing Constance down. He and his wife were ambushed in their home late at night when they returned home. So, in essence, his wages for being a good citizen was death. His pretty young pregnant wife was collateral damage. A shotgun blast sent them both forever into the abyss.

Morgan was young and "cocky", and never imagined himself as a sixty-three year old man sitting on his living room couch in his boxer shorts and a T-shirt, bored into apathetic blankness. Now as Jennifer Lopez twisted herself into an unnatural yet appealing position, purple and gold stage light glistened in her hair like a psychedelic lioness poised to pounce. Morgan's eyes were fixed on her, but his mind had retreated in time a span of thirty-six years, back to 1975.

In addition to the grocery clerk and his wife, Constance

was suspected of killing a second witness in the case. The lead investigator believed he also killed his college roommate in a separate incident. The cases were intricately interwoven with the shoplifting case but the evidence was insufficient to prove the connection. Constance was found guilty of murdering the grocery clerk, his wife, and also their unborn child, but he wasn't charged with the other two murders. He was aggressively interrogated but denied any knowledge of their deaths or whereabouts. Morgan didn't know there were two other victims who had died at Constance's hands, and those stories would never be told.

****

At the time of Constance's trial, the death penalty in Illinois had been suspended, but the legislature was trying to reinstate it. Constance was given a 600-year sentence, but he surely would have fried if the chair had been an option. Soon thereafter capital punishment was resumed but Constance had escaped being put to death. Although capital punishment had been resumed in Illinois, it was constantly under fire from death penalty opponents. Periodically, investigators questioned Constance in prison about the missing persons, but he continued to deny any knowledge of them. In all probability, Constance suspected if he confessed to the two additional murders and revealed where the bodies had been deposited, he would have been tried for those murders. He would be in jeopardy of being sent to death row, so he steadfastly refused to cooperate. The chief detective who investigated the murders worked for years trying to give the families closure, but he retired without ever knowing where the two bodies were buried. In 2011, the Illinois legislature rescinded the death penalty. Three Illinois governors were involved as it traveled through the repeal process. It had been put on a moratorium under Governor George Ryan, and it was a front and center issue with his administration, but he was distracted by corruption charges and eventually went to jail for extorting money and illegally selling license plates to unauthorized trucking companies. It was still under moratorium when Rod Blagojevich took the governorship, but he was distracted by corruption charges, and eventually he was impeached, convicted of lying to the FBI, and was tried for a multitude of other violations. Beyond the time frame of this writing, he, too, was convicted and sent to prison. Under Governor Quinn the death penalty was finally abolished. Quinn's most egregious crime was to display a picture of himself in all governmental offices where he was at least forty pounds shy of his actual weight. Vanity not being an impeachable offense, Quinn survived the process, and the death penalty became a thing of the past.

To Morgan, the question begged, would Constance talk about the missing bodies now that the threat of being executed had been taken away? Maybe he could interview Constance and get him to confess to the other two murders? It was about as likely as jumping a six foot fence with your pants wrapped around your ankles, but the notion had been hatched and weighed on his mind. If he tried and failed, he would at least have a conclusion to his story.

CHAPTER TWO

After Constance was convicted, thirty-six years passed under the bridge while his life dwindled away in prison. Morgan moved on, married Molly, and had two children—a boy, Ryan, and a girl, Alison. He went to college and graduated while working at the police department. The kids grew up and then onto lives of their own. Now the house was empty. Molly was in Milwaukee, and he was there alone reflecting on those ancient memories as though they were only yesterday.

In the beginning there must have been a reason for the madness. Perhaps it was just a wicked thought or a fantasy conjured up and not intended for the real world. It might have been no more than a whim, but it grew into a plan and finally into a twisted reality. It was something only Constance understood. Morgan knew now that Roderick Constance created a deadly and wicked world, and found a way to reside in it without guilt or remorse. He could waste someone's life with less concern than swatting a fly. Those are the kind of thoughts that haunt a policeman's soul long after he has tucked his children in and kissed his wife good night. It stays with you even after hanging up your badge.

Morgan met Constance when he was a Willoughby Hills College student. He was dispatched to take a burglary report at one of the dormitory rooms on the main campus. His memory reverberated through time and his senses were assaulted by the stench of old pizzas and stale marijuana odors. He remembered how several doors crept open as he passed by, with students poking their heads out to make provoking remarks. Morgan was accustomed to the insults and occasional "oinks" and walked on unconcerned, or at least he concealed his irritation. Most of his fellow officers resented calls to the college and avoided them whenever they could. Memories of the Viet Nam War lingered there as fetid as a wet mangy dog. There was anger behind the student's eyes, and they wore it on their faces like a badge of honor. Many officers were war veterans, and the students were the benefactors of anti-war sentiments promoted by previous classes who were active in protests and unrest. Although the war was over and President Nixon had resigned in disgrace, the students were still openly antagonistic toward anyone wearing a uniform.

The veterans were offended by such twisted naivety and ignorance. They had been drafted into the military and sent to a country they knew nothing about, with patriotism in their hearts and love of country as their guiding principal. They endured in a steaming jungle where they fought for their lives and the dignity of their fellow citizens. Ten thousand of their ranks were shepherded into the hereafter, and thousands more were crippled and maimed. When they returned home they were greeted with invectives like, "war monger" and "baby killer." It had been a painful experience for soldier and student alike, but the veterans knew who got the dirty end of the stick.

Morgan would have gotten in on the war under normal circumstances, but for reasons unknown to him he wasn't sent "in country." He stayed stateside, working in the induction station in St. Louis. When he came home he started classes at Willoughby Hills College under the G.I. Bill. He was accepted in the police department and finished school by attending night classes. He was only slightly older than the average student, so he understood their ideals and subsequently he was less annoyed than most of his coworkers.

As he approached the room where he was sent to take the report on that fateful day, he saw a crowd had gathered and were blocking the doorway. The boys parted slowly but not before breaking his stride and delaying his entrance. They wanted to show him and prove to each other that they weren't intimidated by authority. Morgan recognized their sluggish movements just as they were intended. He smiled at each boy as they stepped aside. Morgan had learned early in his career not to take anything personal. It was just part of the job.

Inside the room several boys were milling about. The apparent victim was standing near a window glaring at a broken lock. His hair was wet with sweat and a towel was draped around his neck. He had been to the gymnasium playing basketball and when he returned he found the broken lock and his room a shambles. He was a rich kid, they all were, but that didn't mean they were smart. Getting into Willoughby Hills College was about as hard as getting into a PG-rated movie.

The youthful and somewhat arrogant victim pulled the towel from around his neck and threw it across the room in disgust. "Are you the one who called?" Morgan asked. The boy glared at Morgan with raised eyebrows as if to say "who else?" Morgan didn't wait for an answer. He opened his folder and took out a theft report form.

"When did the theft take place?" he asked. A voice whispered from the crowd, "Hide the dope in there, Kyle." The room filled with laughter, some of it nervous, and some of it just to be annoying. Morgan smiled, knowing pot-smoking was commonplace in the dorms, but he also knew they would have scoured the place before they called for a police officer. There were no Einsteins there, but they weren't stupid. Still they giggled like fifth graders who had just said a dirty word to the teacher in pig Latin. Marijuana in those days was taken a lot more seriously. In 2011, less than thirty grams was a Class A misdemeanor, and anything above thirty was a felony. Being caught with it was no joke. "Knock it off!" the victim shouted. "My stereo's been ripped off. It's not funny!" More snickers.

Morgan realized he should have isolated the victim from the others, but it was only a preliminary report and he would be finished in a few minutes. *Just scribble down the details and get back on patrol*, he thought. The laughter continued as other curiosity-seekers pushed their way into the room. A muscled, shaggy blonde-haired kid pushed past Morgan, giving him a slight nudge without excusing himself. "Man, would I like to pitch to a pair of these," he said, pointing to a Playboy centerfold taped to the wall, simultaneously plopping onto the unmade bed. He was athletic and strong, his declaration predictable. A kid like that had to announce he was important. He was a "jock," a pitcher, a big man on campus.

"Your name, please," Morgan asked politely, directing the question to the victim.

"Kyle Brasky," he spouted angrily. The snickering and ridicule was getting to him. Although he probably hadn't spent a dime of his own money for anything in the room, like anyone in that situation, he felt violated. Someone had broken into the room and rummaged through his stuff.

Morgan had decided in that moment to clear the room. He didn't believe things would get violent, but he remembered that Ed Woodson had responded to a similar call and let things get out of hand. Before it was over it flared into a mini-riot, and it took the entire night shift squad to get things under control. Suddenly it became quiet, and the only sound was the rhythmic smacking of a fist into a baseball glove by the jock while Morgan logged the information into his report. The lull in the bantering was distracting. He glanced up to see a lone figure standing in the doorway, a boy Morgan would come to know as Roderick Constance. The other boys were quietly filing out of the room. He was leaning against the doorframe staring at Morgan with washed-out blue eyes. He was rail thin, clad in an unwashed baggy flannel shirt and jeans with long black hair that clumped in strings held together by weeks of accumulated scalp grease. The knees in his jeans were worn through, his pallid white skin visible through the holes. It was a throwback look popular during the Viet Nam war, but styles were beginning to normalize by the mid-seventies. He looked out of place, on more than one level.

"What's going on," he stated, more as a demand than a question. His piercing stare was focused on Morgan. His cheeks were sunken, and his face gaunt and sallow. He had no reason to be there other than insolence.

"Has anyone shown an unusual interest in your stereo?" Morgan asked, ignoring the boy's question.

"I don't know. Everybody on this floor hangs out in here."

Morgan glanced back to the doorway. The boy's eyes were still fixed on his face, a stare that could only be regarded as a challenge. Morgan's neck was getting a little warm, his brow furrowed, lips tightened as he returned a glare of his own. The boy's lips curled up slightly, turned away from the door, and started off down the hallway.

The fist pounding the leather glove stopped. "Real asshole, huh?"

"He sure is," Morgan agreed.

"He's not real popular around here. You probably noticed how everybody cleared out when he showed up."

"Yea, but he did me a favor, getting those clowns out of my hair," Morgan said. "He's my roommate. His name is Roderick Constance."

12

"I feel sorry for you," Morgan said.

"Hey, how about my stuff? Is it coming back by itself?" Kyle Brasky interrupted.

Morgan ripped off his copy of the crime report, handed it to the contemptuous lad, and headed for the door. "What am I s'posed to do with this?" he asked. Morgan hesitated, wanting to state the obvious but answered politely that CID would be contacting him later in the week for more details. In just a few moments he was in his squad car and back on patrol.

CHAPTER THREE

The November wind whipped through the streets and debris swirled against the red brick building, mounting skyward. When Morgan swung the door open into City Hall, the wind followed him in, scattering parking tickets into the foyer and down the hallway. The matronly woman sitting inside a booth marked *Parking Meter Department* shouted, "All right, now!" and smiled over the narrow ledge that separated them.

"Sorry, Gladdy," Morgan said as he hurried to retrieve the stream of yellow tickets fluttering down the hallway. The tiny room she occupied was no larger than a coatroom. It had been attached to the outer wall of the city clerk's office eight years ago as a temporary parking meter department. Because it also blocked the hallway to the city clerk's office, it was reasonable to expect better accommodations somewhere down the road. But in reality, its permanency was undeniable. Despite her organizational skills and careful planning, the multitude of paper overflowed into the lobby just inside the main entrance to the building. The main door's opening and closing caused the inevitable vacuum and result.

"Burr, its cold out there. It's gonna be another bad winter, Gladdy. It already feels like January," he said as he stacked the loose papers back onto the pile.

"Don't talk like that, kid. I don't think these old bones can take another year like last year," she said. Scientists were talking about a new ice age advancing on the horizon. The seventies had been unusually cold, and each year it seemed to be getting worse. There was even talk about placing a giant mirror in outer space to deflect light onto the earth to warm it up if worse came to worst. Gladys's little office might as well have been right in the middle of the jet stream by the way the cold gusts streamed past her window. For her the ice age was already upon us.

Morgan approached the police department entrance and pushed his foot against the doorplate, but the door was locked. It was designed to open automatically when the doorplate was depressed, but it seldom worked as designed. Willoughby Hills City Hall was built in the 1800's, and although it had served its citizens well, the place was falling into disrepair. The city clerk's office and the police department occupied the lower level while the fire department personnel were housed on the second story. There was a third level, but it had been abandoned years ago and now collected artifacts and one lone enclosure designed as an evidence locker.

Collectively the three departments created a circus-like environment for locals who had to do business there. Enraged sewerage customers arguing discrepancies in their bills, belligerent motorists with parking tickets, and complaints about garbage pickups kept the hallways ringing. There was always a chance of being run over by firemen who were hurrying through the building responding to an alarm, but the police department was the topping on the cake. At least once a week some unruly arrestee had to be wrestled down the hallway from the booking room to the holding cell. Privacy was nonexistent in Willoughby Hills City Hall. It was hard for the average Willoughby Hills citizen to believe that conduct expected on a TV episode of *Bad Boys* could actually occur in their little town.

Morgan continued to stand at the entrance into the police department's squad room. Theoretically, the malfunctioning lock was to release once the doorplate was depressed but as usual it was stuck. A buzzer had been installed to alert the communications officer when it failed. The com officer needed only to hit the remote switch to allow entrance. The system was to be known only to police personnel, but anyone in the lobby would figure it out the first time they saw it in operation. Ironically, the communications officer's desk was situated in a location where all traffic into and out of the squad rooms could be monitored. Roy Helman was the communications sergeant on duty. He had been there since Abraham Lincoln was President, and was quite set in his ways.

Morgan had touched the doorplate with his foot and simultaneously lunged into the door trying to catch it just right, but each time he was denied. Roy avoided eye contact with Morgan for no other reason than stubbornness. Morgan threw up his hands and gaped at Roy who pretended not to see him. "How am I s'posed to get in, osmosis?" he said in exasperation.

Smiling, Gladys got up from her chair, sauntered around her ledge, and pointed a stubby toe toward the steel plate. She touched it lightly, the buzzer sounded, and the lock clicked open. Gladys turned her palms out as if to say, "Nothing to it."

Morgan stomped into the squad room and shouted to no one in particular, "I'll be glad to get back on the night shift where there's not so much bullshit!"

The duty sergeant turned in his chair and looked at Morgan blankly, then said to another officer who was pecking out an accident report, "I guess he hasn't had his ear twisted yet today, Bob." Bob nodded.

Sergeant Wilmert was Morgan's shift supervisor. There were eight sergeants in the department, but everybody called him "Sarge," as though he were the only man with stripes. Even the other sergeants referred to him as the "The Sarge." He was the most respected man in the department and a good leader. He kidded and joked with his men and was known to be a soft touch. He thought people under him deserved the opportunity to develop into individuals who were independent of supervision. Still he could be tough when circumstances called for it.

Sarge was a twenty-five year veteran of the department and had trained some highly successful law enforcement officers. The state police commander had started his career under Sarge as well as the current chief of police. Those were pretty good credentials, but some people thought Sarge was a little lackadaisical. Even though Morgan admired and respected him, he had little fear of him.

Morgan threw his clipboard onto a typewriter and shouted, "Watch out, you old pervert!"

Sarge pretended to be insulted. He would tolerate being called a pervert, but he took offense at the reference to his age. "What do ya mean, old!" he growled. Morgan smiled.

"You kids think you've got a monopoly on youth, but let me tell you something, son, it's only temporary."

Roy had been listening from the radio room. "Youth is a wonderful thing to be wasted on kids," he chimed.

"Sorry, I didn't want to bring AARP down on me," Morgan said and laughed.

Sarge took off his hat and slapped Morgan across the back of his neck. Morgan knew he was outnumbered, so he picked up his clipboard and started looking at his field reports. Sarge, still in a frisky mood, took the clipboard out of Morgan's hand, extended his arm, squinted, and drew the clipboard closer. "Yep, I've still got a few years before I need glasses," he said.

Big Bob, who had been quiet until now said, "You need glasses now." Sarge pretended not to hear him as he inspected Morgan's field reports. He noticed the name *Roderick Constance* written at the bottom of the theft report. "What's this name, this Roderick Constance doing here?" he asked.

"Just some weird kid at the college. He gave me the creeps," Morgan said, his voice trailing off as he returned to the typewriter.

"I know him," Sarge said. "He used to come in here and hang around at the complaints window, bugging the radio operator. He was always asking for police literature." Sarge rubbed his chin and sucked on his pipe. "Remember him, Roy?" A thoughtful expression crossed his face. Roy had wandered back into the communications room. "I caught him stealing a ticket book out of the unmarked squad car right out here in front of the police station. He hasn't been back in here since then. Hell, that was ten years ago. He was just a kid." Roy had stopped listening by then, and Morgan was typing his field reports. Bob had finished his work and had left the building. Sarge cleared his throat with a "uhump" and sauntered into his office.

Back at Willoughby Hills College, Roderick Constance was reliving his meeting with Morgan. From Morgan's point of view, it was nothing more than a weird kid acting tough, but it was something more to Constance. It was a psychological tiff. He had disrupted the police officer's concentration and caused him to lose his cool. He was proud of his power to create uneasiness. He believed his stare was potent, and the police officer wilted beneath it.

Roderick Constance was a failure as a student. His grades were pitiful, and he was on academic probation more than not. He attributed his low grades to inept teachers. He argued with them constantly and disrupted every class he attended. He hated his roommate, John Mason, and referred to him as "the brainless jock." There was nothing about Willoughby Hills College he liked except that he was living in a dorm and not with his mother.

Constance didn't have to live on campus. His mother lived right there in Willoughby Hills. Staying in a college dormitory was expensive, but Constance was attending school on grants and aid. Saving money wasn't a concern. It was a taxpayer burden.

Constance didn't believe in studying, but he liked to lie on his bed and sulk about how unfair the world had treated him. John Mason was in the library as usual, hitting the books, so Constance had the room to himself. He stretched and retrieved a gray metal box from a hiding place behind his bed. He opened it with a small key from a chain he wore around his neck. The box contained a Smith & Wesson .22 Magnum. The .22 was a small caliber, but because it was a Magnum, it could do some damage. Constance cocked the hammer and aimed at the ceiling light. He pulled the trigger and it clicked as the hammer hit the empty chamber. He slowly pulled the trigger again, then again, and again. He aimed at John Mason's family picture sitting on his desk. He pulled the trigger and said, "Bam, motherfucker!"

CHAPTER FOUR

An early winter was in the air, as Morgan had predicted. The sharp November wind whipped through the streets and the flag atop the Lincoln County Courthouse popped crisply. Dry leaves raced across the courtyard and danced in the traffic on Broadway Street. The courthouse dome had the illusion of movement as gray wintry clouds coursed across the sky. The courthouse was the oldest building in Willoughby Hills. It was three stories high and capped with a silver metallic colored dome. There were gigantic clocks on all four sides with Ionic columns supporting a Grecian façade standing as splendidly as the Parthenon on the Acropolis. There were flower gardens at each entrance and even with the icy chill of November the grass was still green. It was obvious by the condition of the courthouse that the Lincoln County citizens valued their public property.

Two markedly different-looking men strolled along the courthouse sidewalk, obviously involved in a conversation. One of them was Ian Rodgers, the Lincoln County state's attorney. The other man was Dan Ingelman, the Lincoln County public defender. Both positions were highly regarded in Willoughby Hills, but the state's attorney was higher on the food chain.

Ian lowered his thick eyebrows in contemplation. He adjusted his heavy winter coat and shrugged his shoulders as he clasped his briefcase under his arm. He pulled his gloves on with his teeth while Dan waited patiently. Ian was in his late forties, his hair was thick but prematurely gray, and he was as fit as an Army drill sergeant. He was wearing an Armani overcoat, and the briefcase under his arm was handmade in Italy. He was a former Chicagoan, graduated from Northern Illinois Law School, and practiced in a prestigious downtown Chicago law firm before moving to Willoughby Hills. His success in Chicago was well known. Everybody in a small town knows everything about everybody else, and there is never a shortage of rumors to substitute when the facts are not known. Ian left prestige and success in Chicago to move to Willoughby Hills to accept a teaching position at Willoughby Hills College. It wasn't merely condescending speculation to say that it was a step down for a man of his qualifications. It was a reality. Teaching at the University of Illinois might have been considered a lateral move, but Willoughby Hills, now *that* was clearly slumming. "Midlife crisis" was the common reticent whisper among his colleagues at the courthouse.

He quit teaching after the first year and accepted an appointment to the public defender's office. Most of his fellow attorneys attributed his move as "coming to his senses," but even the public defender's office was several layers beneath him. When he emerged as the front-runner for state's attorney, the new slant was that it had all been an ingenious plan. Now that he held the position, he was often referred to as "the old gray fox."

Dan Ingelman was as different from Ian Rogers as a man could be. They were both lawyers, but that was the extent of their similarities. Dan had gone to Southern Illinois Law School on the G.I. Bill (a place Ian wouldn't have put a foot into) and returned to Willoughby Hills where he practiced law for thirty years. He made a good living preparing wills, farm lease contracts, and defending drunks and shoplifters. When Ian vacated the public

21

defender's office, Dan was appointed by the chief circuit judge to fill the vacancy. When he took the job his clientele only changed in that the drunk driving and shoplifting cases became more plentiful. Dan was skinny, his hair was lifeless, and he dressed like a pencil salesman. What he lacked in panache he made up in tenacity. He looked like he wouldn't be able to break a pretzel, but he was energetic and fought for every client as though he were defending murder one.

The wind stirred and his comb-over sagged to one side. A quick hand smoothed the flaccid strands before his bare scalp was exposed to the world. Dan turned to Ian and said, "I think you can come up with a better deal than that." He was referring to a case on the next court docket. It was a family fight that turned bad. Now it was in the hands of the lawyers.

"Oh, come on, Dan," Ian interrupted. "I've offered you a fantastic deal—the defendant pleads to armed violence and we drop the attempted murder charge."

"Ian, the entire case is based on the defendant's exculpatory statements, and the Supreme Court has been very clear on that. He has to be given his Miranda warnings regardless of whether he's making a statement in his own behalf or making a confession."

Ian interrupted again. "I've made my offer, but for the sake of argument, I'll remind you that those statements were not made in response to questioning. They were totally voluntary. The police don't have to stop someone from offering an explanation. You know that."

The two men turned and walked toward their parked cars. The conversation continued. Dan was defending a lost cause, but as usual he was trying every trick in the book. He filed motions for discovery, motions to suppress, motions for continuance, and every other legal maneuver he could to muddle the issues in advance of the court date. He seldom thought his clients were innocent, but he believed every defendant deserved a fair trial.

When he was asked how he could expend so much energy on people he knew were guilty, his answer was standard. He had fought the Nazis in World War Two, and they had murdered six million people without the benefit of trials. He would do everything in his power to make sure every person he defended received the maximum protection under the law. He found that a hard line to argue with.

Nothing would be resolved on that brisk November afternoon, but eventually there would be a deal cut before the trial date. Today they would part as friends, not having resolved the matter, but they both knew how the system worked. They needed to dispose of the case before it went to court because that was the way things got done. If every case went to trial, there wouldn't be enough lawyers or judges to try them all.

Chapter Five

Morgan's shift had ended and he was eager to get home. There was a day when he loved his work so much that he lingered in the police station talking to the dispatch officer for an hour after he had been relieved. He still thought it was the best job in the world, but now he had another influence in his life — Molly.

At the moment Morgan was standing in front of City Hall as the occupants of the ancient building emptied into the street. It was Miller time. The cold air was penetrating his jacket as he looked north on Mclean Street, blew on his hands, and waited impatiently. He heard the familiar whine of the Fiat engine in the distance. The orange convertible came around the corner with the top down and Molly's long brown hair flowing in the breeze. Morgan thought she was more beautiful than any woman he had ever known, but right then be believed she might have a screw loose. She stopped at the curb and brushed the hair away from her face.

"Jesus, are you crazy, its twenty-three degrees out here," Morgan exclaimed, slipping into the passenger seat.

"You've been acting a little bored lately, so I thought I'd give you something to think about," she said, giggling softly.

It was a lie. He was as infatuated with her now as he had ever been. "I'm thinking about getting warm right now," he said as he reached over the seat to retrieve the canvass top.

Her face was still glowing from the cold. "Oh, come on! It was fun," she said.

Before he could fasten the latch clips, the Fiat accelerated away from the intersection leaving Morgan gripping the top with his fingernails. He wrestled with the clamps as he eyed the speed odometer. "There's a speed limit, you know," he scolded.

Morgan's admonishment only caused her to accelerate. The Fiat sailed along as the canvass top fluttered in the wind. By the time he snapped the top into place, the apartment was coming into view. Molly made a sharp right turn and the Fiat skidded into the driveway.

Morgan eyed Molly. "Don't say a word," she warned, but then she laughed.

"Hey, I'm a policeman, Molly. What do ya think the neighbors will say when you come sliding in here sideways? I should be writing you a ticket instead of riding with you."

"I'm a special case," she said, flipping her hair as she slid from behind the wheel and started for the apartment. I'm the girl who's sleeping with you."

It was a hard line to argue with. He jumped from the car and chased her inside.

Across town in the college cafeteria, dinner was being served. It resembled an old Army mess hall, with linoleum floors, bright glaring lights, and tables strung out in a row. Students lined up for their evening meal as dishes clattered, tableware clinked, and youthful complaining voices merged into a passive murmur.

In the parking lot, boys made obnoxious remarks to passing female students, basketballs bounced, black kids talked jive, and white kids tried in vain to get the dialect down. The dormitories were empty except for an occasional student dropping off books before heading off to the cafeteria. In Hovey Hall it was quiet and the lights were low. A silhouetted figure appeared at the emergency entrance. He examined the hallway nervously, his head turning quickly left and right. A dirty strand of hair clung to a sunken cheek. A quick swipe of a hand pushed it aside. The frail form was stealthy as he fetched a crooked wire from his jeans. In just a few moments he was methodically fishing a lock in an attempt to gain entrance into a room. The lock clicked, the door swung slowly open, and Roderick Constance slipped inside. He was quick to return with an armful of record albums. These were the days before CDs and iPods. A batch of vinyl was an armful.

Another boy was returning from the dining room to grab some books before heading off to the library. He saw Constance and waited for him to scurry away. He had a long look at him, but a glance was all he needed to recognize him. The witness was Constance's roommate, John Mason. "You thief," he whispered. It was the beginning of the end for John Mason.

CHAPTER SIX

Monday morning brought sunshine to the frigid air. Morgan arrived at City Hall at 8:45 a.m., fifteen minutes early, as usual. He stopped in the hallway as Gladys was hanging her coat inside her office. She rubbed against the wall to get back around stacks of reports and office supplies. When she turned around, Morgan was patting the parking meter tickets smugly, proud of himself for not having sent them flying.

"Now that's better," she said.

He smiled and walked to the complaints window, bypassing the steel-plated door. "Would you hit the switch please, Roy."

"Ahh! You're no fun at all today," Roy snorted.

Ed Woodson was at a typewriter two-fingering out an accident report. "What are you doing here, maniac?" Morgan asked. Ed grunted. He was supposed to be working the four to twelve midnight shift. Eight forty-five was foreign to him.

Ed Woodson was truly a maniac. He loved his job, but sometimes his way of handling things was like a child poking a sleeping dog with a stick. He got results but often as not he turned up a stink in the process. Ed was loud, and there were no filters between his thoughts and his vocal cords. He was as belligerent as a gorilla on steroids, but he was a likable sort of loudmouth. He was Morgan's best friend.

Ed immediately went into a diatribe about how busy his shift had been over the weekend. There were family fights, drunks pissing in the alleys behind the taverns, and burglary reports all over town. By the way he was complaining, patrolling East St. Louis would have been a cakewalk by comparison.

Roy poked his head out of the com room. "Hey, you guys, shut it down in there. All I can hear is Ed's loud mouth blaring!"

"I wasn't that goddamned loud!" Ed shouted in defiance. Morgan just laughed. He knew Roy had to monitor four different frequencies plus the Illinois State Police Emergency Network. A radio voice couldn't compete with Ed's sonorous laughter.

Roy's scolding didn't stick because in only moments Ed was loud-talking again. As he rambled on about being inundated with radio calls, he strayed onto an incident that piqued Morgan's interest. He had answered a call to take a burglary report at the college. The offender's description was similar to the kid he had seen when he was there on Wednesday. Ed called him a bug-eyed, long-haired, weird ass, fucking nutcase. That wasn't exactly how Morgan would have put it, but it was close enough to cause him to think it was the same kid. Was it the same kid who came into Kyle Brasky's room demanding to know what was going on? After a few moments it was clear that he wasn't wrong. Ed's bug-eyed, long-haired, weird ass, fucking nutcase was Roderick Constance. It didn't surprise Morgan. He knew there was something wrong with that kid. Now he was a criminal.

Willoughby Hills College employed their own security officers but they didn't begin patrolling the campus until five p.m. The police department handled everything until five, but after that they only responded to violent situations or serious emergency calls. Everything else was handled in-house. Ed was laughing about getting the call because it was after six, and the student who had witnessed the theft wasn't able to find College Security so he looked up Walter Pieloff, the college president in the phone book, and contacted him at home. Pieloff drove out to the campus and found Jenkins asleep in the security office. Ed bellowed as he described how Jenkins was fired on the spot. Consequently, Ed had to take the burglary report.

Roy barked again for Ed to keep it down, reminding him that he was a sergeant and Ed was still a patrolman. "It ain't a request, it's an order!" he shouted.

"Oh, shit. I think he's mad," Ed said and giggled.

When Ed filed his arrest report, he was scolded by the detectives for releasing Constance on a Notice to Appear, instead of booking him. They suspected him of other burglaries, and they wanted to sweat him a little. There was another reason, too. The kid who reported Constance was John Mason, his roommate. If Constance caught wind of how things went down, Mason would be in a pretty tight spot. Living in the same room with someone you had ratted out might be a little awkward.

Morgan poured coffee into his brown-stained coffee cup. Sarge came through the doorway with the buzzer sounding behind him. Morgan kept the coffeepot in his hand waiting for Sarge to make his way up the hallway. Sarge retrieved his sorry-looking cup and wiped it with a paper towel. Nobody ever washed their cups, they just shook them out and hung them on the hook-lined shelf above the pot. Morgan poured while Sarge moved his cup around in a circle. He watched Morgan's face for a reaction. Morgan raised the pot and performed the "long pour" without spilling a drop. Sarge's expression was pretentiously dour. "I guess we can take you off rookie status," he said.

"I guess," Morgan said indifferently.

He'd been there for about five years, and his rookie status had expired a long time ago, but he thought about that first day. It was as clear in his mind as if it had been yesterday. He had just turned twenty-one. He was wearing a uniform that felt a little too big for him as he walked into the police station. He was self-conscious and as nervous as a preacher who had strayed into a whorehouse. It was almost as though he were an imposter. He didn't know anybody on the police department, and nobody knew him. Willoughby Hills was like many small departments in those days that didn't have their own academy. New recruits were sent to the University of Illinois Police Training Institute where they graduated with a large class of police cadets from all over the State of Illinois. Morgan's first contact with any of the forty-nine men on the roster was at the moment he walked up to the complaints window.

Ron Baird was the first to acknowledge him. Ed Woodson, Stan Hobbs, and Joe Bernard were loitering around a worktable inside the squad room. Roy took off to get Sarge and hummed "new meat" as he passed them. Ed saw him standing at the window like a lost lamb or a high school kid on dress-up day. Ed walked through the com room and glared at him. It was an intimidating and hostile stare. "Goddamn, ain't you green!" he bellowed. "Come and take a look at this, boys. We got us a rookie!"

Morgan still had that fresh-washed glow, and he was probably the most naïve recruit who had ever walked through the door. He had finished first in his class, but now he was standing at the edge of the trenches. Everything he had learned at the academy would have to be put in the hopper and he would start anew.

He didn't know then, but Ed was just delivering the stock rookie-mocking. It was something every new kid had to go through. Starting day was nothing like those big departments, full of ceremony and glad-handing. You just walked in, reported to your sergeant, and started your journey. Morgan relished those first few months in the department because he fit in. They didn't teach you in the Academy how to get along with your fellow officer's. That was something you had to learn on your own. "Breaking in" could be the most enriching or the most humiliating thing a rookie would experience. The results were subject to the recruit's personality. Morgan liked the banter.

Every newcomer to the department had to serve a probationary period as a communications officer. Since Willoughby Hills was small, they seldom hired more than two officers at one time, and it was a practical way to get a rookie warmed up to his new responsibilities. They were required to deal with complaints on the telephone and at the complaints window. They were able to make decisions and get hands-on experience in dealing with the public. It served as a buffer between the rookies and the veterans. By the time they were assigned to a permanent shift, they knew department policies and were ready to go. It wasn't unique to Willoughby Hills, but bigger departments had individual training officers, and recruits were sent directly to the street. In Willoughby Hills, radio duty was a good substitute until they could be assigned to their permanent duty sergeant.

In 1975, political correctness was in its infancy and not yet the animal it would become in 2011. There were rules and etiquette, but people didn't go into convulsions over minor infractions. There were things done in those days that might not be tolerated by a professional police department in the modern era, but it didn't mean they weren't disciplined in matters that were important. In 1975, pranks and bantering were ignored by superiors when it was harmless. That was indeed the case in Willoughby Hills.

Sarge's comment about taking Morgan off rookie status stirred memories of some of the stunts the other guys pulled on him during that first six months. Once they had called in a high-speed chase in progress and reported his car description and license number as the vehicle involved. He was operating the dispatch radio and got a little excited about it but suspected mischief right from the beginning. He pretended to panic, and that made them happy. Once in a while fate distributes a slice of sweet revenge, and Morgan was blessed with a few opportunities during his probationary period for payback. On one occasion he was in the communications room answering the telephone and dispatching radio calls. Ed, Stan, and Bob were in the assistant chief's office loafing because the AC was on vacation and they were treating it like the departmental lounge. Ed thought it would be funny to call in a fake accident report to put Morgan into a little bit of a pinch. Their plan was to ignore a request from Morgan to handle the call, leaving him stumped for a course of action.

There was a standing order not to dispatch the radar units to anything less than a true emergency. Since the three deadbeats were in the AC's office just killing time, if a call came in he would have to run back to the AC's office to find them. They knew he would try to protect them from being caught loafing and would dutifully hunt them down before taking other action. They thought watching Morgan sweat would be comical.

When Ed made the call he disguised his voice, but he had to strain to keep from snickering. Morgan took the call knowing that the only cars on the street were the two radar cars, and the three officers who were loafing would have to hit the street to handle it. Realizing that he would be away from the radio and the switchboard, he flipped on the intercom to access the AC's office.

"What if he dispatches the radar cars?" Stan asked, rethinking the downside of their trickery.

"He won't do that, he's been told enough times not to do that. Here he comes," Ed said, quickly zipping it.

Morgan hurried through the doorway. "I've got an accident with injuries at Sycamore and Broadway," he said.

Ed was sitting in the AC's chair with his feet on his desk. Stan was standing with a cup of coffee in his hand, and Bob was sitting on the floor with his back against the wall.

"Goddamn 'cruit, ain't you ever got any good news?" Ed

shouted.

"It's not my call," Stan said. "I got the last one." He casually sipped his coffee.

"I'm not getting it, Ed has the least seniority," Bob snorted. "It's your accident, Ed."

Morgan was bewildered. "Somebody has to get it. They said there were injuries," he urged. He hadn't come to the point of panic, but an accident with injuries was a serious call. "Somebody has to get it," he said more forcefully.

Morgan was concerned about being away from the radio and switchboard. Roy had made a supply run and the com room was unmanned. He waited for a response but the three officers just sat there ignoring him. Fearing that someone might have come to the complaints window or an emergency call was coming in on ISPERN, he dashed back to the radio desk to check. He intended to go back to the AC's office and get a little more insistent, but when he entered the com room he could hear the three officers laughing on the intercom.

"Did you see his face?" Stan snorted.

"I thought he looked a little mad when we said we weren't taking the call. Did you see how he glared at me?" Bob giggled. They were very tickled with themselves. It was a carnival, a literal celebration of his gullibility.

"What if he dispatches the radar cars?" Stan asked again.

"He won't do that. Rookies always do what they're told," Ed spouted.

The com room was empty, and the radios were silent. The complaints window was quiet, and Morgan could see Gladys sitting at her ledge gazing out the window. He cut the intercom to the AC's office, went to the coffeepot, and retrieved his cup from the hook-lined shelf. He poured a cup and walked down the hallway to the AC's office. He entered as casually as a man going through yesterday's mail.

Ed was puzzled by Morgan's lack of concern. "What happened to the call?" he asked. Now he was concerned.

"I took care of it," he said. He blew across the hot coffee as steam rose into the air.

The three ill-behaved officers glanced sheepishly at each other. "How's that?" Stan said.

"I put out the call—accidents with injuries—both radar cars volunteered to get it, but the chief was just leaving a meeting with the mayor, and he said he'd go down there to aid the injured," Morgan said. "He asked where you guys were, so I covered for you. I said you were busy."

"Fuck," Ed gasped. The other two just stared at Morgan in disbelief. "You know you're not supposed to dispatch the radar cars!" Ed shouted. The fact that the chief was heading for a nonexistent accident with injuries put a little urgency into his deportment.

"I know, but what else could I do? You wouldn't get it," Morgan stated defensively.

They all looked at each other again, then Ed dropped his feet from the desk and scrambled for the door. Stan was right behind him.

Bob watched them but he stayed sitting on the floor. "It was a prank call, Ed. There's no accident. What the hell!"

"The chief doesn't know that, does he! We gotta get moving before he gets there—Jesus Christ, you fucking rookie! How in hell are we gonna cover this?"

Bob decided the other two were right, so he started to panic too. All three stooges went tearing down the hallway, banging into each other and lunging for the door. Ed kicked the doorplate, but the lock stuck as usual. "Goddamn it!" The buzzer seemed to be a little louder than normal, a hysterical squawking in fact.

"Hit the switch, Cooper!" Ed shouted. Morgan just stood there smiling. He was smug and confident, not at all like the novice he was supposed to be.

"There's no accident, Ed," Morgan said, suppressing a laugh.

Ed stared at him with eyes seemingly about to pop out of his eye sockets. His lips were drawn tight, and his jawbone twitched. "What?" he said, somewhat puzzled. He hesitated and then spouted, still not up to speed. "I know that, but you put out the call!"

"No, no, I really didn't." Morgan sipped at his coffee.

Stan smiled slightly and Bob snickered. Ed's brow was still furrowed, but a vague sort of grin emerged at the corners of his mouth. "So you didn't put out the call?"

"No accident, no injuries, no radio dispatches to the chief, just three guys with egg on their faces," Morgan scoffed.

Ed tried to keep his annoyed expression, but relief and embarrassment made it impossible for him to maintain his anger. He walked back up the hallway slowly. "I guess you think you got us," he said."

"No, no, I don't think I got you, I know I did," Morgan laughed.

Morgan continued to stare into his cup. Sarge snapped his fingers. "Earth to Cooper," he said.

Morgan was back in the present. He sipped his coffee and smiled vaguely. "Sorry, Sarge, just thinking about the good old days."

"Yes, and I don't think they're all over yet," Sarge said sourly.

The conversation about Roderick Constance was forgotten. It was as routine as a traffic stop. No one in that squad room could have predicted how the inferior-looking college student would affect their futures.

CHAPTER SEVEN

November ended with harsh winds and bitter cold. The days grew shorter and December was flush with holiday glitter. Pedestrians dressed in their winter coats, mittens and scarves, filled the downtown streets carrying colorfully wrapped packages as they hurried from one store to another. Shopping malls at that time were not yet a dynamic in small towns, and downtown businesses were still the major retail power.

It was a quieter atmosphere inside the Lincoln County Courthouse first floor misdemeanor court. Dan Ingelman was standing at the prosecutor's table with State's Attorney First Assistant Gary Winstead. They were having a conversation about a case going to trial on that date. It was December 7, 1975. Gary thoughtfully scanned through a manila envelope containing subpoenas, motions, and police reports. It was the State of Illinois vs. Roderick Constance. Ian Rogers didn't handle misdemeanor trials, but Dan, Ian's counterpart, wasn't so lucky. Any case requiring a public defense was totally Dan's responsibility. The only time he had the luxury of an assistant was on major cases, and even then they had to be appointed by the chief circuit judge.

The courtroom opened and Roderick Constance stepped in. He pointed to the defense table and asked, "Is this where I'm supposed to sit?" Dan nodded an affirmative.

Ed Woodson was in the corridor. He was there to testify if necessary, but he was oblivious to the surroundings. His laughing and bellowing could be heard as the door was closing. "Did anybody notice a little nip in the air?" he shouted. His words echoed off the high ceilings but silence was restored when the door clicked shut. The court reporter, a Japanese-American, scowled and leaned over trying to see who had made the remark.

The two attorneys approached each other. Dan was first to engage. "I'm willing to plead my client guilty if we can have court supervision, Gary," he said.

"I think Ian and I discussed this one when we disposed of the Renchler case," Dan said, vying for a plea agreement for Roderick Constance.

The younger attorney licked his finger and turned a page. "Dan, I wanted to revisit this case with you. Ian advised me that you and he had reached an agreement for supervision, but there's an unforeseen problem."

"What problem could there be. This is his first offense — and a few record albums, I mean, give me a break!" Dan said.

Gary interrupted. "That's precisely the problem, Dan. Our records indicate that he has a prior retail theft conviction in Will County. The judge won't allow supervision when there's a prior."

"What! A shoplifting charge?" Dan asked glancing at his client.

"We've got a certified copy of the conviction right here," Gary said, tightening his upper lip and looking over his glasses.

Dan inspected the document.

"There's no mistake, Dan. If you didn't know about this, I'd say your client's been lying to you," Gary said.

The courtroom was beginning to fill with defendants whose cases would come up during the morning session. Coughs, whispers, and nervous shuffling were an indication of how intimidating the courtroom was to first-time offenders waiting nervously for their cases to be called. Roderick Constance slouched in his chair. A beam of sunlight had settled on him, shining through a window on the east side of the courtroom. He was as relaxed as a cat lying on a window sill soaking up the sun.

Dan chewed on his lower lip. He was a patient man but not completely without ire. He shot Constance another disparaging glance. Dan believed in doing everything possible for his clients and he didn't care about their guilt, but the one thing he wouldn't tolerate was being lied to. He crisply shot up from his chair and motioned for Constance to follow him. By the time they reached the lobby, some of Dan's anger had dissipated, but still his expression was as rebuking as a Catholic nun who had caught a fourth grader chewing gum in class. From a distance Constance looked like a schoolboy getting a well-deserved tongue-lashing.

When they returned to the courtroom, Gary was instructing a witness on another case he was handling. He too lacked the convenience of having only one case to prosecute. The defendants would be marching into the criminal record books throughout the day. He glanced at Dan, then patted his witness on the shoulder, uttered a few encouraging words, then headed for the defense table.

"Well, what's your offer?" Dan asked.

"We want thirty days in county jail, two years' probation, restitution for the record albums, and counseling with Lincoln County Mental Health."

Dan looked shocked. "This is a simple theft, for crying out loud!"

"Dan, the truth is we've been getting some feedback from the detectives on your client," Gary said calmly.

"Does Ian know about this?" Dan asked.

"He's the one who stipulated the terms," Gary shot back hastily, offended that Dan thought he might have been able to deal better with Ian.

"We can't take that," Dan stated firmly. "I'll take this to trial. We can't do worse than that."

"That's your call, Dan. Just don't call for a pow-wow in the middle of the trial looking for a deal," Gary said, still scanning the material inside the manila envelope, trying to look complacent and disinterested.

The judge's chamber door opened. Chairs scooted and silence fell across the gallery in anticipation of his entrance. "All rise," barked the bailiff. Judge Feldman hurried into the courtroom and took his seat behind the bench. The bailiff cleared his throat. "Hear ye, hear ye, hear ye, the Eighth Circuit Court of Lincoln County is now in session."

The judge sat erect in his chair. "Why are we here, Mr. Winstead?"

"Your Honor, the State of Illinois charges that Defendant Roderick Constance entered upon the property of Willoughby Hills College and into room number 308 of Hovey Hall, also the property of said college, and did unlawfully exert control over property therein with the intent to permanently deprive the owner of the benefit and use of the property."

"Mr. Ingelman, how does the defendant plead?"

"The defendant pleads not guilty, Your Honor, and requests a trial by jury."

The Judge scribbled into his docket sheet and handed it to the court clerk, stating, "So be it. The defendant will be here in this courtroom on March 3rd, 1976, for a trial by jury. Please call the next case."

It was a watershed moment. The citizens of Willoughby Hills were cheerfully going about ringing in the Christmas season, while snow was softly falling on wet brick streets. It was so serene that Norman Rockwell himself might have been sitting on the corner with a canvass and easel, painting a picture of the least likely place on earth for evil to fester. Still, at that moment a malevolent chain of events had been set in motion. The thought might not yet have been hatched, but certainly it was the beginning of something minatory.

CHAPTER EIGHT

Jumping forward in time to October 7, 2006, thirty years after Constance was arraigned, the Chicago Police Department arrested Calvin Washington, the owner of Heaven's Gate Funeral Home and Cemetery. An investigation was initiated by the Illinois Department of Health and Human Services in response to a request from the Cook County Department of Vital Records. It all started when a team of young clerks were assigned to update burial records from Cook County funeral homes and cemeteries. The assignment was to transfer records from the original hardbound books onto computer files. The process was tedious and the books were flush with mistakes. Often when errors were discovered and taken to superiors, the miscues were written off as impeachable content, an asterisk added, and the information was posted without comment.

Almost every funeral home and cemetery in the county had errors, but few were suspicious. Most didn't require an audit or an investigation, but Heaven's Gate was laced with numerical errors or deliberate manipulation of statistics. After reviewing records all the way back to 1885, there were several hundred bodies listed in the same burial plots. In shorter terms, there were more bodies than graves. A reasonable conclusion might be that grave sites were being sold more than once with bodies piled upon bodies. Double and triple sale of one plot was easy money.

The records for Heaven's Gate were impeccable from the late 1800's up to about 1975. At that point everything went haywire. The Department of Health and Human Services filed a complaint with the Chicago Police Department and the State of Illinois Department of Law Enforcement. Investigators were dispatched to audit the books and inspect the facilities and grounds.

By 2006 the funeral home was rundown, with paint peeling, broken steps, and cracked windowpanes. The grass had recently been cut but huge clumps of grass left the lawn looking like a hay field. Grass clippings covered the sidewalks, and the shrubbery was overgrown. Inside the home they found the carpeting worn threadbare, the ceilings spotted with yellow stains from numerous leaks, and the wallpaper had grown dingy from years of neglect. Investigators were immediately stunned by the distressed condition of the home, but they would be mortified by what was to come.

Heaven's Gate was built in 1883, and like many old structures, the basement had stone walls and floors brought in from rock quarries and laid by hand. That was normal, but Heaven's Gate was like a dungeon with moss and mold in every crevasse and corner. The crematory furnace looked like an ancient steam engine boiler—black, rusty, and burnt-out. Ashes from the dead were in heaps alongside the door and in places where they had trickled out of split seams opened by the wear and tear of intense heat. There were several concrete rooms where human ashes were piled to the ceiling and left to soak up the moisture percolating up from the basement floor. It wouldn't have been more mortifying if dead souls had come back for their bodies, haunting the ruins and seeking a respite from the horror.

The cemetery had been mowed but the grass was no more than chickweed and clover. A pond under the hill past the gravestones was found to have bodies anchored beneath the water and bones left there from antiquity. Hundreds of bodies were stacked in the same graves, and others were buried without a vault or coffin.

Calvin Washington was found in his apartment above the viewing room, high on heroin, covered with filth and vomit, and nearly dead. He denied any knowledge of the conditions of the cemetery and argued that he hadn't buried a body in seven years. Later his attorney would argue that he was on drugs and mentally ill. Many observers thought that if the same thing happened in the suburbs, Washington would have gotten a life sentence. Of course he was already old and a lengthy sentence would have been for pretext only. The other argument was that if it had happened anywhere besides the inner city of Chicago, it wouldn't have gone unchecked for forty years. The judge gave him twenty years, and he died in prison three years later.

Sometimes a twist of fate doesn't smack in the face of destiny, but it creeps along quietly down the road unnoticed until it's pertinent only in condescending mockery. That was the case with Calvin Washington. Although he was dead, there would be a time when his pathetic life and existence would have a sardonic reemergence. A sixty-three year old Morgan Cooper would be the legatee of his restoration.

CHAPTER NINE

On December 10th, 1975, thirty-one years before Calvin Washington was arrested, Roderick Constance and another student from Willoughby Hills College by the name of Tyrone Hightower left Willoughby Hills. They were headed for Chicago. Hightower was from the city and could have traveled home every weekend, but this was his first trip back since school started in September. He had ten brothers and sisters from the ages of thirteen to forty-one, and he just didn't like the crowd hovering around the homestead. He was no more interested in school than was Constance, but he wanted to do a little business downstate, and going to college at the government's expense was like getting a small business loan. His mother had a new place in Aurora, having been a recipient of a home from Habitat for Humanity. Before that she was living in the Taylor Homes on the south side of Chicago. That was where Tyrone spent most of his younger years. His grades in school were awful and he actually seldom attended, but he got a good education just the same. It just wasn't about math and science.

He had started his criminal life hustling clients for a local dealer, Leroy Barber, who set up shop in the Taylor Homes when Tyrone was about eight years old. He patrolled the sidewalks in front of the abandoned Saint Mary and Joseph Catholic Church at

South Michigan Avenue and 75th Street. Little Tyrone and several other children his age would bark at the traffic like little carnies, seeking out potential customers.

Saint Mary and Joseph was a grand fixture made of sandstone blocks, sturdy enough to withstand an atomic blast, but it couldn't survive south side poverty and crime. The gigantic steeple still jutted skyward, and the walls equipped with flying buttresses were as solid as the day they were put in place, but now it was grimy, the grounds were littered with refuse, and the grass was worn down to solid earth. Magnificent stained-glass windows were boarded up with plywood and decorated with gang signs and graffiti. It was dark and hopeless, like a dank and empty medieval castle.

The church had a tier of concrete steps leading to the entrance where Barber would sit at the top level, and his fifteen to twenty underlings were scattered on lower steps according to their status in the organization. Once Tyrone or one of the other children got a bite, Barber's minions would descend on the prospective client, deliver the drugs, and collect the money. Barber had only to sit and wait for the payoff to come to him.

Barber was a dangerous, brooding man. He and his subordinates occupied the church steps dressed in black hooded sweatshirts with the hoods shading their faces. They were a menacing entity in the neighborhood and to challenge them was suicide. Anyone who was dealing in that part of town had to have Barber's approval, and that was never given without a hefty percentage of the profits.

Little Tyrone Hightower had a secret—a dangerous secret. He had risked his life on several occasions by making deals without Barber's approval or assistance. He had fallen into good luck, as long as he didn't get caught. There was a middle-aged man who ran a funeral home about ten blocks south of 75th Street just off of South Michigan Avenue. His grandfather owned the funeral home and a small cemetery behind it. It was like a little park in the middle of the ghetto. The place looked like a grand ole southern mansion. If it weren't for the dead bodies occupying the grounds, Tyrone thought it would have been a nice place to live. In 2006 it would not resemble the beautiful place as it now existed.

The man's name was Calvin Washington. He was a mortician, his father had been a mortician, and his grandfather and two generations before him were morticians. Calvin's father died from a dreaded infection contracted from one of the bodies he embalmed. Calvin was left with his eighty-one-year-old grandfather to run the family business.

Calvin lived a secluded and lonely life. Occasionally he walked up the street in the evenings to find little Tyrone. At first he bought marijuana, but after a while he advanced to speed, crack, and then heroin. Little Tyrone was able to furnish him with whatever his habit demanded, but all transactions were privy to the two of them.

Now, fifteen years later, Tyrone was branching out. He couldn't do business in south Chicago, that is to say, if he valued his life. Leroy Barber was bigger than he had ever been, plus there were several of his lieutenants who had their own interests in the neighborhoods. Drugs were what he knew, so setting up shop in another part of the state seemed to be a good option. He already had a few regular customers on campus at Willoughby Hills College. The only reason he came back to the city was for his lifelong client, Calvin Washington. Washington would pay anything for a fix.

Roderick Constance and Tyrone Hightower weren't friends. Constance had never had a friend in his life, but he thought Hightower was interesting. Hightower was loose with his tongue. He talked about business as openly as if he were discussing poker rules. He didn't know that people in a small town never turned their heads to drug-pushing and criminal activity, and they weren't afraid to stand up and point an accusing finger when they were called upon to do it. The police department wasn't overwhelmed by gang activity and they were more than ready to put a collar on people they suspected of tarnishing their community. Business in central Illinois was a lot different than on the south side of Chicago.

Constance had a car, and Hightower needed a ride to Chicago. Constance saw it as an opportunity to learn, to find options, to expand his horizons. Hightower wanted to start an acquaintance with Constance because he thought he was a self-deluded moron he could use. Business was business, and sometimes you had to associate with people you didn't like.

It was after eleven p.m. The lights from the city were glowing off low-hanging clouds and the cold wind was blowing debris across the street. Constance was quiet as Hightower talked about how people had the wrong impression of the streets. Living in the Homes was good. There was always someone to hang with, and the sound of basketballs bouncing and police sirens wailing in the distance were as comforting to him as a family picnic was to people in Willoughby Hills. Hightower was never afraid to walk down the streets or go out at night. If you knew your place, you were never in danger. Some people got shot, but some people deserved it.

He was still talking, stopping only to direct Constance to turn as they made their way through intersections and traffic lights. They turned off 75th Street and drove east to South Michigan Avenue. In the middle of the block Constance slowed and entered into a long concrete driveway. A green florescent sign identified the funeral home as Heaven's Gate. Hightower directed Constance to stop in the driveway at a side entrance where a single lightbulb was shining. They both got out of the car, Hightower opened the door, and they entered. There was a small room immediately inside, then a hallway leading into the viewing room. A casket was mounted on a carriage in front of the altar. The lid was open, exposing a body dressed and ready to go to its final resting place. Constance gawked, but Hightower gave it a quick glance and hurried on. The sweet smell of flowers permeated the room. The lights were low and shadowy, but Hightower moved quickly through the room, familiar with the surroundings. He passed through the viewing room and down another hallway to a door leading to the basement. They descended the stairway with the pungent smell of damp earth and moldy stones increasing with each step. It resembled a medieval dungeon. At the bottom of the stairs an older black man stood watching them as they came down. He was wearing a white lab coat and gloves. A body was lying on a steel slab at the door of the crematory. Constance could see inside the furnace where fire streamed a bright blue intense plume like a colossal gas range. The man shoved the slab forward, and a searing sound emanated from the furnace as the flames began to consume the corpse. The stench of burning flesh mingled with the dank smell of the basement.

Hightower laughed. "Calvin, you need to get a new stove, man!"

"It's all right. It does the job," Calvin said quietly. He looked at Constance. The long hair, sallow skin, the strange quiet manner — Constance made him nervous. His face twitched, he blinked and sniffed. He looked at Hightower with raised eyebrows.

"He's cool, man. He's wit me."

"Did you bring the stuff?" he asked. Calvin wasn't looking for conversation. He wanted the horse, the smack, the big H. It didn't matter what they called it, he wanted it.

"You got two grand, Calvin?" Hightower asked, smiling.

"I've got it, you know I've always got it."

"Then get it," Hightower said sternly. The smile was gone. It was all business now."

Calvin led the way as they walked up the stairs, down the hallway, through the viewing room past the dressed-up body, and into a small office with a window overlooking the driveway. He opened a small safe and retrieved twenty one-hundred-dollar bills. In only moments the deal was done, and Constance and Hightower were back in the car, northbound on South State Street.

Hightower gave directions as Constance drove. It was past midnight. The streets were empty and quiet. It was as dreary as a Polish concentration camp. As they reached South State and Pershing Road, Hightower said, "Stop."

Constance stopped right in the middle of the street. The twenty-three high-rise apartment buildings called Robert Taylor Homes stood like a huge brown foreboding prison, lacking only a twelve-foot fence capped with a string of barbed wire to qualify as a correctional facility. Trash and debris floated on the breeze as the wind swirled between the buildings. It couldn't have been more depressing if it were on the face of the moon.

Hightower gazed out the window as if he were viewing something heavenly. He sighed and turned his cap sideways. "Beautiful," he said.

Constance watched him quietly. He wasn't familiar with most of the city, especially the slums, but he was comfortable and at ease. He waited for Hightower to speak again, but Hightower continued to stare out the window. The envelope containing two thousand dollars was lying on the seat. Constance glanced at it.

"It looks like shit," Constance said, reverting back to Hightower's comment that it was beautiful.

"It looks like home to me," Hightower said. "I be safe here, bro," he added.

"Not really," Constance said.

Hightower laughed and turned to look at Constance. He was still smiling when Constance shot him between the eyes.

Hightower slumped into the seat. Constance reached across his body, opened the passenger door, and pushed Hightower out onto the street.

Chapter Ten

Five days later Molly Peterson gazed out the living room window. Snow fell in large flakes creating a flawless blanket of white that stretched out past the driveway into the street and finally became an endless misty blur. A car creeping along 18th Street was the only thing moving. Molly was thoroughly lost in her thoughts. Her expression was dark and troubled.

Morgan watched her from the bathroom sink. He wiped the shaving cream from his face and walked into the living room. "What's going through that pretty little head now?" he asked.

Molly tilted her head, threw back her hair, and looked at him. "Do we have to go?" she asked, referring to the annual police department Christmas party.

Each year on December 15th, the Willoughby Hills Police Department threw a drunken bash and disguised it as a Christmas party. It seemed impossible for the forty-nine member department to get together, have a few drinks, exchange Christmas presents, and go home. It always turned into an alcohol-induced Donnybrook. The infusion of many different and aggressive personalities linked with spirits created a very volatile atmosphere.

In those days there was an expression called "last dogs," applied to those people who traditionally closed the place down.

They huddled in small groups as the chairs were being placed facedown on the tabletops in order to broom the trash out. They were always the people who were still there in the early morning hours while the bartenders sat at the end of the bar smoking and waiting for them to take the hint that the party was over. Men were more likely to be last dogs than women, but they usually subjected their wives and girlfriends to the tradition. Everybody in the department wanted to be known as a last dog, but few of them earned the distinction. It was more fun to rehash the experience than it was to live it.

Last year Peggy and Norman Lewis (traditional last dogs) disrupted the party by creating a ruckus right in front of the band. Norman wasn't a police officer, but he was a legendary police buff. Even Sarge couldn't remember when Norman started following the police department. Norman owned the Topper Restaurant and Bar. The Topper was Willoughby Hills' finest restaurant. It was known throughout Illinois, drawing clientele from Chicago and Springfield where political parties and events were commonplace. Every year on each officer's anniversary he rewarded them with an all-expense-paid dinner. The gesture was nothing less than a shameless gratuity but coming from Norman no one questioned the motive. The Topper was a first-class eating establishment, and the five-star extravaganza was nothing to sneeze at. Norman spared no expense when it came to his friends in blue. In exchange Norman expected to be invited to all police functions and to be treated as an equal. He made no apologies for his fondness for police officers—he was proud of it, and he defended them as though he were one of them.

Peggy shared Norman's affection for the men in blue, as she did everything else in his life. She worked relentlessly with Norman to establish the Topper as downstate's finest restaurant. Even now she worked every weekend just like she did when they were struggling. She didn't need to work but she loved the restaurant.

Peggy was a clever woman who wore bright, colorful dresses and expensive, flashy jewelry. She was beautiful in her younger years, and aside from being a little flamboyant, she had aged gracefully. Norman and Peggy were dedicated to each other, but they frequently argued in public, treating the community as though the whole town were members of their family and privy to their barneys. When they were drinking, neither of them could do anything to suit the other. Their arguments were seldom serious, but last year at the Christmas party things went a little farther awry than usual. The rumor was that Norman threw Peggy into the drum set as the band played, "Hit the Road Jack." The truth was that Peggy shoved Norman, but because Norman was so much bigger than Peggy, and totally immoveable, she lost her balance and stumbled backward into the band and rattled things a little. After Peggy regained her balance, she and Norman lashed out a string of obscenities worthy of two drunken sailors on a three-day furlough. They were finally separated by the chief and his wife.

Morgan, a traditional last dog, witnessed the event. He bragged that it was a once-in-a-lifetime opportunity to see the upper crust groveling in conduct usually reserved for drunks of an ordinary strain. This year there would probably be something to equal it. There always was.

Morgan glanced out the window. The streets were nearly deserted, and the snow was accumulating rapidly. A snowplow roared by with a curtain of white mist spraying into the air.

"Why don't you want to go?" Morgan asked. He wasn't considering not going, not in the least. He would go alone if he had to, but he was curious about her concerns.

"Oh, I don't know...you said they always have trouble," she said.

"We have fun too," Morgan said. He watched her face. He

knew her too well. She was apprehensive about meeting new people. She wanted to be that feisty girl who drove the Fiat with the top down in freezing weather, but she was actually fragile and breakable. She leaned on him for support. She was beautiful, with baby-soft skin, large brown eyes, and thick, radiant brown hair. She was intelligent and had nothing to fear from anyone. Morgan had seen other women fade in her presence, but still she was afraid. She could stand up to people and she knew how to fight. It was friendship she feared. The thought of meeting new people terrified her.

"Come on," Morgan said. "What's the real reason?"

Molly bit her lip. "Morgan, I don't know these people...I mean, here we are living together. They know we're not married."

"Molly, nobody cares about that stuff anymore," Morgan said. (In 1975, premarital cohabitation was beginning to become accepted, but in conservative communities it was still frowned upon).

"We're living in sin, young man," she protested.

"Lavishing in it is more like it, I'd say," he laughed.

Molly rested her elbow on her knee and her face in her hands. "Okay," she said softly.

The American Legion Hall had been acquired for the party again this year. It was traditionally chosen because it was reasonably priced and didn't look like a big empty banquet hall like most locations they could afford. It was divided into two sections—a dining room which doubled as a meeting room, and a separate, modern-looking sports bar. The veterans of the department all belonged to the American Legion and they treated the place like they owned it. Policemen are unruly when they're under the influence of alcohol, even belligerent. They don't deny it or try to cover it up, but they do try to justify it. The old standard excuse is that they handle all kinds of situations when they're on duty, and they can't respond with aggression or anger. It bottles up, and when they get a few drinks in them, hostility bubbles to the surface. They're very cliquish, and they hang together even when they have personality differences. Policemen don't have to cover up for bad behavior or deny something they've done. Their fellow officers will do it for them.

The low lights seemed to dim when Morgan and Molly entered the bar. The band was already playing and a few brave souls were dancing. Policemen were standing at the bar, and their wives were behind them making small talk. Some of the guys had already slipped their wives and were cruising around the room talking shop. They never got tired of talking about the calls they answered, the lunatics they had to deal with, or the dangers they faced. It was better than having a therapist on call.

There were built-in pitfalls linked to having a Christmas party, as surely as there were dangers in dark alleys, handling drunk calls, and burglar alarms. One of them was hosting attendees who weren't really in the clique—people who didn't understand that hate-love bond they shared, the one that caused them to wish they could tear each other's guts out, but when they found one of their own drunk behind the wheel of a car at a stop sign, taking him home and lying for him was the first option. Gladys's son-in-law, Leonard Wilson, was one of those outsiders. He was the meter service man. He collected the meter money and repaired the parking meters. He was a natural-born chin-wagger, and he had unlimited access to the police station. The policemen despised him because he gossiped about them. It made him feel important to have the inside "skinny." He eavesdropped on their conversations, soaking up information, feeling elevated knowing things about policemen that outsiders didn't know. The demon—alcohol—possessed their tongues and caused them to rattle and wag, spilling their secrets, and sending them into fits of unmitigated disclosure. Leonard Wilson was there to soak it up and pass it on.

Morgan glanced around the room. He shook his coat and stamped his feet to shake off the snow. Harold Santino, the Department public relations officer, waved to him. Harold and Morgan were in the same morning coffee klatch, and good friends. "I'm glad you made it," he shouted with a hand aside his mouth as though that would limit his shouting to the two of them.

"A little snow can't keep me in," Morgan said.

Harold scooted between crowded tables to make his way to the door. "Hello, Ms. Peterson. You're looking beautiful, as usual," Harold said through a big public relations-type smile. He had already been to the bar, Morgan mused.

"Thank you," Molly said politely.

Ed Woodson came through the door. "Hey, get the hell out of the way, Cooper!" he shouted. "It's cold enough to freeze the nu—"—he stopped— "off a brass monkey, you know." He stomped his feet and smacked his gloves together.

"You're like a big cow," Harold scolded. "You're taking up too much room and you're making too much noise."

"I love a party," Ed exclaimed. "It's just that I have to watch my language until everybody gets drunk. That takes about a half hour." He chuckled. His face was beaming and his features clearly concurred with his declaration. He did indeed love a party.

That's why you're the first one drunk," Harold said. "You can't talk without cussing, so you're pounding beers." He laughed and slapped Ed across his back.

****

At that same moment beyond the city limits, a stringy-haired college student was northbound on a hazardous snow-covered highway, heading for Riverside, Illinois. His eyes were glued to the road, his mouth was drawn tight, and determination was fixed on his face. The steering wheel bounced as the tires followed the ruts already cut in the heavy snow. The windshield wipers dragged leaving ice residue on the glass. The weather was fierce, the snow was blinding, and traffic was crawling at a snail's pace.

The frigid wind was brutal, but no colder than the ice in Roderick Constance's veins. He had put a .22 Magnum bullet into Tyrone Hightower's head without even a dash of guilt, but it was even more remarkable that he did it without a modicum of anxiety or fear of being caught. Now he was headed for Riverside, Illinois, with treachery in his heart. His association with Hightower was no more than strangers passing in the night, but he had a real dislike for his roommate, John Mason. The thought of killing Mason turned his blood from cold to boiling hot.

****

Back at the VFW hall, Leonard Wilson walked past Ed with a drink in his hand. Ed faked a move at the drink and smiled. "Hello, Nerd," he said.

"Hi, Ed," Wilson mumbled as he retreated, expecting Ed to jostle the drink from his hand.

"I'll take it," Ed threatened flippantly, again reaching as though to separate Wilson from his glass. Wilson walked into the crowd, watching Ed over his shoulder.

Ed sauntered into the bar, still rubbing his hands together. Molly focused on Ed with curiosity. She was acquainted with him through Morgan, but she didn't really know him. He was Morgan's best friend, and that made her want to like him, but she didn't connect with him. A guy like Ed was as alien to her as little green men from Mars.

"People seem to really like him," Molly said, unknowingly exposing her skepticism.

Morgan wasn't surprised. Molly and Ed were as different as a potato and a plum. "Some people can be brash and get away with it," Morgan said. "But Ed's different. He trash-talks, but there's a hefty seam of benevolence running through him. He'd give you the shirt off his back."

They were still watching him as he walked through the crowd, slapping people on the back, pinching others, and laughing louder than anyone in the place.

"On the other hand," Morgan continued, "if he thought you were trying to get over on him, he'd shut you down just like that." Morgan snapped his fingers. "People like me never push the outside of the envelope, we never just spit it out, we let things ride. When we reach a point where we have to straighten someone out who's been jerking us around, they hate our guts just for stopping them. Ed just says no, right from the get-go. People know right from the beginning where he stands. They expect him to lay it out there and they never get mad at him for it."

Molly listened as though she were being introduced to his inner reasoning for the first time, but she knew it was true. He was easy, but at the same time strong—as strong as anyone she had ever known. Her eyes were fixed on his face as she held his arm. She depended on him and borrowed from his strength. She was excited just to be there with him. If he needed to mingle, which he often did, she wouldn't object. She wanted to be by his side because she was uneasy around strangers, but that wasn't the reason she clung to him. She truly loved him.

Morgan suppressed the urge to walk around. He saw Stan and Jim standing at the bar, and for an instant he wanted to join them. They were laughing, apparently already having gotten their noses wet. Ed walked by and belted down a mixed drink. "I hope I don't have to go see Ralph tonight," he said. Morgan looked baffled. You know, Rrraaaalllph," Ed said, drawing it out in a gurgling growl.

"Oh, yea, I get it," Morgan said.

They were shuffling through the crowd scanning the dining room for a vacant table. Molly was becoming anxious. There was no such thing as assigned seating, it was totally helter-skelter. Molly didn't like awkwardly standing in front of all those people, not knowing where they would sit. Several people invited Morgan to sit with them, but after assessing the table location and seating arrangements, he graciously declined. Molly would have accepted anything just to be in a place where people couldn't stare at them. Finally, Morgan spotted Harold waving frantically. "Over here, over here," he shouted. Molly clenched Morgan's hand as they made their way through the pack.

"Why didn't you say you didn't have a table," Harold scolded. "I've been saving these chairs for my brother-in-law, but the hell with him!"

At that point Molly spoke up. It wasn't the private, confident Molly, but a superficial persona she used when she was uncomfortable. "Are you sure we're not imposing?" Her voice was even different.

"Heck no, Morgan's my buddy. I want you to sit here. I don't even like my brother-in-law." He laughed. His wife Nancy turned and slapped him across the shoulder. "That's a lie," she spouted.

"She doesn't like him either," he teased.

"Harold!"

Morgan squeezed Molly's hand. She looked across the table and forced a smile. Her hand was clammy. "How about a drink?" he asked. She nodded that she did. He scooted his chair out and headed for the bar.

Outside the snow was still falling. Sirens were wailing in the distance. The night shift was working shorthanded because of the party and they were jammed with accidents and snow emergencies. Sarge and the assistant chief had volunteered to work because they were both teetotalers and wouldn't have attended anyway. Morgan wondered how Sarge was doing. He probably handled three or four accident calls a year. By now he must be biting off the end of his pipe.

Morgan ordered drinks and watched the table while he waited. Molly was chatting nicely with Harold's wife. Harold was up greeting Ian Rogers. Ian grabbed a chair from a nearby table and scooted in.

****

Roderick Constance was cruising north on I-55. Although the snow had subsided, the highway was still extremely slick. In spite of that he was making good time. His headlights illuminated the highway sign indicating Riverside was sixty miles away. His pallid eyes were tumid and his brow furrowed. The dim light from the instrument panel made his face look wicked, like someone possessed by satin himself. The emotion he bore for John Mason was unnatural. He hated Mason so much that he envisioned killing him in gruesome, torturous ways. He wanted to cut his throat and listen to him gurgle and gasp for air. He thought it would serve John right to douse him with gasoline and set him on fire. His adrenaline was hot as it surged through his veins. He felt strong and invincible. He wanted to butcher Mason, but he knew it would be best to do it swiftly and without disruption. Just kill him and be done with it.

****

Morgan rejoined the others at the table. Molly breathed a sigh of relief. Nancy Santino was a nice woman and she and Molly were communicating well, but still she wore that very detectable uneasiness. Ian studied Morgan for a moment. "Hello, Morgan," he said.

Morgan was happy to see that the state's attorney had chosen to sit with them. "Out rubbing elbows with troops tonight, I see," Morgan said.

"I wanted to compliment you on the gun shop burglary investigation you handled. Your methods were good, and the way you made the arrest was superb," said Ian.

"Just doing my job," Morgan said.

"He's being modest," Molly piped in, almost in her private, confident character. "He talked about it for a week." Morgan was pleased that she was opening up, but a little embarrassed that she "outed" him for crowing about his accomplishments.

The gun shop burglary had put a feather in Morgan's hat. It was a case that should have been handled by a detective, but CID had blown off a tip he had given them, leaving him holding the bag. If an informant handed you a tip and you failed to act, you surely wouldn't get another one. Sarge gave Morgan the go-ahead to follow up on the information when he learned the detectives had snubbed the lead. The chief detective, Ernie Linehurst, was on vacation, so things were being put on the back burner. Sarge didn't think the detectives were overworked and secretly hoped Morgan would humble them with a good collar. Morgan followed up on the lead, questioned the witnesses, tracked down the suspect, and made an arrest. When he made the stop, the suspect had one of the stolen guns on him. After an eventful interrogation he had a confession and recovered over two hundred guns. When Ernie returned from vacation he had a lot of praise for Morgan and harsh criticism for his crew. Morgan never intended to embarrass them, but Sarge was a little amused to see them eat crow.

Talking about it with Ian Rodgers made him a little uncomfortable. Handling compliments was harder than dealing with good-natured bantering. When Ed heard about the arrest he called Morgan and said, "Even a blind hog gets an acorn once in a while." They both laughed, but that was Ed's way of saying "good job." Morgan was a lot more comfortable with that kind of acknowledgment.

Right at the moment Morgan just wanted to avoid the subject, so he took Molly's hand and headed for the dance floor. Molly was strikingly beautiful, and Morgan was athletic and strong. They looked good together. Several people watched them as they worked their way inside the pack. Molly wanted to blend in, to be as discreet as she could be.

The band was playing "Brown Eyed Girl". The lights seemed instantly lower, and all the distractions were gone. Molly clung to Morgan not because he was strong or that she needed protection, but because she loved him, and it was shining in her eyes. The affection he felt for her at that moment was growing as they swayed to the music. He looked into her eyes. Her gaze was penetrating, but so soft and warm that he could almost feel it seeping deeply into an indescribable place he didn't even know existed. Her face was glowing. She had light, delicate freckles and her skin was like silk. She hated her freckles, but that was a mystery to Morgan. He thought they were beautiful, as was everything about her. How could such a beautiful, witty, and sophisticated woman have feelings of inadequacy? This must be how elegant women begin. They know they have something special, something desirable, but it frightens them. It's something so ever present that they can't run away from it. They want to stay in the background, afraid to be visible, knowing that someone will point them out and try to analyze them. Eventually they learn how to control the mystique and slowly it evolves into something powerful. Molly was one of those people but she didn't yet know it.

Morgan felt a little diminished when he thought about everything Molly had going for her. He was just a mere policeman. Sometimes he thought Molly could do better. He didn't have to fret about it long because his thoughts were interrupted by shouting. "There's trouble at the bar!"

Morgan glanced around to see Ed standing near a table in the barroom. His eyes were wild looking and a raging anger was burning in his features. Merle Bartels, the sixth ward alderman, was standing near Ed, all puffed up like a little red-faced blowfish. Bartels was the finance committee chairman, and the city council's resident bully. Morgan couldn't hear the conversation, but he was sure Ed was on the receiving end of an ass-eating. Morgan excused himself and hustled to intervene.

"You're a disgrace to the city," Bartels snorted. Morgan pushed his way through the growing crowd.

"Get Ed outta there," someone said.

Morgan took hold of Ed's arm but he pulled it away. "Don't, Morgan, this son of a bitch called me an asshole!"

"I never called you an asshole, I called you an ass," Bartels interrupted in a condescending sneer.

"People call you worse than that all the time, hell, I call you an asshole," Morgan said.

"Well, that's you, not this stuffed shirt son of a bitch!"

Bartels was a constant pain to the police department. In addition to being on the city council, he was an attorney and owned the largest accounting agency in town. He was born with a silver spoon in both ends and he knew about as much about the working class as he knew about the center of the earth. He hated the police department because they had power. Even the least of them could make him obey speed limits and pull him over for running stop signs. He believed they were inferior to him, and it was insulting that they possessed that kind of authority. He often called the dispatcher and ordered them to send cars to write parking tickets that were routinely overlooked. He pestered the chief about ordinance violations so obscure they were hardly known, much less enforced. The policemen recognized his nit-picking for what it was—a rich blowhard throwing his weight around.

Anyone with a modicum of foresight could have predicted trouble when Ed and Bartels occupied the same establishment at the same time. Ed would take criticism from his friends but he didn't extend the same privilege to others.

"Come on," Morgan urged.

"No!" Ed snapped through clinched teeth. "I wanna know

who this son of a bitch thinks he is!" He reached out and grabbed Bartels by his lapel and jerked him forward. Bartels blinked and sputtered as if someone had put a rattlesnake down his pants. He squirmed to free himself but he was no match for Ed. Whatever restraint Ed possessed had left on the evening train. A naïve searching was etched in the rage, a rummaging in his psych to try to understand how one human being could feel so elevated. Ed wouldn't tolerate it. He wanted Bartels to learn humiliation.

"You prick, this is the American Legion, not the fuck'n Ritz or the Château Le Bullshit! What are you doin' down here anyway, asshole!"

Morgan yanked Ed's fist loose from Bartels coat. "He'll be all right," he said turning Ed toward several policemen who were waiting to help restrain him.

"The hell he will!" Bartels shouted, shaking with anger. "I'll have his job!

"If his job is that easy to get, you can have mine too," Morgan said.

"I will! I know you, Cooper. What's that other asshole's name? I want his name and his badge number."

Morgan didn't answer. The onlookers were dispersing. Bartels was enraged. He jerked his coat and straightened it out. "I'll have their jobs," he huffed to a few people who were left, watching him in astonishment.

Norman Lewis stepped forward. "No, you won't, Bartels. What happens here, stays here—got it?"

Bartels was shocked. He glared at Norman. "I suppose you think the chief will overlook this kind of conduct? And I might even talk to the state's attorney over there to get a battery complaint started."

"I think the state's attorney will ignore it, and I don't believe the chief will hear about it," Norman said leaning into Bartels and glaring into his eyes. Bartels watched him in disbelief.

Norman continued. "You're a bully. You talk down to these men like you're something special, a regular little Lord Pomeroy. You got what you deserved and I have to say — it was entertaining to me." Bartels studied Norman, sensing there was substance in his words.

"I'll make it a little clearer. If you start anything over what happened here tonight, you'll never be the mayor of this city. I'll use every penny I own to make sure you're not." With that being said, Norman turned crisply and walked away. He knew how to handle men like that. Bartels was so puffed up on himself that any responsibility to do the right or moral thing wasn't even in the equation. It made him feel good to look down his nose at others. Self-aggrandizement was his motivation. Norman knew he would swallow his pride because he wanted to be mayor. Any ethical problem he had with Ed's behavior was insignificant. His feathers were ruffled and he wanted revenge, but weighed against the damage Norman could do to him politically, he would keep his mouth shut.

The band struck up a new song and people shuffled back onto the dance floor. Morgan followed some of the other policemen to take Ed into the kitchen where he would finally settle down. The ruckus was over, and he was thinking about the serious trouble he and Ed might have gotten themselves into as he and Molly made their way back to the dance floor. He looked down at Molly and saw a tear trickle down her cheek, but she was smiling.

"Why are you crying?" he asked.

"I've got the most wonderful man here," she said, impressed with the calming affect his presence had made. She didn't know that breaking up a fight or taking charge of a volatile situation was as routine to him as taking out the trash.

With that said, he forgot about feeling diminished and his troubles were put aside.

****

A green sedan sputtered onto the service drive of a gas station in Blue Valley, Illinois. A scruffy attendant sat at a table peering over a paperback novel. He pulled a tight sweatshirt down to cover his bulging belly. Roderick Constance got out of the car and waited. He paced and stared at the robust attendant. "Hey, buddy, I need gas," he shouted. The obese attendant rose from his chair, waddled to the window, and pointed to a sign that read, "Self-Serve." In 1975 self-service had just been implemented in Illinois. Prior to that, pumping your own gas was illegal.

Constance shot him a disdainful glance before starting to pump gas. When he was finished he left the car running and went to the telephone booth at the edge of the service drive. His breath was hot and steaming. It turned to ice as it made contact with the glass. He fished for a dime inside his pocket, and then dropped it into the coin slot. He pulled a torn piece of paper from his coat pocket. He dialed and waited. The phone clicked on the other end, and then, "Hello, John," he said. A long pause followed. Constance turned to check the clock on the service station wall. It was eleven thirty p.m.

Willoughby Hills College was on break for the holidays. Kids were home with their parents, wandering the streets of their hometowns, finding old friends, reminiscing old times, and catching up on their new lives. Graduating from high school, starting college, and beginning permanent jobs was monumental in a young life, but in reality they were only a few hours and a couple of late mornings in their own beds away from being just as they were before. Only their expectations had changed. John Mason was the exception. When he answered the phone that blustery winter night, his fate had been altered forever.

The conversation didn't take long. Constance wanted to know what Mason had told the police investigator about the burglary. Constance had been scheming against Mason even before he "ratted him out" on the stolen records, and he had evidence that Mason had possessed and used drugs, thanks to the late Tyrone Hightower. He threatened to expose him to the police department and report him to the school administration. Mason wasn't really a heavy drug user, but he had dabbled a little. He was ashamed of having been involved in drug use and would have changed if he had it to do over, but Constance knew about it and now he was paying for it in spades. He idolized his dad, and even the implication that he was a user struck fear into his heart. Constance wanted a meeting with him in a secluded location where they could discuss a deal. Mason agreed.

****

The snow had stopped in Willoughby Hills, but it was drifting against cars and filling up the alleyways. Morgan and Molly were breaking tradition as they hurried to Morgan's car. He was giving up his last dog status for the night. They had slipped out the back door and were headed home. Harold stuck his head out of the door and yelled, "Where ya goin'? The fun's just getting started."

Morgan pulled his coat tight against his ribs. "We're en route to the homestead," he shouted as they got into the car.

"Party pooper," Harold said as he waved good-bye.

****

Roderick Constance smacked his hands together and shifted from one foot to the other, fighting off the stinging cold seeping through his shoes. The wind whipped through the steel girders and swirled in gusts along the Kankakee River. Headlights appeared on the bridge above him. Brakes squeaked and a car came to a stop. Constance shined his flashlight as an athletic silhouette hurried down the levy. Soon John Mason was standing in front of him in the darkness.

"Okay, what do you want, you weird bastard?"

"I'll ask the questions, John. You'll answer 'em—got that!" Constance snapped. Mason waited, knowing that Constance held

67

all the cards. The sky had cleared and the moonlight glistened off the ice-covered river. It was as bright as midday but as eerie as a graveyard in the blackest of night. He felt vulnerable and weak standing there on the riverbank. Constance was in the shadows, now silently watching him.

Mason was getting nervous. He kicked the snow and waited. The silence was broken by a clicking sound. At first Mason was puzzled, but suddenly he realized that Constance was holding a gun. Mason tried to stay calm, to hide the fear, but it was raging through him like a freight train. "I'll take that gun away from you and stick it up your ass," he growled.

Constance stepped closer to him. "Sure you will," he snarled. There was no fear in Constance, no resignation about what he was going to do. Mason looked into those distorted features. His eyes were fixed but strangely empty—a miasma tic glare.

"Come on, Rod, somebody could get hurt," Mason said.

"That's the plan," Constance hissed.

John knew he was in trouble—more trouble than he had ever been in before. His heart was pounding with blood surging through his veins as he turned to run. He burst through the heavy snow and made a dash for the levy. A shot rang out and echoed across the river. John fell as blood gushed from a wounded thigh. Constance walked unhurriedly along the hastened tracks left in the snow. John whimpered and floundered, writhing from the pain. Constance approached him and cocked the gun again. John looked up into those hollow eyes. "Don't kill me, please. Please, Rod, don't. I don't want to die, please!"

His plea was in vain. Constance pulled the trigger, the shot fatal.

It was the end of John Mason.

CHAPTER ELEVEN

Golden sunshine glistened through ice crystals on the window. Molly was lying in bed washed in sunlight. Morgan pulled on his rubber boots, stood up, and inspected himself in the mirror. Molly watched him as he adjusted his belt and shoved the nine millimeter into his holster. She was usually gone by the time he was off to work, but because of the holidays she was sleeping in. Molly was a court reporter for a private firm, but most lawyers didn't like to schedule depositions close to Christmas, and she appreciated the time off.

Morgan snickered to himself as he thought about the expression on Bartels' face when Ed shook him like a rag doll. Morgan was like most policemen. It was his job to handle violent situations, to keep the peace and make arrests, but he thought there were times when violence was just as necessary as a plea for calm. The incident with Bartels was one example. Bartels had been hassling the police department like an agitated little Pomeranian. Ed had most likely put an end to it. He would be a hero to the patrol division, and Morgan thought the top brass would have a secret admiration for him too.

Morgan kissed Molly on her shoulder and headed off to work. When he stepped out into the bright sunlight, he saw Roderick Constance walking down the sidewalk. He recognized him instantly but didn't remember his name. His stringy, limp hair was flying feebly in the wind. His sallow skin was glaring in the bright morning sun. Morgan watched him as he approached. He waved and said, "Hey, officer, last night I ran my car off into a ditch over on 56th Street. It's been there all night. I didn't call it in because I had to walk all the way to my mom's house on McCleary Street." He didn't say, *I murdered my roommate last night.*

It wasn't a complete lie. He had run his car into a snowbank, but it was deliberate. Having a disabled vehicle was a real convenience under the circumstances. Happening upon Morgan here, although coincidental, it was perfect for his alibi.

"What time was that?" Morgan asked. He was suspicious of Constance, but he would treat him just as he would any other citizen reporting an incident.

"Oh, I guess it was about ten," Constance said.

Morgan guessed that the night shift was too busy to check that area because of all the snow-related accidents. They may have seen it, but maybe it just wasn't a priority to check it out. Morgan studied Constance. "Was it off the road?" he asked.

"Oh, yea, I wouldn't have left it there if it wasn't safe," he said. "I was just stuck in the ditch. No hazards or anything like that." Constance was as amiable as the greeter at the local Walmart.

Morgan looked at his watch. "The night shift had their hands full but they wouldn't have ignored a disabled vehicle unless it was safely off the road. "I'll run by there before I report in, and if it's not a hazard I'll give you till noon to move it. Maybe you could get your friends to push you out. Save some money."

"I will, officer. Thanks."

Morgan opened the door to the Fiat and started to get in, but as an afterthought he shouted to Constance as he was walking away. "What were you doing down there anyway? That's pretty much an out-of-the-way place."

"Just driving around," Constance said, still walking away.

Morgan surveyed the driveway. The landlord had cleared the snow and put down salt. There were dark places showing through to the asphalt. The Fiat spun and fishtailed until it hit the dry pavement on 18th Street. The deep ruts in the snow caused the car to swerve erratically from one furrow to another until he turned off Lincoln Avenue onto 56th Street where he saw the green Chevy sedan sitting sideways in a snow-packed ditch. He stopped and looked at the car for a long moment. He remembered that Constance had said he was stuck at around ten p.m. There were beads of ice on the windshield, but there wasn't any snow on the car. If it was just sitting there hung up in the ditch, there should have been snow accumulated on the hood and rooftop. He scribbled down the license number, made note of the discrepancy, and went back to his car.

When Morgan arrived at City Hall, he flung the door open and the parking tickets swirled into the air. He gathered them and put them back into the pile. He expected Gladys to complain about his carelessness but she was quiet. Her head was lowered and her expression was gloomy.

"Hey! Lose your best friend," he said.

Her face didn't brighten. "Morning, Morgan," she said.

"What's the matter, Gladys?"

"Oh, that bastard of a son-in-law beat on Milly after they got home from the party last night. She's got a black eye! That no good…" She stopped before she broke into a rant.

Morgan tried to comfort Gladys, but she was as any mother would be in a situation like that. She cried a little and bemoaned the fact that her daughter had caught a losing hand. She knew Leonard would be fired if a police report were made, leaving things in a bigger mess than they were now. Morgan promised to have a talk with Leonard off the record, and that made her feel better.

Morgan stood at the entrance into the squad room. He saw

Roy sitting at the radio desk. He was wearing a long face too. He gave a swift kick against the steel plate, the buzzer released a small blurp in protest, and the door swung open. Roy glanced over his glasses apathetically.

"What's wrong with everybody around here? I can't even get a rise out of Roy," Morgan said peeking around the corner into the com room. Roy looked over his glasses again but didn't speak. The buzzer rang again and he spun around and hit the bypass switch, trying to beat the forcible entry.

It was Ed pushing his way past the squad room door. "Damn, it's cold out there," he snorted. Generally, Ed was as rumpled as a Cabbage Patch doll, but today his uniform was freshly starched and pressed. His brass was shining like a new dime and his leather was glistening.

"Where we having coffee, partner?" he said.

"What do ya mean, *partner*? You're eight hours early, aren't you?" Morgan asked.

"Didn't they tell you, Morg, old boy, we're teaming up!"

"What are you talking about?" Morgan asked suspiciously.

"They cracked up two cars last night. Too many cops, not enough cars. They wanted volunteers to double up so I did the honors," Ed said.

Morgan grinned. He thought it had more to do with the Bartels incident than with damaged police cars. Most of the time when there was trouble hanging over a young cop's head, they sent him to Sarge — back to the henhouse to take refuge under his wing.

"What's with the good uniform? It wouldn't have anything to do with going in front of the chief this morning, would it?"

"Hell no! If I was going in front of the chief, I'd have worn my black commando pants and high water boots. The chief don't scare me," he piped.

Morgan changed the subject. It was futile to talk seriously

about the Bartels incident with Ed. He probably didn't remember most of it anyway. "Do you remember that kid you arrested at the college last month? The one with the stringy hair and skinny as a pretzel."

"Which one? I arrested a shit-pot full of 'em. They all look alike to me."

"The one whose roommate called the college president at home," Morgan said.

"Oh, yeah, his name was Roderick Constance," Ed said without hesitation.

"Yeah, that's it," Morgan said as he turned to go into the radio room. Morgan handed a sheet from his note pad to Roy. "Run this, it's a car in the ditch over on 56th Street."

Roy pecked out the license number on his Western Union teletype, a piece of equipment that was on its way to becoming a thing of the past. It took about three minutes for most inquiries, and that was considered a modern marvel five years earlier, but now it was obsolete. The new CR-2's could get the same information in about ten seconds. Morgan suspected it was just the beginning of computer use in law enforcement. Willoughby Hills wouldn't be receiving the new technology until they moved into their law enforcement complex in 1979.

Roy cut the tape and inserted it into the machine. It rattled and clattered as the record search was being sent. Morgan waited. When it was returned Roy ripped off the printout and handed it to him. He studied it looking for anything unusual, but it only confirmed that it was a 1972 Chevy sedan belonging to Roderick Constance. Morgan explained the situation to Roy, advising him that he had given Constance until noon to remove the car from the ditch. "If there are calls on it, tell 'em we've got it covered," Morgan said as he sauntered back into the squad room, unaware of the importance of the information he had acquired. The more critical bit of information in Morgan's early morning contact was that Constance had stumbled upon the place where Morgan lived.

Bob Fulmer came into the squad room and took a boxing stance. "Hey, it's Muhammad Ali," he said, addressing Ed.

Ed rolled his eyes and laughed. "News travels fast," he said.

"I was there, Ed, but I guess you were too drunk to know it."

Sarge came into the squad room and the three officers fell silent. Sarge stamped his feet on a frayed rug near the doorway to his office. He walked over to the coffeemaker, casually retrieved his cup from the shelf, and wiped it with a paper towel. Roy's radios crackled in the quiet. Sarge poured coffee into his cup and sat it on a worktable. He glanced into the com room. "Morning, Roy," he said.

Roy acknowledged him. Morgan and Bob slurped their coffee. Ed wore an anxious expression. Sarge tamped the tobacco into his pipe and lit it. The smoke circled around his head as he puffed. He sniffed and bit down on the mouthpiece. Holding the pipe between his teeth, he finally spoke. "I guess you guys want to know if I've spoken to the chief and if he knows about Bartels. Weellll, he called me this morning, and to dispel any doubts you might have, he knows it all. He said he knew it last night even before he went to bed. Fortunately, it wasn't Bartels who told him."

Ed snorted as he tuned to refill his coffee cup.

Roy continued. "He wasn't happy, to say the least, but there's a bright side. He's not bringing Ed up on charges unless Bartels presses the issue, so let's just hold our breath."

Ed looked at Morgan and huffed. "Hell, I've been holding ever since old Moses kicked off his shoes!" Nervous laughter permeated the room.

Sarge laughed too. "I'm glad I wasn't there, but it doesn't matter, you guys always cause trouble for the old Sarge anyway," he stated wryly. Sarge started for his office but looked over his shoulder. "It might not be a bad idea if you three weren't in here drinking coffee when the chief comes in."

Morgan slapped Ed on the back and said, "Let's go get 'em, partner." They hung their cups on the hook-lined shelf and headed for the door.

Harold was coming in as they were leaving. "Hi, champ," he said. Ed rolled his eyes.

They were off to the squad car and then onto routine patrol. The sunshine sparkled through snow-filled tree branches, and kids threw snowballs at each other at the bus stop. The sky was blue all the way to the horizon, the air had lost its chill. Water ran out from under snow piles and trickled into the gutter.

Ed slumped down in the car seat, tilted his head back, and pulled his hat down to cover his eyes. "I didn't get a hell of a lot of sleep last night," he said.

Morgan eyed him curiously. "You don't really think you're going to sit over there and sleep, do you?"

Ed opened one eye and peered out from under his hat. He looked like a fat lazy cat trying to ignore a ruckus in the room. A city snowplow rumbled in from the opposite direction, pelting the windshield with a gusher of snow. Morgan swerved and Ed was thrown against the door. His hat bounced around the car and finally lit on the floor between his feet. "I guess not," he said as he sat upright.

The day wore on as Morgan and Ed chatted between calls. There were a few accidents left from the backup log—a neighborhood quarrel over a smoking garbage fire, and an ambulance assist from a slip-and-fall in front of the library. It was a day of small incidents. Ed's headache was gone. His recovery started once he heard that the chief was ignoring the Bartels episode. With that out of the way as far as they were concerned, arguing over their favorite greasy spoon for lunch was the most pressing issue on their agenda. Morgan wanted the Tiz Right, and

Ed was vying for Franky's House of Eats. Before they could settle the issue, they were dispatched to take a report at the Lincoln County Developmental Center.

"Ahhh, shit!" Ed moaned. "I didn't want to go to the state school before lunch," he bellowed.

Morgan stared at his friend. "Ed, sometimes you can be a real asshole," he said, taking sides with the mentally retarded.

"Don't lecture me, Cooper, I know my faults, I admit it. I hate them crazy sons of bitches!" He rolled his eyes and tightened his lips over his teeth. His features revealed an expression as if to insinuate there was honor in his position.

As they arrived at the state school, an iron gate swung open and a blue-clad security guard waved them through. (In 1975, the mentally handicapped were treated like prisoners). The brick streets inside the high chain-link fence had already been cleared. The neatly packed snow ridges alongside the curb was evidence that the residents had been diligent in getting the snow removed. Several patients now stood resting on their shovels breathing steam into the air. Their empty faces seemed hollow but still revealed an innocent curiosity. Their eyes followed the squad car to the administration building where it stopped in the circle driveway. Handicapped students were gathered in a group nearby motionlessly studying the squad car. One middle-aged man with sunken cheeks had a stocking cap pulled down so tightly on his head that his huge ears were bent into a fold. Ed watched one of the students approach the car. He stuck out his tongue and wrinkled his nose. The resident tried to match Ed's expression. He came close to getting it right but his eyes bulged and his brow furrowed into an expression, leaving the impression that somewhere in the back of his mind he was asking himself what the hell he was doing.

Ed turned to Morgan and said, "Man, he's crazy."

"He's a retarded kid, Ed," Morgan protested. He didn't want

to find humor in Ed's asinine comments, but the corners of his mouth were twitching to grin. (The word "retarded" in those days had not been tarnished by political correctness).

"Yeah, he sure is," Ed said. Morgan gave him a bewildered glance. Ed thumped his knuckles against the window to regain the kid's attention, placed his thumbs in his ears, and wiggled his fingers. The student followed suit. Ed cackled and Morgan suppressed a smile.

"Awh, come on, Morg, it's fun. This kid's funny, man! Look at him, he thinks this is a sideshow!"

Morgan shook his head disapprovingly. Ed grinned.

"Let's go take the report," Morgan said.

Ed argued that someone had to stay with the squad car to be sure the students didn't tamper with it. Morgan went inside alone. As he disappeared inside the doorway, Ed was making a face at another student. The student's arms drooped at his sides and saliva drooled from his lip. Ed smiled and bugged out his eyes. The student stared at him indolently.

Ed tired of making faces and turned his attention to a huge icicle hanging from the downspout on the administration building. His thoughts were interrupted when a well-aimed snowball smashed into the passenger window at eye level. He instinctively pulled his neck in like a turtle and recoiled. He turned quickly as a lethargic-looking resident was brushing snow from his gloves.

"I'll be a son of a bitch," Ed said aloud, cocking his head in disbelief. A second snowball soared in from a different direction and spread across the window.

"I don't believe this shit," Ed sputtered as he peered through the slush. The students were screeching with laughter. One kid held his side as he bent over in hysterics. Ed rolled the window down and the laughter went silent. The students went completely somber as quickly as a light leaving a room at the flick of a switch.

"Knock it off," Ed ordered.

A student reached down to retrieve a handful of snow. In a quick jerky movement he flung the snow into the air. A mist floated through the car window and settled on Ed's face.

"You goddamned hardhead, no wonder you're out here in the nuthouse!" Ed exclaimed. The same student went for a reload. "Hey, don't do that," Ed warned. The student let fly with an accurate toss. Ed's shoulder was covered with snow. Ed tightened his lips and grimaced. He jumped from the car and stamped his foot in an intimidating gesture. The students dropped their arms to their sides and stood inertly. Their faces were as innocent-looking as the family dog after a long weekend of ravaging the house while the folks were gone. Ed counted eleven of them. "What are you guys doing, ganging up on me?" They looked at each other in quick spasmodic movements, each of them searching the other's faces, excited by the endeavor but completely puzzled at the same time.

Ed was satisfied that he had the last word as he turned to get back into the squad car. Just then he was smacked in the back with another well-thrown icy sphere. The residents howled with laughter. Some cheered and clapped feebly. Ed reached down and packed snow into a firm round ball. The students just stood there like ducks in a row. There wasn't a smile on any one of their eleven faces. They could descend from giggling fits to complete despondency in a tick.

Ed watched them sympathetically. Finally, he said, "Ah, shit," as he dropped his snowball to the ground. As soon as he did, several residents picked up snow and he was hit with another barrage. Ed chuckled. "All right, you guys, I give up. Truce, truce, you savie? I quit, you win." He took one of them by his hand. "Here, gimme five," he said. The student strained to understand. "Gimme five," he said again. "Go ahead," he urged. Steam rose from the nostrils of the onlookers. They cocked their heads and studied Ed. Finally, one of them tapped Ed's hand lightly.

"Goddamn, you did it," Ed shouted. The students laughed. Ed turned to the larger part of the group. "Come on, gimme five," he said with an outstretched hand. One by one the students approached him and slapped his hand. They giggled and hooted uncontrollably. One reluctant kid ran up and slapped Ed's hand, at the same time turning to make his retreat. Ed laughed. "And they say you guys are crazy, huh?"

As the last student crossed his palm, those who were first had already lost interest. Ed brushed off the snow and stamped his feet on the brick pavement. Morgan had finished his report and was returning to the squad car. "How'd you get your good uniform wet?" he asked.

"I don't know," Ed said.

Morgan looked at him suspiciously. "You weren't outside playing with the kids, were you?"

"Hell no! You won't catch me playing with them crazy bastards," he spouted.

As the squad car rolled through the metal gate, several students waved and pointed.

After Ed was initiated into the mentally handicapped snowball club, they busied themselves on routine patrol. They wrote a few stop sign violations and towed an abandoned car left in a snowbank. Like most of their days, it was winding down without much ado. There was an old saying that police work was "hours of boredom and moments of horror." Most days were just hours of boredom.

Morgan hadn't told Ed that he intended to have a private talk with Leonard Wilson. He knew that Ed would insist on being with him when he did it, but Morgan wanted to go solo. He was confident that his methods would get results, but he didn't know if there would be fallout. He was nervous about it. Morgan wanted to be a model police officer. He had high expectations of himself, but what he was about to do didn't fit into that persona. He was about to have the infamous "talk" that policemen frequently have with wayward citizens.

As he walked into the city garage, he was blinded by the sudden change in the light. The garage was dimly lit, the smell of old oil and faint gas fumes hung in the air. There were motor parts and tools laying haphazardly everywhere. As Morgan's eyes adjusted to the light he saw two squad cars with broken headlights and crumpled bumpers. Bob Crabbits was wedged beneath one of them grumbling about a stubborn bolt that wouldn't break loose. There was a single lightbulb on the end of an extension cord shining from beneath the car providing the only light. Bob was covered with grease and oil, and his face was a burnt umber of grime. "Hey, Morgan, what's happening?" he said.

Morgan didn't make small talk, he just asked if Leonard was in the meter repair room. Bob said that he was. Morgan walked to the back of the garage, negotiating fan belts, hanging tailpipes, and stacks of used tires. Leonard had his back to him, standing in front of a workbench beneath a hanging lightbulb. He was examining a Playboy centerfold. When he saw Morgan he recoiled and tried to conceal it. The fact that he was looking at a picture of a beautiful naked woman was the least of his flaws.

"Look what I found in the garage trash, Morgan. I think Bob put it there," he said.

Morgan stopped for a moment, trying to decide if he really wanted to descend into a pool of self-righteousness. He vowed that he would never do anything overbearing because he had the authority to do it. But now as his eyes were fixed on Leonard, his thoughts were on Gladys and the hopeless expression she was wearing when she talked about Leonard battering Millie. He remembered seeing Millie on occasion wearing bruises on her face, avoiding eye contact with him, embarrassed that she was a victim. That image towed him over that invisible line. Morgan stepped into the room, grabbed Leonard by the shirt collar, and with an open hand he delivered a swift blow across Leonard's face. A "bitch slap," the most humiliating assault one man can bestow upon another. Morgan didn't like the feeling rushing through him. It excited and disturbed him at the same time. It made him feel stronger, more powerful, but wild and out of control. Leonard cowered away in fear.

"Is that how you hit Millie!" he growled. He didn't recognize his own voice.

"I never hit her," Leonard cried.

Morgan shifted his grip from Leonard's shirt collar to his throat. "You're a fuck'n liar," he barked. He had forgotten the invisible line defining right from wrong. He tightened his grip as Leonard gasped for air. "If you ever hit her again, I'll tear your throat out!" he shouted. He wanted to hit him again. He wanted to beat him bloody, but more than anything he wanted him degraded.

Leonard spoiled his plans by begging. "I won't, Morgan. I'll never hit her again. Don't hurt me," he whined. He looked at Leonard for a long time, trying to decide whether to hit him again, finally restraining himself and releasing his grip.

That was it. He had done what he thought he would never do, but now it was over and he swore to himself that he would never do it again. He left the garage, knowing he was different now. He wasn't the same man he had been when he went in.

Later, when Morgan told Ed what he had done, he was ashamed. Ed didn't think it was a big deal. He was jealous that Morgan had gotten the honor.

Chapter Twelve

In a small brown house at 1811 McLeary Street, Roderick Constance scanned through the *Chicago Tribune*, glancing at the subheadings. He licked his fingers and turned the pages. There wasn't even a footnote about John Mason's failure to return to his family after his late-night visit beneath the Kankakee River Bridge. Constance didn't know whether to be relieved or to feel neglected that his handiwork hadn't made it into print.

The Constance living room was drab and dingy. The curtains were drawn with the only light discernibly creeping in around the curtains. Constance brushed back his stringy hair and sighed. He dropped the newspaper on the floor and crossed the room. Frances Constance entered the room and raised the shades. She glanced inquisitively at her son. "Why do you sit here in the dark, Rod?" she asked.

"It's so damned dirty in here, I'd rather not be able to see it," he snapped. His impudence had no bounds.

"Well, I have to work, son. I'm tired when I get home," she said defensively.

"I'd rather stay at school all the time, then I wouldn't have to look at this dump," Constance snorted.

Frances retrieved a moldy, half-eaten sandwich from the fiberboard coffee table where Constance had left it on a previous visit. She wrapped it in a napkin he had discarded on the floor. "You could help by picking up after yourself, son," she said almost diffidently.

"I do that at school," he snorted.

Frances lowered her head and continued to tidy up the small living room. "I don't see why you can't just stay here and drive to school. And that business with the police — the charges about those record albums they say you took — I know you have the public defender, but I have to take off work...and the money..." she moaned.

"Christ!" Constance snapped.

Frances glanced at her son, not surprised by his insolence. "I want to be in court with you," she said.

He stared at her with a distant look in his eyes, pondering something beyond the dreary walls. "You don't have to go anymore," he said. She hesitated in her halfhearted attempts at cleaning, perplexed by his declaration.

"They don't have a case. I only have to go to the next hearing because they're dropping the whole thing. Ingelman says I should be there. They don't have a witness. John Mason's run away from home — left the country — flew the coop," Constance said.

Frances watched her son, confused by what he was telling her, but she believed him. She was blind to his dishonesty, or at least immune to it. She had lived her entire life for him, and her wage for it was pain. Her attempts to save him from himself garnered nothing but disrespect and disobedience. She had started out with two strikes against her, and now had bottomed out. Although Roderick wasn't the sole reason for her unhappiness, still he was like an anvil on her back. She had begun her life in Willoughby Hills' poorest section and had never gotten out. It wasn't like the slums of Chicago, but poverty here was just as incapacitating. She quit school when she was sixteen and started waiting tables at the Glasgow Inn, a dinky little dinner owned by a Scottish immigrant. She married the first man who came along, and unfortunately it was Roderick Constance, Sr. He was a construction worker who drifted into town looking for work. Frances invited him to stay with her, and he accepted because he was desperate. He needed a place to sleep and fill his stomach. The combination was predictable. A short courtship, a marriage that lasted only a few months, an unwanted pregnancy, and a woman left alone in despair. Now she had a brown tar-papered house, monumental debts, and a son who provided nothing but discourtesy.

Roderick hadn't come to discuss his criminal case with Frances. There was something else motivating him. He needed her to remember the date and to know the details of December 15th. As far as he was concerned, she was a moron who was too stupid to live, but he needed her.

"Mom…Mother…*Frances*," he said sarcastically, pausing each time he called her by the three different names, resolving not to imply that speaking to her parried a modicum of respect or affection. "Last night was December 15th, I was here watching *Dallas*, just in case the cops come calling."

It was embarrassing to lower himself from his lord-like psychological perch to implore a favor, but he struggled through it.

"Rod, my television is broke. You know that," Frances said meekly.

"Frances, if the cops start asking questions about me, I was here watching *Dallas*!"

"Okay, son, I'll remember."

CHAPTER THIRTEEN

December was harsh with relentless cold and mammoth snowstorms. Enormous piles of snow engulfed everything. It had turned dirty after endless days of subfreezing temperatures and looked more like gray ash heaps scattered across the city. All across the state dry snow was carried over the prairie unobstructed, burying small towns and making travel impossible. It was a busy time for the police department. Cabin fever had become an epidemic as family disputes became a nightly occurrence. Sarge's shift now included Ed after the chief determined that he needed some of the old Sarge's influence.

They were just beginning their first month on the night shift. Tony Marcelli was the night shift's communications officer. Joe Bernardi was the crime prevention officer, whose position was a combination of detective and concentrated crime patrol officer. Joe had an elaborate crime prevention van with all the latest equipment. He had eavesdropping devices, which were illegal without a court order; a nightscope with infrared lens, still packed in the shipping parcel; fingerprint equipment, which he was not qualified to use; and other various crime-fighting devices that had never been utilized. The van was loaded with spotlights on both sides, high powered alley lights, and strobe lights pointing in every direction. The crime prevention van had more candle

85

power than the utility company. It was equivalent to a modern day CSI mobile investigative unit.

Joe's assignment was to assist the Criminal Investigations Division with stakeouts and other necessary details. The rest of Joe's time was spent helping the night shift answer radio calls. Joe was the crime prevention unit, part and parcel. The concept behind the crime prevention unit was good, but the problem was that Joe was too lazy to do his job. Instead he spent his time at the complaints window gassing away the hours with Tony. Ed had dubbed them Tony "Macaroni" Marcelli, and Joe "Brainyard" Bernard. Neither the patrol division nor the detectives claimed Joe, and he considered that an advantage.

It wasn't unusual for large departments to "lose" or bury their incompetents, but the Willoughby Hills Police Department was too small to effectively obscure their inferiors. In Joe's case they had tried. They had given him a title, some equipment, and presently they were ignoring him. Joe was fifty-two years old and marking time to retirement. Joe had no interest in the department and was delighted when he was shuffled aside.

Joe's hours were permanent. He worked the eleven to seven shift Monday through Friday. On weekends he took the van home with him, theoretically to restock it and clean the equipment. Since he never used anything in it, his weekends were his own.

Joe's only real responsibility was to be the "keeper of the keys." It wasn't an official title, but again a phrase Ed used when he was referring to Joe. "Where's the keeper of the keys?"

The response was always the same. "Awh, he's somewhere goofing off."

He had a key to every municipal building in the city. The city clerk's office key was on his substantial key ring along with the jail key, the city garage, and the dog pound. The only two keys he used frequently were for the door to the jail kitchen and the Coca-Cola machine in the hallway.

Naturally the jail kitchen was posted off limits, but the coke machine key was obtained by honest means. Napoleon Bonaparte Jones, the black Coca-Cola serviceman, had given Joe a copy. Since both the day shift and evening shifts were routinely gypped by the battered machine, Napoleon thought free Cokes for the night shift was a fair exchange. Joe was equally generous. He provided sandwiches from the jail kitchen two or three times a week and complementary Cokes.

It was late in December, and the apples, oranges, and other goodies local citizens had delivered to the officers for Christmas had diminished. The empty orange crates were proof that it had been a good Christmas season, but now the pickings were getting lean. With all the candy, fruit and baked goods lying around the squad room during the holidays, Joe had been dormant in his role as gofer. Tonight he was preparing to resume his duties.

At shift change Joe met Ed at the squad room door. "Hey, Ed, I'm taking orders tonight, want anything?" he asked.

"Brainyard, you know me, by two a.m., I'd eat a fried pig's asshole."

Joe took a stubby pencil from his shirt pocket and pretended to write on his hand, "One pig's asshole," he said and chuckled, quite amused at himself.

Morgan and Sarge both arrived at the entrance to the lobby at the same time. Morgan held the door while Sarge balanced his briefcase, his pipe tobacco pouch, and his checklist in one arm. In the other he carried a cardboard box filled with twelve clinking bottles of Scottish whiskey.

"I could have helped you with that," Morgan said as he made a feeble attempt to take some of Sarge's load.

"You've waited too long now, it's easier to do it myself," Sarge said as he pulled away from Morgan's grasp. They went through the same production when they reached the squad room door. As they continued up the hallway, the load was slipping and swaying as though it were alive, trying to escape Sarge's grip. Morgan tried again to assist but Sarge spewed out an animal-like snarl and bit down on his pipe.

"You hardheaded old—" Morgan stopped and Sarge glared at him over his newly acquired glasses.

Sarge dropped the box and the whisky bottles rattled inside. "Wilson's Wrecker Service sent this as a New Year's present. Sign your name and take one," Sarge said. "And if somebody wants mine, they can have it too. I never touch the stuff."

"I'll take yours," Joe piped. No one objected. Morgan donated his and Joe graciously accepted that too.

"It's a wonder the tires on the van hold up with all the perishables he totes home," Morgan said, patting Joe's stomach.

"You kids will learn when you've been around as long as I have that you get what you can take out of this job," Joe spouted unrepentantly. Joe knew every establishment where cops were given a discount or a free meal. He never took anything illegally, but he never passed up a free offer either.

"I never turn anything down. I don't want to hurt these waitresses' feelings, you know," Joe said.

"Harold better keep an eye on you, Joe, with such sauve' you might just nose him out of a job," Sarge said facetiously. These were the days when a free apple for a beat cop was the rule, not the exception. Sarge accepted things as they were, but he didn't approve. He didn't like gifts from the wrecker services, free coffee from friendly waitresses, or an apple from a fruit vendor. He didn't like it, but he didn't confront the issue either. It was a problem that needed to be addressed, but Sarge didn't want to be the man to do it.

"Public relations! I coulda had that job," Joe snorted.

Morgan glanced at him. It was probably true. Joe could talk the cigar right out of the mouth of a wooden Indian. Morgan mused that it was such a waste. How could a man devote his time and energy so diligently to such bullshit?

"How fucking long has it been since you had a court case, Brainyard?" Ed asked.

"Two years," Joe said without hesitation. The others laughed. Joe's inactivity was a joke. He hadn't handled a serious call for so long that he'd forgotten how it was done.

Joe cocked his head in thought. "I'll tell you guys something. I quit going to court for a good reason." They all smiled and waited. "When Ian Rogers was elected state's attorney, he had a unique viewpoint about law enforcement. One night I had the opportunity to sit down with him over a drink. He was down at the Rusty Bucket rubbing elbows with the less fortunate. I just happened to be there.

"The beer was probably free," Bob snickered.

"As a matter of a fact, Ian picked up the tab," Joe said proudly. He went on to state that he and Ian spent most of their time talking about what needed to done to make the police department better. "Of course that was before you kids came on and straightened everything out," he said.

It was common knowledge that Ian had the opinion, in his first few years in office, that light sentences and social services were the way to go. Exposure to the job and introduction to the criminal element had hardened him as time marched on.

"Back then Ian thought we should use Notice to Appears for almost everything, and whenever we could we should release violent juveniles to their parents," Joe said. "He even thought we should just cut some people loose without charges on some offenses, unless of course they were recapitulators."

Sarge sucked on his pipe and eyeballed Joe suspiciously. "So what does that all mean, Joe?" he asked.

"Well, I thought if that was the deal, then why bother making an arrest? I'd just save him the trouble," Joe said.

Sarge smiled and rolled his eyes.

Ed said that Joe's story had made him tired and he was considering going home. He pretended to head for the door.

"Not so fast, Ed, I've got a call coming in," Tony shouted from the radio room. He jotted down the information in his logbook. "There's a man at 890 Loren Street holed up in his bedroom, says he's going to kill himself."

"How many of these are we going to get this month?" Morgan snorted.

Ed smiled. "Since we're getting so good at this stuff, we'll take it, huh, Morgan."

Joe glanced at Sarge. "I'll go along and take care of these boys for you, Lloyd," he said, punching Sarge on his arm.

"Sure, sure," Sarge said, thinking Joe was only kidding. When the three officers were halfway down the hallway, Sarge realized that Joe was actually volunteering to answer a call. "He's really serious, so keep the old walrus out of trouble," he called after them.

When Joe left the station his lights were visible all throughout the downtown area. The red and blue beams bounced off the shop windows like a prism. His siren wailed as he careened through traffic recklessly. By the time Morgan and Ed arrived, Joe was standing alongside his van waiting for them as though he had been there since noon.

When Morgan started toward the house, Joe asked him somberly what he wanted him to do. He was as solemn as a rookie on his first call. "I don't know, Joe. Just listen and jump in if you think we need help," Morgan said.

Morgan studied the house. It was small and had a front porch. He tried to analyze where inside the bedroom might be located. There were lights shining through the windows on all sides. He hoped the man wouldn't be able to see them coming. He had never been on a threatened suicide where the person making the threat didn't think it was a good idea to take a cop with him.

At that point Ed approached him. "There's two windows on each side of the house and a rear entrance. I'll go inside and you two cover the windows. If he comes out shooting, give me a chance to get out of the way," Morgan said. He was starting to get a queasy feeling in his stomach. Sometimes these things went bad.

When Morgan reached the front porch he peeked in the window. There was a stubby overweight woman pacing in the living room just inside the door. She chewed her fingernails and wore an expression as if the end of the world was only moments away.

Morgan pecked on the glass and she flinched at the sound. Her eyes widened with fright, but in a flicker they filled with pleading. She rushed to the door and opened it with shaking hands. "Please hurry, I think he's gonna kill his self," she moaned.

"What kind of gun is it?" Morgan asked.

"I don't know, it's just a little short gun. Please hurry."

Morgan stepped into the living room. It was dirty with plenty of stuff to stumble over. He pushed a TV dinner tray aside with his foot. "Turn off that TV," he said, pointing as if the woman might not know where it was.

He examined the layout of the house. There was an empty room off the living room and a dining room between them and the kitchen. The bedroom was adjacent to the dining room.

"Our bedroom is right through there," the woman pointed. Ed and Joe entered the house and were waiting for instructions.

A cat circled Joe's leg, oblivious to the danger. "Scat, goddamnit!" Joe barked, kicking the cat a good two feet into the air.

Both Joe and Ed were senior to Morgan, but his judgment was keen. Ed trusted him, knowing his decisions were always sound. Joe had forgotten everything he had ever learned and was grateful that Morgan was giving the orders.

"Ed, go back outside and come in through the back door. When I call him out he'll have to come into the dining room. If he turns toward me, you rush him from behind. If he turns toward you, I'll hit him from this side," Morgan said. Ed nodded and hurried to do as Morgan had suggested. Joe stayed with Morgan, nervously rubbernecking over his shoulder.

After an ample amount of time passed for Ed to get into position, Morgan entered the dining room. He could hear his heart beating softly in his ear. He glanced over his shoulder and saw the chubby woman following him. Her hands were trembling and her cheeks wet with tears. "Go outside and wait," Morgan ordered in a whisper.

"Please, he's all I got," she pleaded. "He wouldn't do this if he wudn't drunk," she said.

"Okay. We'll take care of him, now go outside," Morgan said, this time more sternly. The woman watched him through tortured eyes. "We won't hurt him, ma'am," Morgan assured her. Joe took her by the arm and guided her through the living room and deposited her on the porch. He tiptoed back inside to rejoin Morgan.

Morgan listened intently. He could hear mumbling coming from the bedroom. He cocked his ear, thinking he heard the clicking sound of a revolver being cocked. His eyes searched the kitchen for Ed. "What's keeping you, Ed?" he muttered under his breath. A cold gust of air streamed through the room. Morgan glanced to see the plump woman standing with the outside door open. She wanted to do as she had been told but couldn't restrain her emotions. She shivered and bit her lip in a nervous fit.

"His name's Bob Turner," she said, trying to be helpful. Morgan shook his head approvingly but held his hand up, signaling for her to go back outside. She held her ground in the doorway.

"Mr. Turner, this is the police, would you come out of the

bedroom, please? We need to talk to you," Morgan said. There was silence. Morgan could hear a clock ticking somewhere inside the room. He waited for a reply. He could hear Joe breathing. His own breath was coarse and deep.

Joe's eyes were wide in anticipation. "You guys can have this shit. Now I remember why I left the patrol division," he said.

Morgan glared at him in disbelief. "Shuuuuh," he scolded.

At that time the bedroom door creaked slowly open. A balding man in his late sixties clad only in his boxer shorts, filled the doorway. An enormous stomach hung over his underwear and his eyes floated behind thick glasses. His eyes swam around inside the frames, scanning the room looking for his petitioner, and finally his gaze fell upon Morgan.

Morgan sized him up. His balance was poor, and he swayed like a bowling pin about to topple. No doubt he was in a drunken stupor. Morgan wondered if he should just rush him, but he chose to wait. He had been in many situations just like this and a good blitz was as effective as anything.

"Who invited you here?" he barked. Morgan glanced through the kitchen. Still no Ed.

"Your wife did, Mr. Turner. She's worried about you."

"She worries too much," Turner growled.

Morgan was worried too. It was time for Ed to be in position. Something must have gone wrong.

"Have you got a gun?" Morgan asked.

"Fuck yes, I got a gun," the fat man growled. His hand was obscured by his huge belly.

Morgan gingerly moved his hand to his nine millimeter, just resting his palm on the holster.

"Well, put it down and come on out and talk to us," Morgan said, using a firm and calming voice.

The man shook his head stubbornly.

Joe touched Morgan's shoulder. "Let's just leave him here.

Give him some space."

Morgan shot Joe a glance that would have said, *Shut the fuck up*. Joe shrugged as though he had just made a viable recommendation and had been inappropriately slapped down.

"Where is Ed?" he snapped, still not taking his eye off the obese man.

"If he makes a move, duck into that empty room over there, Joe," Morgan said. He was beginning to feel uneasy about Joe's presence there. "Fuck, I don't need this," he whispered to himself. Bob Turner wobbled just a little. Morgan sensed that something was about to go down. He stepped closer to the archway separating the two rooms. Suddenly the man's enormous stomach swung around and a fat hand popped up and there it was—a 357 Magnum! Morgan instinctively reeled, unholstering his nine millimeter. He pointed it at the man's chest. "Halt!" he shouted.

Turner stopped but kept the gun aimed at Morgan's face. "Put down the gun," Morgan ordered. Now the sound of blood was pounding in his ears.

"I won't put it down," Turner slobbered, taking another step in Morgan's direction.

"Stop!" Morgan shouted again. He searched the kitchen for Ed. Time had slowed down. Everything seemed to be moving at a snail's pace. The old man took another step in his direction. Morgan's eyes widened. He could feel them bulging in his eye sockets. "Put the gun down or I'll kill you," he yelled.

"Go ahead, kill me! I'll kill you!" he shouted defiantly. Morgan aimed at Turner's head, simultaneously cocking the hammer on the nine. He made the decision to shoot. He had no other choice. He shouted incoherently, "Stopppppp!" He waited endlessly for the discharge. Then just as quickly as he had decided to fire, his finger withdrew from the trigger. He was no longer acting on logic but on instinct alone. The old man had staggered and dropped the gun to his side. Before he could even think,

Morgan was reacting. He moved rapidly to a position behind the archway. He retrained the gun on Robert Turner's chest. Turner was regaining his balance and his control of the 357.

At that same instant Ed charged from the kitchen with his shoulder lowered. He struck Turner in the lower torso like a defensive back with a full head of steam. The gun flew across the room and bounced endlessly, making clunking sounds like a loose cannon. Morgan was so glued to Robert Turner that he could see his eyeballs bouncing around inside his eye sockets. His glasses popped off his nose and splashed into a goldfish bowl. Morgan and Joe were on him like two blue tick hounds on a bone. They smashed his face into the filthy carpet and pinned his shoulders to the floor.

"Ooweee," he cried, clutching his back.

Morgan grabbed the gun and emptied the cartridges into his hand, then rolled Bob over and handcuffed him. He moaned pathetically, but Morgan had no sympathy for him.

Mrs. Turner returned to the dining room trembling violently. "Is he hurt? Is he hurt?"

"Sit down, ma'am, we're getting an ambulance."

"Oh, Lord, is he hurt?" she cried tearfully.

By then the frustration had finally gotten to Joe. "Do what the man said, goddamn it," he shouted.

Morgan smiled, then he snickered. "I almost shot that old son of a bitch," he said, glancing at Ed. "You guys will never know how close I was," he added, breathing a sigh of relief.

Ed poked around on Turner's back assessing the injury. The old man moaned.

"Where were you, Ed?" Morgan queried.

"I had to break the fuck'n door down. The SOB was locked in," he snorted.

"Man, I had the trigger pulled all the way through when he stumbled. I don't know how I kept from shooting him," Morgan said, eluding back to his near-kill. It made him shudder.

The old man on the floor moaned again. "You yell'n son of a bitch, you throwed me off my guard or I'd a killed you."

Morgan breathed another sigh and looked at Joe. "Joe, you did okay," he said. Joe beamed.

"That's one of them recapitulators Ian was talking about down at the Rusty Bucket. He don't get a Notice to Appear."

They all laughed.

CHAPTER FOURTEEN

The ambulance attendants rolled Bob Turner's drunken carcass onto a backboard as he moaned. Morgan, Joe, and Ed retold the story to each other as though they were telling it to someone who wasn't there. The cold air turned their breath to steam as they crossed the street to the idling squad cars. Several bystanders who had gathered to rubberneck were dispersing, walking slowly away from them. Joe spoke to them as he passed. He was wearing a satisfied expression. He was pleased with himself. Morgan watched him strolling to the crime prevention van wearing a half smile. Joe sensed that Morgan was analyzing him. He glanced over his shoulder and said, "Hey, Morgan. If a slot comes open for a sergeant in the patrol division, maybe I'll put in for it."

Ed ran to his squad car and scooted into the driver's seat. Morgan's thoughts were still lingering on the earlier incident. He wondered if he had reacted quickly enough. If Bob Turner had been more capable and not a fat, clumsy lout, maybe he would be a dead cop by now. If Turner hadn't lost his balance he'd be a hunk of dead meat. It was only luck that things ended as they had.

Red and blue lights from Joe's van bounced off houses like lights from a carnival wagon. They went dark when Joe hit the kill switch. A lone lingering bystander in a heavy winter parka approached him.

"That's quite a setup you have there," he said. Back in those days people were used to seeing squad cars with a lone single bubble atop the roof. All that light was a spectacle.

"Crime prevention van," Joe stated proudly.

The bystander studied Joe momentarily, building courage to pry. "We saw you coming all the way from over on 13th Street. It must have been some kind of real emergency, huh?"

"Not really," Joe said flatly.

"What was the problem?" the nosy citizen persisted.

"Just a man who needed a little help," Joe said as he grabbed the headrest to assist in hoisting his heavy frame into the driver's seat."

Just as he was settling in he stopped as though he had been hit by a lightning bolt. He jumped back out of the van and stood on the pavement. "Damn it! Damn it!" he howled.

Ed punched Morgan on the arm and pointed at Joe. "Son of a bitch, he's started a quarrel with a citizen," Ed snorted. They both hurried to join Joe.

"What's going on, Joe?" Morgan asked.

The confused onlooker turned his gloved hands outward and shrugged. "I didn't do a thing," he said defensively as he backed away.

"Someone's stolen the keys," Joe moaned.

"The keys to the van?" Morgan asked, looking inside the van to the ignition switch, noting that they were dangling on the steering column.

Ed caught on instantly. "Jesus Christ, Brainyard, you didn't!" He gasped. "The keys, Morgan, the keys!"

"Oh, the keys. The keys to every municipal building in town—those keys," Morgan said. He climbed into the van and started scouring under the seat and then into the passenger compartment. Still there were no keys. After several minutes of searching, Morgan suggested that they would just have to contact the city manager to have the locks changed. It would be an expensive annoyance, but Joe was in no danger of losing his job. Their main concern was for Napoleon Bonaparte Jones. The Coca-Cola key would fit every Coke machine in town.

"I know Coke will fire his old ass," Joe said pitifully. He was totally concerned. They were good friends and drinking buddies. Joe loved Napoleon like a brother.

"Maybe you left them at the station," Ed said, trying to be encouraging.

"Fat chance. In fact, I thought about them as I was getting out of the car. I even thought about them being stolen. I should have locked the car," he said.

Morgan walked across the street and questioned a group of stragglers who had waited to watch Bob Turner be loaded into the ambulance. When they were asked if they had seen anything, they all shook their heads no.

They searched the van again, and then the dirty snow for several more minutes before eventually accepting the fact that the keys were most likely stolen. Other than being insulted and embarrassed that someone may have taken keys from the police van, their main concern was for old Napoleon Bonaparte Jones. They didn't want him to suffer for Joe's negligence. They knew too that recovering the keys was not likely.

As they pulled away, a green sedan slowly left the alley. Roderick Constance twirled Joe's keys on his finger as he watched them drive away.

Chapter Fifteen

When Morgan's shift ended the next morning, he hung around the police station until the day shift personnel reported for duty. He went to the detective's squad room to talk to Ernie Linehurst. Without an explanation about the stolen keys, Morgan thought it would get a good laugh, and the incident would be forgotten. He could imagine how they would snicker about poor old Joe screwing up again, but never giving a serious thought about someone actually having the balls to steal right out of a police vehicle. Most of the guys would think Joe had only lost them somewhere while taking a nap. "Most likely they fell out of his pocket while he rolled around in his sleep. He probably kicked them out onto the ground when he stopped for a free doughnut."

Morgan had his doubts too, and in reality it wasn't a high priority. Still, losing the keys to the city was something the detective squad should know about. Aside from that, Coca-Cola might look upon Napoleon Bonaparte with a jaundiced eye.

The chief detective was a talkative man, down to earth, and easy to be around. Unlike some of the other detectives, he didn't believe he was better than the guys on the beat. A patrolman's responsibility was to answer radio calls and patrol the streets. Ernie's job was to follow up on crime reports and handle investigations. He didn't consider his duties more important, just different.

Ernie was short and stocky and in good shape. He smoked a cigar and wore a rumpled tan-colored raincoat. Some of the men called him Columbo, after the popular TV detective.

Ernie was the fifth child in a family of ten. He had five brothers and four sisters. He joked about being John Boy from Walton's Mountain and sleeping two to a bed, but everybody knew he was proud of his family and his upbringing. He bored people with stories of his childhood, growing up in the hills of Ste. Genevieve, Missouri. He might have been dismissed as just a "good old boy" if it weren't for the fact he was really good at his job. Ernie was the best detective the department ever had.

At the moment Ernie was articulating a story from his past to Larry Riley, the department training officer. When Morgan entered, Ernie raised a finger, implying a pause, and said, "Come on in, Morgan, I was just finishing a story here."

Morgan took a seat in a beat-up leather chair. Ernie talked while Morgan looked around the office. The drab olive walls were lined with black and white photographs from antiquity. One picture was of an attractive dark-haired woman standing at the rear bumper of a Model T Ford. She was thin and willowy, and her eyes bore a strong resemblance to the chief detective's eyes. The photograph was frayed and yellowing around the edges. It had been hanging in that same spot as long as Morgan had been in the department. There were other pictures too, of men in double-breasted suits and wide printed ties. Morgan knew they were Ernie's relatives but they looked like mobsters from the 1930's. Ernie's office was a museum.

Morgan glanced at Ernie as he was waving a hand over his head in a circular motion, emphasizing a point he was trying to make. He was animated as he simulated, looking nervously in all directions, and incorporating his actions into his story. He was talking about the barber shop incident. Morgan had heard it before. Ernie and two brothers, Glen and Joe, were working on a construction job in a small town in Missouri. They had taken their lunch break and decided that the youngest brother, Joe, needed a haircut. When they arrived they found the shop unattended with the door open. Glen manned the shears while Ernie stood guard. In just a few moments Joe's head resembled a chimpanzee's butt. That was long before Ernie took up law enforcement but still a frequently iterated tale in his repertoire.

Larry glanced at Morgan and smiled. He too had heard the story before.

"We lathered Joe's neck and shaved him with a straight razor. We swept up the loose hair and dropped a quarter in the cigar box," Ernie said, and then he remarked as he always did when he finished a story, "Boy, those were the days."

Morgan thumbed through the incoming reports on Ernie's desk. Having finished his tale, the chief detective turned in his swivel chair and waved as Larry went out the door.

"So what can I do for you, Morgan?" Ernie asked.

"We had a little problem last night," Morgan began.

"I heard about it," Ernie interrupted. "Bob Turner again, huh? We used to answer calls to his house back when I was still in uniform. He's been threatening to kill himself for years. It's a wonder you didn't shoot his blubbery old ass," Ernie said.

Morgan stared out the window into the gray morning light, contemplating Ernie's comment. It was true. The police department continually answered calls to the same addresses year after year. They listened to the same arguments and settled them with the same words they had uttered before. The majority of citizens were law-abiding people who stayed within the boundaries for no other reason than common decency. Still there was the small portion of the population that committed crimes over and over again. Usually the offenses were against each other, and they resented police interference once the situation was defused.

In Bob Turner's case he would be transported to the emergency room, examined by a doctor, then shipped to an alcohol detoxification center. When he was released he would go before a judge, be found guilty, and he would be placed on probation. The order would stipulate that he refrain from the use of alcohol, but he would violate the order within a few days. Maybe someone would kill him in a situation like Morgan had stepped into, or maybe he would actually kill himself.

"Yeah, sometimes I get sick of my own words. We just keep using the same old lines," Ernie said as though he had read Morgan's mind. He rolled the cigar in his cheek. "Well, what's your problem, Morgan, I know you're not here to revisit the barber shop story?"

Morgan explained the missing key situation, emphasizing the part where Napoleon Bonaparte had entrusted Joe with the Coca-Cola machine key without the approval of his superiors. Ernie assured Morgan that he would put a junior detective to work calling all the service stations and laundromats to alert them to the problem. The key Joe had lost was a master key and would open any Coke machine in the city. If a small effort saved Napoleon's job, it was the least he could do. Ernie was like everybody else — he didn't think it was a big deal. It was a petty crime to break into a soda machine. Still, it relieved Morgan's fears.

Chapter Sixteen

The Coca-Cola key was less important to Constance than it was to Morgan. Of course he intended to use it, but it wasn't planned. He simply saw an opportunity to steal the keys and took it. It was exhilarating to be so intimately close to danger. Stealing from a squad car — that was as good as it gets. He was like a moth circling a flame. The urge to get close was too strong to resist. It was astonishing that Constance had greater emotional stimulation from stealing a key ring from a squad car than he had from gunning down John Mason.

His dishonesty wasn't thought out or planned, but he was constantly on the prowl for opportunities. He would use the Coca-Cola key when he needed money. All through January he roamed department stores smoothly tucking items under his coat. He loved cold weather. It was easier to shoplift in heavy clothing. It was no task at all to walk into a store and pick up a camera or a tape recorder. He often took things and went straight to the return counter for a refund without ever leaving the store. January ended on a high note, definitely in the black.

On a bright February morning, Constance was cruising Keokuk Street looking for a record shop where he could try out a concealment flap he had sewn into the lining of his coat. It was a little larger than a record album cover. Albums were hot merchandise and he was having little trouble unloading them. He drove the Chevy up to the curb in front of the Wind Mill Record Shop. The Chevy's front wheels locked on the icy asphalt and skidded up onto the sidewalk. He went into the store and in just a few moments he was back with a stash of marketable goods.

Constance was still living at Hovy Hall, but for all practical purposes he had dropped out of school. He hadn't attended a class for an entire semester and had been given straight W's for grades. He didn't care about school, but he liked having the room to warehouse his loot. Now that John Mason was gone he enjoyed complete privacy. He wasn't paying for the room. It was a responsibility of the federal government to pay the bill, and as long as the college was getting the money, they would turn a blind eye.

Constance had heard the rumors that John dropped out of school during the Christmas break, or that he had simply disappeared. It was a sure thing that he wasn't coming back, but Constance was the only one who knew the truth. He never got involved in the conversations about John because he didn't want to defend anything he had said if the police came calling.

Constance lay in his bed smiling as he thought about it. There was satisfaction in knowing something that nobody else knew. There was a growing sensation within his depraved reflections that having power over life and death had made him superior. He reminisced about killing John Mason, and it made him high to think about it. The fact that John begged him was stimulating.

Chapter Seventeen

Morgan guided the squad car into the parking stall in front of his apartment. He loved working the night shift, but now he was back on days. Life was more normal when he was on days. Molly was usually gone before he got off work so he spent his days knocking around the apartment alone. He liked the witty little notes she left on the refrigerator and pinned to his pillow, but he preferred her warm body lying next to him in their bed. He had been on patrol when he saw her car parked in the driveway. She was supposed to be making a deposition in Springfield, but now she was home in the middle of the day. He was happy to see her there and his curiosity caused him to stop and inquire. He radioed in that he would be on the portable, left the car running, and went to the door. He found the door locked so he knocked and waited. The frigid wind streamed down his collar as he danced on the doorstep. Soon he heard footsteps. When Molly opened the door her shoulders were bare. She was wrapped in a yellow towel and her hair was wet. She beamed when she saw him. "What are you doing here?" She laughed.

"We got a call that a woman in 7-A was exposing herself to some schoolchildren," Morgan said.

"Seven-A, that's our number," she said seriously. Morgan laughed, and then Molly giggled at her own gullibility.

"Two little girls reported it. They said their thirteen-year-old brother went back for a second look," Morgan continued to tease.

Molly slapped him on the arm. "Quit kidding, why are you home?" she asked.

"I'll ask the same of you," Morgan said. Molly turned and walked back into the bathroom. The yellow towel dropped to the floor. Morgan followed her putting his hands around her waist.

"Not now, you're on duty," she said as she gently pushed him away. "I'm glad I can do that to you," she said, believing it would be a shame if she adored him as she did and he was only lukewarm about her.

"My deposition was cancelled so I decided to come home and wash my hair," she said. Morgan watched her blow-drying her hair. She turned her head to the right, flinging her hair across her shoulder. She combed it back tilting her head to one side. She flipped it to the left and repeated the process. Her green eyes were fixed on her hair in the mirror but she sensed Morgan's gaze. She smiled. Molly was becoming very content with her life.

Morgan got up and went to the refrigerator and inspected the contents. He wasn't hungry, but he poured a glass of milk and drained it. "You know what they say about milk drinkers, don't you?" Molly asked as she watched him through the mirror.

"No, what do they say," Morgan asked.

"They do better than the udder guy," she laughed. Morgan looked at her only half smiling. "Come on, laugh, it was funny," she urged.

"Where did you hear that one?" Morgan asked as his smile turned into a twisted little grin.

Molly glanced at him with a wry smile. "One of the attorneys told it to me after the deposition yesterday. I've been waiting for you to go to the refrigerator just so I could use it. I thought it was funny," she said.

"That goes to show how little humor some of those lawyers

have," Morgan said grumpily.

Molly's eyes sparkled as she watched his face turn somber. "Morgan, you're jealous that I was sitting around with a bunch of attorneys listening to dirty jokes." She giggled.

"I wouldn't exactly call a joke about a cow's udders a dirty joke," Morgan said.

"That's only because I didn't tell you the rest of it," she laughed.

At that moment their coquettish goading came to an end. Roy came on the radio and advised him to report to his car. Once he was in the squad car he was directed to proceed to 829 Lyndell Street on a Code One (emergency lights and siren.) He hit the emergency switch and accelerated, dodging traffic and taking side streets until he saw Ed stopped at the curb on Lyndell Street. He was sitting there dark and motioned for Morgan to cut his lights. Two other squads were at the end of the block.

This was a neighborhood where a railroad track ran alongside the road on one side with small white houses on the other. The structures were all similar, with wide white aluminum siding and little black shutters. Most were dented, worn, and tarnished looking. Some of them had driveways, but most cars were parked alongside the street. They were occupied by factory workers and people with blue collar jobs.

Eight-twenty-nine Lyndell was located off the street a good distance with a brick driveway cluttered with children toys. The house was dimly lit and the neighborhood was quiet. Ed wanted Morgan to join him and instructed the other two officers to take positions triangulating the property line. They had every angle covered before Morgan and Ed approached the house. There wasn't a squeak or groan coming from the house, but still they were cautious. "If this is a Code One you'd think you could hear yelling and cussing, dishes breaking, stuff like that," Ed said.

It was still quiet when a small boy darted out the back door and ran to the alley. He was naked from the waist up, and barefoot. He was carrying a brown paper bag as he skipped through the snow, the cold stinging his feet. He slung the bag into a garbage barrel before darting back to the house.

"This ain't no Code One," Ed snorted. He walked to the side window and peeked in. "There's a woman in there mopping the floor," he exclaimed. Morgan joined him and looked inside. A woman with witch-like, black stringy hair, dressed in a full-length brown dress swayed as she stroked the mop across the floor. She mumbled and growled incoherently. Two small boys watched her. One of the boys was dressed in dirty pajamas and the other was bare except for blue jeans. He was the boy who made the trip to the garbage barrel.

"What the fuck is going on here?" Ed moaned. A neighbor from the next house stepped out onto her porch. "I'm the one who called," she said, glancing around as though she didn't want to be seen. "It sounded like they were killing each other over there."

After a moment Ed proceeded to the door and rapped it with his fist. The neighbor was still watching them. "Don't tell them I called, please," she said. Ed nodded and she stepped back inside.

The first rap on the door didn't get an answer, so Ed stepped back up and knocked harder. When that didn't get a reaction he yelled, "Open up. It's the police!"

The door slowly creaked open. A small boy with tear-filled eyes stared up at them. "May we come in?" Morgan asked. The boy didn't answer but continued to gaze at them. Swathed in fear, the innocent face pleaded for relief. Ed lightly pushed the door open and stepped inside. The stringy-haired woman continued to swab, never turning to look at them or to acknowledge their presence. Morgan examined the substance on the floor. It was dark and had formed in a pool. "What is that?" Ed demanded.

The woman didn't answer. She sloshed the mop across the murky-looking substance in trance-like movements. Morgan walked to the yellow bucket she was using to wring out her mop. Ed watched him until he stopped and was staring into the receptacle. A disturbed expression emerged on his face. "Hey, that's blood," he said, simultaneously grabbing for the mop handle.

"Leave me alone!" The woman screeched as she tried to pull the mop away from Morgan. Ed grabbed it and she fought, but with a strong hand he relieved her of it. Morgan jumped over the blood and went into the bedroom. A skinny, naked man lay sprawled across the bed. His skin was ashen, his eyes were half open and expressionless. His legs dangled from the bed with dry blood caked on his left calf. A stream of coagulated blood trailed from the bedroom to the pool where the woman had been mopping.

"Ed, get her away from the blood. It looks like she's killed him," Morgan said. The two little boys stood in the doorway with their small little feet touching the bloody pool. Their expressions didn't change. Morgan had only confirmed what they already feared. Morgan raised the portable radio to his lips and said, "Roy, call the coroner and get Detective Linehurst out here as soon as possible."

Roy acknowledged, "Ten-four."

Ten minutes later the scene had radically changed. There were five squad cars with lights flashing red and blue all along the street. An ambulance was parked in the driveway. Sarge had been dispatched to take command of the scene, and several other officers were scouring the neighborhood for witnesses. Flashbulbs were blinking inside the house as the sun dipped behind the western horizon. Nosy people milled about outside the yellow police tape trying to find out what had happened. As darkness descended, the flashing lights grew brighter. The woman with the witch-like hair sat in the backseat of Morgan's squad car with her face buried in her hands. The squad car was equipped with a wire mesh, and the windows were unbreakable glass, but it wasn't likely she would try to escape. She was so drunk and despondent that the criminality of her act had not yet soaked in.

Inside the house, Ernie Linehurst kneeled beside the pool of blood. He snapped a stainless steel spoon from a sterile package and dipped it into the blood. He placed the specimen into a container and gave it to the evidence handler. The bottle was marked with the time, date, location, and the evidence handler's initials. This was a "pat case." Even Joe Bernard could have handled the investigation, but still Ernie was careful. He approached each case with the same consideration that he would have given to the perfect crime. He believed in doing things right no matter how insignificant it seemed. Ernie hated being surprised in court and went to great lengths to prevent it. Morgan watched Ernie until he paused. "I've questioned the next-door neighbor, and Ed and Jim have talked to everyone on both sides of the street all along the block. I've got notes right here," he said. Ernie instructed the evidence handler to take the notes and enter them into his evidence log. The evidence handler sneered. "They're only notes," he protested.

"They're original notes," Ernie corrected.

The evidence handler relieved Morgan of the folded yellow sheets. "I suppose you'll have to sign them out of evidence to write your report," he said curtly.

"Sit down here with me, Morgan," Ernie said. Morgan knelt down beside the senior officer. "What do you think happened here?" he asked.

Morgan looked at Ernie blankly, then lowered his eyes in thought. "Well," he started. "It looks like they got into a fight and she stabbed him to death."

"That's good. But how did she do it? What happened?"

Morgan looked around the room then said, "I don't know. I

haven't talked to the kids yet."

"Neither have I, but the story is presenting itself to us right now," Ernie said.

Morgan watched with interest as Ernie continued. "You said when you came in here one of the kids went running barefoot out to the alley. Has anyone been back there yet to see what he threw away?" Morgan advised that a search had in fact been made. Ernie went on. "I'll bet there was a broken knife handle in that bag he tossed," Ernie said. He glanced at Morgan over his glasses. "I know that because I see the blade over there under the kitchen counter. It separated and fell away from the handle. Would you go over there and circle it with this yellow marker and bring it back to Sam." He handed Morgan a small tong and a pair of rubber gloves. Morgan rose and carefully went to retrieve the knife blade.

"As a matter of fact, it was a knife handle," he said half smiling.

"It didn't take a lot of deduction to make the connection. Do you see those potatoes over there on the kitchen table? Only half of them are peeled." Morgan was silent. Ernie continued to verbalize his suspicions. "There's also a whiskey bottle with only a sip left in it. It sort of appears they'd been drinking for some time. The old gal was peeling potatoes and getting ready for dinner when the jawing started. He was probably beefing about something he didn't like. Did you notice the scratches on his face?" Ernie asked. Morgan shook his head no.

"Well, he had some, and she had blood under the fingernails on her left hand. It looks like they started arguing in the kitchen and fought right into the bedroom. I would say she was getting the best of him. She was swinging with both hands. I would imagine she was holding the knife in her right hand. My bet is that she forgot she had it." Ernie stopped for a moment glancing at the corpse. "Did you see the location of the wound?" he asked, again looking at Morgan over his glasses.

"Yes," Morgan said. "It was right below his left knee. He just laid there and bled out."

"Well, he was in a drunken stupor, he probably didn't even feel it," Ernie stated. "She finally backed him up and he fell backward into the bed. That's when he started kicking her. She stuck him in the knee. Hell, she probably didn't even know she stabbed him. I suppose they fight all the time," he added. Morgan nodded in agreement.

"When he stopped kicking her, she just went back into the kitchen. She probably waited for a while, cooled off, and then went back in to check on him. That's when she saw the blood." Ernie sighed. "You know, if his legs had been elevated he'd be alive right now."

"But why was he naked?" Morgan asked.

Ernie rubbed his chin. "She must have panicked when she saw all the blood. She stripped him down trying to find the wound. She probably thought the knife blade was still in him."

Morgan thought about everything Ernie had told him, and it made sense. She would have seen the knife handle and believed the blade was still in him somewhere. It was reasonable to believe that was the reason she had the kid run the knife handle back to the garbage. In her drunken state she probably thought if there was no handle it would be harder to connect her with the crime.

"In her drunken condition she was probably stripping him down just to find the wound. She was trying to save his life," Ernie said.

He stood up and looked around the room. "Okay," he shouted to no one in particular. "Clean 'er up. I'm through here. Lock her up on aggravated battery." He rolled the cigar in his cheek as he snapped his evidence case shut.

CHAPTER EIGHTEEN

Morgan walked with Ernie as they proceeded back to their squad cars. Morgan was impressed with Ernie's analysis. He might have come to the same conclusions Ernie had, but it was easy to visualize what happened once Ernie had laid it out for him. He thought elucidating the details from scratch might have been a little more problematic. The fact that Ernie directed them to arrest the woman for aggravated battery instead of murder demonstrated a moral power too. A lesser person would certainly have pushed for a murder charge, knowing that more notoriety would be generated, placing himself in a brighter light. Ernie's decisions were always fair and never self-inflating.

As they walked on slowly, Ernie twisted the cigar in his cheek. Trouble was etched in his expression. Not dark, but pensive and considerate. Finally, he said, "You know, Morgan, I've been on this job for the better part of my life and I've seen a lot of death—on the street with all the accidents, and now with stuff like this. But you know, I don't think I'll ever get used to it." Morgan watched him quietly and did not reply.

"I'll go home tonight and not be able to sleep. I'll think about how that body was getting stiff, how lifeless it was. What happens to the person? Where do they go? The split second after he died we could have pumped blood into him and massaged his heart until it thundered, but it was too late. It wouldn't have made a penny's worth of difference. What gives us this consciousness and warmth and mobility we call life?" he asked glumly.

Morgan merely watched Ernie. He had his own views about life and the hereafter, but he didn't think the time was right to talk about it. He could see Ernie's disquiet, and he valued his friend's introspect. The fact that Ernie wasn't hardened by the job made Morgan respect him even more.

Ernie seemed to realize they had descended into a gloomy pall, and after a few attempts to get onto another subject he just stopped and stared into the darkness. It wasn't until that moment that Morgan realized Ernie was a lonely man. He knew that Ernie had been married when he was very young, but he didn't know he was still haunted by a relationship that had slipped through his fingers. Ernie never mentioned her name or talked about a disappointment that was so deep it tortured him. The pain he endured was his burden to carry. He thought about it every day, many times a day, but he masked his pain with cheerful conversation and yarns from the past. Morgan didn't want to feel sorry for Ernie. He had too much respect for him, but he didn't like the thought of Ernie going home to an empty house after investigating a tragic death where he would contemplate how fragile life really is.

Morgan suggested that they have a few beers at his apartment. He wanted Ernie to meet Molly, and he was happy and surprised that he accepted. They signed off together.

Chapter Nineteen

The sun shone brightly on Wednesday morning as Ian Rogers entered the courthouse. Gary Winstead came through an opposing door, and the two attorneys met at the elevator. Ian addressed Gary first. "Looks like we're getting a break from the weather this morning," he said.

Gary looked thoughtfully at Ian. "Did they call you about the homicide last evening?" he asked.

"No, but I heard about it on the news while I was on my way in this morning," Ian replied. The elevator door opened and the two men stepped in. The door began to close when an arm lunged into the opening and the doors separated. The janitor, Byron Wilson, Nerd Wilson's brother, hopped in.

"Whee, I just made it," he exclaimed as if there was some urgency attached to getting that particular lift. Smoke swirled as Ian glanced scornfully at the no smoking sign. Byron was oblivious to his disapproval, sucked on the Camel non-filtered, and exhaled an unhealthy haze into the air.

"The girls in your office were complaining about the sink in the bathroom draining a little slow," Byron said, flipping a plunger in his hand. He directed his remark to Ian and watched Ian's face implacably waiting for an answer.

Ian didn't want to look at Byron, but after a long pause he

finally said," That's fine, Mr. Wilson."

The stubby man turned a can of Drano in his hand as he read the instructions.

"Did you hear about the murder yesterday, Mr. Rogers?" he asked. Gary watched Ian's face, suppressing a slight smile. Gary knew Ian disliked Byron and his brother Leonard. He thought they were small-minded little gossip-mongers. Ian had ordered his staff to be discreet about office matters when Byron was lingering there. His exact words were, "Be careful when that little weasel comes around."

Ian eyed Byron suspiciously. "I only heard about it on the news this morning, but you can't place much credence in those early breaking news reports," Ian said.

"Well, I guess it was a hell of a deal," Byron declared. He gawked at Ian again waiting for a response. Ian stared at the lighted numbers on the elevator wall. When Ian ignored the remark, Bryan persisted, "You know Morgan, don't you?" he asked.

"Morgan who?"

"Morgan, the policeman."

"Of course," Ian replied impatiently.

"Well, I guess he caught the murderer right in the act," Byron said.

Ian displayed a derisive frown. "Is that right," he said. He might have been looking at a pile of horse manure by his expression.

The elevator door opened and the three men stepped off. Byron hurried to keep up with Ian. "They say she axed her husband to death and that Morgan saw the whole thing."

Ian stopped and faced Byron. "Is that the restroom you were talking about" Ian asked pointing to the third-floor ladies' room, his face a burnish pink.

"Yep, it sure is," he said.

"Then I suggest you get started on fixing it. This office is quite busy during working hours, and when the girls get an opportunity to go to the ladies' room it certainly should be operable," Ian stated firmly.

"Sure thing, Mr. R, sure thing," Byron said, totally oblivious to Ian's irritation.

Ian walked into the secretarial pool, which he had to pass through to get to his office. The typewriters were clattering away. "Good morning, girls," he hailed as he walked into the library, not waiting for an acknowledgment. Ian peeled off his raincoat and reentered the secretarial pool. "Tina, have we received the police reports yet?" he snarled.

"Yes, Mr. Rogers," she replied. She hopped to fetch the police reports and handed them to him. Ian disappeared into his office.

"Wow, is he in a bad mood this morning," she said as Gary was walking by.

"No, he's not in a bad mood, it's just that he rode the elevator with Byron Wilson. He's probably anxious to find out about the homicide last night too," he added.

The clattering typewriters stopped in unison. "What homicide?" Tina asked.

Gary looked puzzled. "Didn't you get a homicide report?" he asked. Tina scanned through her crime reports. There were several reports but the most serious was an aggravated battery charge.

The office door swung open. It was the second assistant, Tom Spencer. "Did anyone hear about the murder yesterday evening?" he asked. Tina was still scanning her report log. Tom didn't stop as he headed for the coffeepot.

"Only what I heard on the radio, and from Byron—you know, our resident reporter," Gary said and laughed.

Tom was the youngest assistant, and only six months out of law school. He disappeared into the law library, blowing across his hot coffee. Ian walked back in. "Tina, get Tom and tell him to come into my office."

Turning to Gary he said, "Gary, you too. I'd like to go over these reports and review the jury calendar for next week." The typewriters started again and the three attorneys walked into Ian's office.

Inside Ian's office chairs scooted as the two subordinates arranged themselves for the meeting. "First of all, the homicide report is right here in front of me. Detective Linehurst did the preliminary report. It looks like the defendant stabbed her live-in boyfriend with a paring knife. Evidently he was too drunk to realize he had been injured and he bled to death," Ian said. He filled the other two in on the details as he read. When he finished, he checked the report with a red pen and handed it to Gary.

Tom studied Ian's face, then he said, "Wait a minute, Tina said there were no homicides." His brow furrowed as he spit the words in a challenging demeanor.

Ian looked at Tom as though he had just insulted his mother. Tom sensed the irritability. "I mean, ah, you know, she said there were no homicides, and now you say there is," he said suspiciously.

Ian presumed Tom was bewildered over the charges, and he didn't approve of his attitude. "Ernie charged her with aggravated battery — a felony," Ian said flatly. Tom glanced at Gary, then back to Ian. He shook his head openly showing his disappointment. It was easy to see he wanted a more serious indictment.

"Don't you agree with the charges?" Ian asked.

Tom hesitated. "I don't understand it. I mean, the defendant killed the victim while committing a felony. The Illinois Revised Statutes and the Supreme Court concur. It's murder," he said.

Ian thought about it for a moment. Tom certainly knew his law. He was bright and eager, and combined with his youthful exuberance he was a worthy adversary. But he wasn't an adversary, he was a subordinate. At the moment Ian viewed Tom as a little dog nipping at his heels.

"I think it was the proper charge, and I'm glad to see that at least one detective over there has the moral fortitude to put personal acclaim aside and make the proper charge in an instance like this," Ian snapped.

Tom was still not satisfied. "Don't you think we should have at least charged her with manslaughter, and then we'd have something to bargain with?" he said. At that moment Tom knew he was stepping on Ian's toes, but after all it was a common practice to load up the charges and work your way down. Every pre-law college student knew that.

Ian was annoyed. "Dan Ingelman knows what I'll bargain on. I've made that clear to him down through the years," he said. Tom didn't object but his jaw was set and his eyes were fixed, staring at the desktop in front of him.

Ian glanced at Gary to get a read on his impression of the conversation, or maybe just in disbelief. Ian still wasn't through. "When I took this office I said I was going to represent all the people, and that includes the defendant. The woman was drunk! She was probably just holding the knife, swinging wildly in the heat of the fight. If you want a murder change out of that, maybe you should re-examine your sense of right and wrong," Ian said acrimoniously.

Tom looked like he had been slapped in the face. The argument was over. Ian examined the papers on his desk. "Tom, you can have all the traffic cases this month. That along with your shoplifting cases will keep you busy." He looked up glaring at Tom as if daring him to say another word. Tom was quiet, realizing that Ian had a little volcano smoldering inside him, only a few mutinous syllables away from an eruption. Ian stopped and rubbed his chin. "Gary, on second thought, mix up some of those traffic charges and give Tom some of your criminal cases.

We've got to try those two attempted murder cases, and this agg. Battery will probably take some trial prep. I thought Dan was willing to deal on a couple of those misdemeanors, but he didn't have the good sense to plead them out. We'll have to take some of them to trial."

Gary thumbed through the files and handed a portion to Tom. Tom took them without looking up then he left the office. He clearly had not recovered from his clash with the boss. He had to be asking himself if he had lost his mind. Tom knew there were times when he was his own worst enemy. This was one of those times, but he was young and saw things from a different perspective. He wanted a good old-fashioned murder trial. There wasn't much mileage in a run-of-the-mill agg battery.

After he was gone, Gary looked at Ian and said, "He's good, Ian. Imagine how aggressive he'll be after about ten years in this business." Ian placed his elbows on the desk and rubbed his face with both hands, but he didn't speak.

"That's the first young attorney I've seen get under your skin," Gary said.

"Well," Ian said, obviously coveting a desire to break into a tirade. "They come out of law school, buy themselves a vested suit, start drinking Scotch, and call themselves lawyers..." Ian stopped, smiled at himself, and glanced at Gary. "He is good, that's what infuriates me about him. He'll be influential someday. I just hope his values are worthy of his talents," he said.

Gary laughed and thumped his fist on the desk. "I'm going back to work, boss," he said.

Reassigning some of Gray's cases to Tom was the first brick in a wall that would obstruct crucial information necessary in bringing a maniacal murderer to justice in a timely manner. Tom approached the counter in the secretary's office. "Jenny, would you pull some of Gary's cases for me? I need William Billingsley, Thires Jones, Andrew Dupage, and Roderick Constance."

Jenny was the witness coordinator, and she recognized the names. "We're having a problem with the Constance case. We can't locate the eyewitness," she said.

Tom was thumbing through another file but stopped and looked at her. "What have we done to locate him?" he asked.

Jenny scanned through the file reading the entries from different dates. "We sent a subpoena to the Cook County Sheriff's Department, but it was returned, not found." She grimaced.

"That's not unusual. Sending a subpoena to them is about as effective as throwing it out the window. What else?" he asked.

Jenny turned the pages in the file. "We sent a subpoena certified mail, and I see here that I attached a note asking him to call our office as soon as he received the subpoena to let us know what's happened to him since we last talked." She hesitated then said, "It looks like I made an entry here asking his father to contact us. His father called and said his son has been missing since December 15th."

Tom continued to scrutinize another file. Jenny rolled her eyes, irritated by his attitude. Tom scribbled notes, licked his thumb, and turned a few pages. "Did you check his story? Maybe he's had a change of heart. Maybe he just doesn't want to make the trip down here for the trial."

Jenny stopped to think. She handled hundreds of witnesses throughout the year, and it was remarkable that she could put her finger on the information Tom was so indignantly requesting. She remained composed and after a moment she said, "I called the communications sergeant and he confirmed a missing persons on him. His name is John Mason. See, its right here in the file."

Tom snapped the file shut, glaring at Jenny as if she were responsible for John Mason's absence. He walked into his office and closed the door.

CHAPTER TWENTY

John Mason was missing, but only the most cynical-minded person would suspect such a cruel manifestation. At some point in the future John's tragic ending would become relative in connecting an entire series of cruel manifestations, but at the moment he was merely a component necessary to bringing a misdemeanor offense into the courtroom. It wasn't unusual for witnesses to vanish before trials. Often they moved without giving notice, and at other times they just skipped out to avoid testifying. Either way if the witness was vital to the prosecution and the witness could not be found, the case was usually dropped. Dan Ingelman counted on such things. When the State had a strong case he would often delay the trial as long as he could. He knew the longer it took to get the case into court, the more likely it was that the witnesses would forget, lose interest, or just move without leaving a forwarding address. Dan worked the system continually. If the state's case was a little shaky, he would file a speedy trial motion hoping he could pressure them into making mistakes. He played each case by ear, keeping up with every detail and changing his strategy whenever necessary.

In Roderick Constance's case, the State was completely dependent upon their only eyewitness. Without John Mason, a guilty verdict was virtually impossible. Dan was on top of the case, and he knew that Mason was not available for trial.

On March 3rd, the weather had broken but there was still a chill in the air. Gray clouds rushed across the open sky while the sun intermittently shined through, softening the nip in the air. Roderick Constance walked across the courthouse lawn, right past the sign stating, "Keep Off The Grass." His long hair flying in the wind, his gate was brisk, revealing an air of pure arrogance. His hearing was at eleven o'clock, and he was certain he would make a one o'clock appointment he had made with a college girl who wanted to buy some of his record albums. The thought of going to jail was the furthest thing from his mind.

Constance reported to the clerk and was instructed to take a seat in the witness waiting room. He was there for fifteen minutes before his name was called. When he entered the courtroom, Dan rose to greet him. The jury watched him as he walked to the defense table. The clerk called the case, and Tom Spencer gathered his folder and approached the bench. He held the folder in front of him as he addressed the judge. "Your Honor, the State moves for a continuance in this case," he stated.

Dan interrupted. "The defense objects to any request for a continuance."

The judge glanced at the file on his desk. "What are your grounds for a continuance, Mr. Spencer?" he asked. Tom explained that the State's key witness could not be found, and he restated his request for a continuance.

Dan wouldn't stand for a continuance without a fight. This was just what he had hoped for. "That's not the fault of the defendant, Your Honor," he stated sternly.

Tom studied the judge's face. "Without this witness we have no case, Your Honor. We need more time," he said.

"What's the reason for his absence, Mr. Spencer?" the judge asked.

"I don't know. Only that the Cook County Sheriff's Office

returned the subpoena not found,"

Tom said. Dan interrupted again. "Your Honor, the defense has reason to believe that the witness has been reported missing by his father. He hasn't been seen since December 15th of last year. We have a police department printout right here indicating his status." Dan handed the printout to the judge. The judge examined the report. "He's been missing for three months, Your Honor. There's no reasonable expectation for his reappearance now," he continued.

The judge lowered his glasses and looked at Tom. "Mr. Spencer, I can understand the State's position, but we can't expect the defense to keep returning here for a trial because of the State's missing witness. There's no indication he will resurface. On the contrary, it seems he doesn't want to be found. The motion for continuance is denied."

"Your Honor, the State cannot present a case without this witness," Tom said with frustration audible in his voice.

Dan closed his folder. It was over and he knew it. "In that case, the defense moves that the court find a verdict in favor of the defendant," he said. The judge jotted down notes in his case log. "The court finds that the State has not proven the elements of the offense. The case is dismissed for lack of prosecution." He handed the file to the clerk and the case had come to an end. Constance shook hands with Dan and walked out of the courthouse a free man.

Chapter Twenty-One

Less than a week after Roderick Constance was acquitted on a directed verdict, he was in his room with Julie McBride, a Willoughby Hills college student from Libertyville, Illinois. She was going through his stolen record collection, buying them at a bargain price. Julie's father was a financial consultant with offices in Chicago and St. Louis. Money wasn't a problem for Julie. She had her own checking account, credit cards, and cash. She didn't need to buy records from Constance, but she liked the idea. She knew they were stolen, and that made it even more interesting. Julie wasn't overly bright, she wasn't attractive, and she didn't look rich. She was fat, she wore clothes that were ill-fitting, and her face was pitted from pimples she squeezed incessantly.

Roderick Constance was friendless and Julie learned he would talk to her as long as she did all the talking. Constance didn't like to talk but he would listen to her ramblings. Julie learned right away that he was violent, so she was cautious not to cross him. As time passed she accepted that disagreeing with him only invited his loathing.

Today she was curious about his court hearing, but she was proceeding cautiously. She had read in the newspaper that he was acquitted. She beat around the bush several minutes before finally asking him how he beat the charges. Constance's answers were short, but they weren't hostile, so she persisted. He told her that the State didn't have a case in the first place. He said there was a young punk who prosecuted his case, simply trying to make a name for himself. He told her the judge threw it out.

"I heard there was a boy in this dorm who ratted you out," Julie said. Constance just looked at her placidly. The corners of his mouth turned up slightly. It was as close to a smile as he would ever furnish. He had an evil grin that he used at times when he wanted to coerce someone, but there was nothing genuine about it.

"He was your roommate, wasn't he?" Julie asked.

Constance walked around the room picking up packages of T-shirts, stacking them on John Mason's bed. "I got a good deal on these," he said. Julie giggled. It was no secret how good the deal was. It doesn't get better than free.

Constance seemed to be less agitated today than normal, so Julie decided to tread a little less lightly. "Come on, Rod, how did you get off those theft changes? It was all over school that your roommate called the cops on you. Details, details," she said laughingly.

Constance looked at her and said flatly, "John Mason disappeared so they had no case. It was that simple."

"Did you kill him?" Julie asked, releasing a nervous laugh. She covered her mouth and waited for Constance to smash his fist into her face. Her attempt at humor suddenly seemed idiotic.

Constance didn't go into a rage as she expected. The corners of his mouth curled again and he said, "Yeah, I killed him." He then laughed — a totally uncharacteristic expose'.

Julie was so relieved that she horse-laughed, blowing a mist into the air. "You're so funny," she squealed.

In a world where people will believe the worst in others, a declaration that you've killed someone will still generate a hefty portion of doubt. Most people can't imagine a soul so polluted as to murder a fellow human being. Murderers frequently walk into police stations to confess to horrendous crimes, but they are never believed until the facts bare them out. When Constance's admission was followed by a lighthearted laugh, Julie assumed it was a rare attempt at wittiness.

After a rousing excursion into jocularity, Julie had come up hungry. Humor made her hungry, as well as serious dialogue or any other activity in her life. She hadn't reached 175 pounds by staving off her appetite. She had seen an electric skillet stashed beneath John Mason's bed. After another probing conversation about its procurement, Constance admitted that he had gotten a deal on it as well. Julie offered to unwrap it and stir up a home-cooked meal. It was against school regulations to cook in the dorms, but rules were like armpits to the two of them—everybody has a couple of them, and some of them stink.

The Kramer Super Market was just off campus so they cut through a residential area to go for groceries. Constance told Julie to leave her purse in the room since they wouldn't be needing money. When Constance entered the front door, the store manager, Matt Corgliano, saw him. Julie peeled off to the magazine section and Constance strolled around the corner to the meat counter. Matt knew Constance was a thief. He had been watching him for several months without catching him in the act. Matt stomped down the aisle to the assistant manager's office. Jack Fink could hear the heavy footsteps. Matt was coming to get him to watch a shoplifter. Jack knew too that *"this little bastard is robbing us blind!"* It was comical how Matt lamented about shoplifters. Jack was pouring over a mountain of paperwork, but he placed his pen on the desk and waited for Matt to storm into his office. The door swung open, Matt stuck his head inside, and roared, "Come on, Jack. I want you to watch someone for me!" He grumbled incoherently for a moment, his face was distressed, and his teeth were clenched. "This is the sneakiest little bastard

I've seen in a long time!" he snorted.

Jack smiled. It was a rerun of the last time he had been called upon to be the security agent for the store. He grabbed his coat and headed for the floor. He found an aisle near the meat section, pushed a shopping cart, and tried to blend in as much as possible. Matt was in the crow's nest watching Constance from behind the mirrored glass, biting his lip, stewing over the sneaky little bastard lingering in the meat department. He had lost over ten thousand dollars to shoplifting in 1975 alone, and he was bitter toward college kids in general. He had a violent temper and had even once slapped a young pilferer. It was a transgression he regretted. He had to release the kid, write an apology, and dole out a two hundred dollar gift card to avoid prosecution and a civil suit.

Matt had been the Kramer store manager for seven years. Prior to coming to Willoughby Hills, he was the assistant manager in the Joliet store. Matt was raised in a rough neighborhood and worked at Kramer's as a carry-out boy. Without them he would have found himself working in the Joliet Foundry where his father and brothers were employed. Kramer's had made him a successful man and he was loyal to them. When the store's profits were affected by theft, he considered it a personal injury.

Meanwhile, Jack had located Constance who was glancing around checking for store personnel, not at all nervous. In Constance's trivial mind he probably thought he was invulnerable to detection, but his actions were predictable. He selected four steaks from the refrigerated meat counter and started toward the front of the store with a bounce in his step. Halfway down the aisle he fumbled with the steaks and they dropped to the floor. He clumsily leaned over to recover them and when he came up, two steaks had disappeared. Jack knew where they were. They were in the kid's coat. Constance might have believed his sleight of hand was worthy of Houdini himself, but Jack had seen that trick a hundred times. Jack knew he was headed back to the meat section to put two steaks back into the meat tray as though he had changed his mind. Constance wanted steaks, but he wasn't satisfied with a two for one "five-fingered discount." He wanted them free. The two steaks were well hidden inside the flap in his coat, and the other two went back into the refrigerated display. Jack signaled Matt in the crow's nest. Matt in turn called the police department. When Constance joined Julie at the magazine rack he saw Matt and Jack coming. Matt stomped along like a mad bull, leaving little doubt about what was going down. Constance saw the squad car coming into the parking lot. He and Julie headed for the door. Constance leaned into Julie and whispered, "Run." Matt and Jack gave chase.

Morgan was driving into the parking lot. He had been on many calls just like this and he recognized instantly they had a runner. The slender boy cut between two cars leaving the two older men in the dust. Morgan knew he would cut across the parking lot and head for the residences where bushes, trees, and fences were plentiful. Morgan swerved, accelerated, and beat him to his escape route. He bailed out and ordered the boy to stop. Constance darted around the squad still trying to escape. Morgan lunged for him, bringing him face down on the asphalt.

Matt and Jack ran up puffing. "This son of a bitch ripped off two steaks from my store," Jack shouted.

"I didn't steal anything," Constance barked.

"The fuck you didn't, you idiot, you've been stealing my stuff all winter!" Matt growled.

Morgan had a firm grip on Constance so he guided him around, getting between him and Matt. "Come on, let's settle down," he said.

Morgan handcuffed Constance and pushed him against the car. He pulled his feet out so that his weight was rested against the car door, leaving him immobile. Morgan recognized Constance from his encounter with him at the college and again on December 16th after the snowstorm. He also knew he had skated on the theft charges Ed had imposed.

"Don't you pigs ever get tired of hassling people," Constance snarled.

Morgan ignored him as he patted his jacket pockets and then down his legs. There were no weapons, no steaks. He glanced at Matt with raised eyebrows. "He probably gave them a pitch," Matt said. Morgan lifted Constance, guided him around the squad car, and deposited him in the passenger seat. He began the process of retracing the young thief's steps. Matt followed him berating every college student who had ever lived. "This is a false arrest," Constance shouted after them.

As they searched between cars, Morgan shined his flashlight on the ground. A middle-aged perky, little lady approached them. "Is this what you're looking for, Officer?" she asked. Self-satisfaction gleamed in her eyes. "He threw these under my car," she said, extending her arms with two steaks in her hands. There were muddy blotches on her knees from kneeling on the asphalt as she plucked the meat from beneath her car.

Morgan thanked her and took the steaks. He gave them to Matt, informing him that he would have to get pictures of them before they were returned to the store. He retrieved a pen and small pad from his pocket. "I have to ask you for your name and address, ma'am," Morgan said.

"Oh, I won't have to go to court, will I?" she asked. Her sense of accomplishment drained as an anxious expression crept onto her face.

"It's possible," Morgan said.

"I didn't know I was getting myself into this or I would have left them under my car," she snapped.

Morgan smiled. "Well, ma'am, these shoplifting charges are often settled before they get to court. You know—restitution and stuff like that."

Matt glared at Morgan. A low growl radiated from down in his throat.

"My name is Irene Stokes, I live at 1801 McGavin Street," she said as she brushed the mud off her knees. Morgan jotted down the information and then went back to his squad car.

Matt followed him, still berating every college kid he had ever seen. "I guess these punks can just walk in and take the whole damned store, and you guys will shuffle them through the system with a slap on the hand!" he said.

Matt was 5'11" and weighed about 190 pounds. He had huge hands, layered with callouses from hard work. His hair was black, his skin dark, and even without the name Corgliano, everything about him said Italiano. His eyebrows were lowered and his jaw twitched as he bit his lip.

When they reached the squad car, without warning Matt threw open the door and shouted, "You fucking punk, if you ever come into my store again, I'll break your goddamn fingers!" Matt was like a bulldog with the hair raised on his back, his lips curled with teeth glaring, standing over his prey.

Morgan slammed the car door and pushed Matt away from the car. Matt didn't resist. Morgan looked over his shoulder at the young arrestee in the backseat of the squad. Constance was a cornered wild animal who was poised to do battle. His hands were cuffed behind his back, but he wasn't intimidated. His back was straight, his jaw was set, his eyes glaring in defiance. "You son of a bitch, I'll kill you!" he snarled.

"Don't make me laugh, you fucking punk!" Matt yelled.

Jack moved in to pull Matt away again. Two other squad cars were driving onto the parking lot with emergency lights flashing. Ed drove up beside Morgan's squad car. He cut his emergency lights and rolled down his window. "What's going on out here? The radio operator's been trying to get your status for fifteen minutes."

"We had a runner. I didn't have time to radio it in," Morgan said.

Ed glanced at Matt and said, "Hi, Matt, what's going on?"

"Fuck, don't ask," he barked as he turned and marched away. Ed rolled up his car window and slowly left the parking lot. Morgan called in his status and transported Constance to the police station where he was processed for retail theft. Constance was later bonded out by Julie McBride. It was a routine shoplifting arrest—not much different than a hundred other cases Morgan had handled. He turned Constance over to the jailer and went to the squad room to write his report.

CHAPTER TWENTY-TWO

It was quiet and peaceful in Willoughby Hills. Cabin fever was on the decline. The dirty snowdrifts were gone and warm breezes sailed across the prairie in a calm rushing harmony. Still, at any moment the quiet might instantly change. In Illinois the weather in springtime is irregular and wearisome. It might be crystal clear with crisp white clouds floating lazily across a cobalt sky, but beyond the horizon a mega-storm will be advancing like a frenetic monster spawning destruction in its wake. Rain in Illinois is usually accompanied by fierce lightning and winds plunging from the clouds, breaking tree limbs and sending roofing shingles into gyrations. A gentle rain was as unlikely as finding gold in your backyard with a metal detector. But now in Willoughby Hills when the weather was quiet, another menace was materializing in the shadows. Roderick Constance roamed the streets making observations, plotting his next malicious endeavor. His devious mind was working overtime. Now murder was his number one trial prep against criminal charges. John Mason had not died in vain. His death served to free Constance from prosecution. If nothing else, it was handy. Now it was someone else's turn.

He wanted to get into the police files. There were names and addresses in those files that he needed. Constance had been stalking the Kramer store employees, studying their habits.

Getting to them would be easy even without their personal information. He could do without the info altogether, but if it landed in his lap, that would just be dandy. His main concern was the woman who had returned the steaks. He didn't have a clue about her. She was the problem.

In in all of history atrocities are committed in bulk. The Chinese murder their citizens for their body parts. The Irish Republican Army during the 60's regularly bombed unsuspecting innocent people in coffee shops and restaurants to make a political point. Hitler and the Third Reich murdered six million people for having done nothing more than being born to a certain ethnic group. Nothing can ever mitigate the grimness of that, but dying en masse alongside ten or ten thousand is no more an atrocity than dying alone beneath a bridge on a lonely snow-covered riverbank, or having a bullet ravage your brain in a downtown city slum. A life extinguished at the hands of another without justification is an impiety — an infringement upon God Himself. Every life counts. Constance didn't get it. The sanctity of life was never a consideration for him. His selfishness was limitless. If the witnesses against him had to die so he could walk, then so be it.

When Constance was arrested for shoplifting, the processing room at City Hall was in use, so the jailer took him to the third floor evidence room where he was fingerprinted and photographed. He saw the junk, the artifacts and outdated supplies, but most importantly he saw several rows of file cabinets lining the walls. The jailer pulled his file and stapled the Polaroid pictures he had taken to the folder and then returned it to the cabinet. Constance knew right where the witness's names and addresses were being stored. Now he was determined to find a way back into that room. Constance had studied the dilapidated building until he knew every inch of it, and he had a plan.

On March 15th, it had been warm throughout the day, but as the sun was setting, huge billowing clouds were building in the western sky. Morgan stood in the apartment doorway watching the clouds with fearful interest. As darkness descended, lightning was streaking in violent bursts, setting the sky ablaze. Morgan pretended to be looking into the darkness from curiosity only, but fear was treading on his peace of mind. He didn't want Molly to suspect his apprehension. He was embarrassed by his uneasiness.

Morgan had been a policeman for five years, and nobody would ever accuse him of being chicken or being afraid. He had disarmed men who were bigger than him—men who were enraged, wielding knives, and brandishing guns. But he handed their asses to them, and he never backed down. No one could call him a coward, yet here he was, unnerved by a pending thunderstorm.

The lightning sizzled again and he turned from the door, startled by the abrupt light and vociferous sound. He thought about his childhood and how his father was terrified of thunderstorms. When the clouds rolled in from the west and the slightest wind stirred, his family was hurried into the storm cellar, to huddle like scared rats. Those childhood memories lingered into his adulthood. His father was the bravest man he had ever known, and if thunder and lightning were that awesome, it surely was something to fear. It was clearly a phobia and he tried to cover it up, but still when the weather turned foul, he was as nervous as a kitten in a dog kennel.

Molly watched him from the living room. She knew he was anxious, but she was careful not to embarrass him by pointing it out. She walked to the doorway and joined him. "Oh, boy, it looks like we're in for a good storm," she said. She tried to sound frightened. Morgan always had a hefty portion of guts when others were depending on him.

The lightning crackled again. Every nerve in his body went on alert. He placed his arm around Molly and hugged her as the thunder rumbled in the distance.

On the other side of town in Hovey Hall, Roderick Constance was preparing to go out into the night. He was dressed in black, wearing a stocking cap with a heavy sweatband to prevent rain from pouring into his eyes. He carried a nylon rope around his neck and a flashlight fastened to his belt. He opened the door and peeked into the hallway. When all was clear, he scrambled down the hall and pounced into the pouring rain.

The wind swirled as Morgan resumed his lookout at the living room door. The leaves in the trees across the street rustled as the sky turned greenish-black. Morgan suppressed the urge to go to a place of safety. Molly came back to check the sky. This time she had a worried look on her face. She felt a genuine fear when a stiff gust bent the small trees earthward, and the wind howled across the utility wires.

Morgan had been in a small tornado when he was in his teens, and although his perceptions were fogged by fear, he at least had that experience to draw from. Now as the wind howled, he recognized this was only a thunderstorm, just straight winds. Molly was alarmed, but now his concern was diminished. Morgan had found that when things really became treacherous, he was much better at dealing with them than when there was ambiguity or doubt. Now as the storm raged he would watch and analyze it logically. The anxiety inside had gone away. Morgan was afraid of what he couldn't see — now his nemesis was out in the open.

Roderick Constance scuttled through the darkness, often blinded by lightning flashes, and wind-blown debris. The civil defense sirens were wailing, activated by sixty-mile-per-hour winds, but still he forged on, unafraid. As he approached City Hall the rain fell in torrents. A transparent wall of water and wind stretched into the limitless darkened sky. Constance sprinted to the building next door where the radio lab was located. There was a steel radio tower with a ladder leading to the roof. City Hall was three stories tall and impossible to scale, so he would climb onto the radio lab rooftop to use as his base. From there he would make his way to the top of the ancient red brick administration building.

Thunder clapped and lightning hissed as he jumped onto the steel tower to make his ascension. He stopped momentarily considering the possibility of being electrocuted. The thought only hastened his pace as he scurried up the ladder like a rat running from a sudden light. When he reached the rooftop, Constance studied the rusty fire escape hanging from the side of City Hall. It was bent and crooked, eroded by rust and time.

Constance rung out his stocking cap and pushed back his soggy hair. The fire escape hung only three feet above his head. He neared the edge of the rooftop and measured the distance he would have to jump to catch the bottom rung. He tiptoed and stretched to find he was only inches away from touching it. He could easily have lunged for the rusty iron and grabbed it, but he was forty-five feet from the ground. Not fear but logic caused him to back off and attach safety ropes to his belt. He tied the rope around his waist and threw the other end around the fire escape. When it was secured he hopped from the radio lab onto the fire escape. He scurried up the rusty iron steps onto the rooftop of City Hall.

Wasting no time, he went to the chimney, tested its stability, and then tied the nylon rope around it. He peered over the gushing rain gutter to locate the window he wanted to enter. He stopped to insert the end of the rope into a section of garden hose that was the circumference of his waist, and then wrapped it around him. He fetched two hooks from his pocket, attached them to the rope, and then pulled tight. The hours he had practiced doing this would have to pay off, or he would be left dangling helplessly in midair. Slowly and carefully he backed down the wall like a spider on a web. The bricks were wet, and twice he slipped and scrambled like a cat to reposition himself just in time to avoid catastrophe. Although the hooks were authentic mountain-climbing gear, the rope was a local hardware variety more suitable for household duty. The garden hose would protect him from rope burn by allowing the rope to freely slide through it, but in a fall when the rope ran out, the jolt would break every bone in his body. Still, the thought of death didn't worry him. Minutes later, which seemed like an hour, Constance had reached the evidence room window. He had estimated the distance perfectly and rested, cradled on the garden hose as casually as sitting on a playground swing.

While Constance was dangling sixty-five feet from the ground, Joe Bernard was just coming on duty. He drove to City Hall with the intention of goofing off with Tony Marcelli, but it was pouring and he didn't want to get wet. While waiting out the rain, Joe was driving around the downtown area pretending to be doing his job. He was cruising the alleys, shining his spotlight at windows and doors as though he were looking for broken casements or busted locks. He drove through the alley behind the radio lab. He pointed his spotlight one way and then another. Unknown to Joe, his spotlight was shining right on Constance hanging on the rope in front of the evidence room window. If he had glanced up to actually examine the buildings he might have seen Constance suspended there. A mere glimpse at Constance and even he would have known something was slightly askew. Constance froze. There was nothing he could do except wait for the officer's next move. He was surprised when he saw the police van moving slowly out of the alley. It turned onto Mclean Street and disappeared around the corner.

Constance waited for a long moment, his mind churning out possible excuses for why he was hanging like a dummy on a string on the outer wall of City Hall in a thunderstorm. Nothing but the truth would be believed. Miraculously he wouldn't need a reason because nothing happened. There was never an alarm, no flashing red and blue lights, no fat cops with bullhorns demanding he come down, only the rumbling of thunder as the storm was departing slowly to the east.

Once he realized that the cop was either blind or stupid, Constance replaced his leather gloves with surgical gloves. He sliced the windowpane with a glass cutter, taped across it with duct tape, and waited for a thunderclap. When Mother Nature accommodated with a rumbling from above, he thumped the glass with his elbow. The glass popped and splintered but held together in one large piece, the result of having been secured with duct tape. Methodically he taped and thumped until he cleared a hole large enough to get through.

He hopped inside. The shadows and creaking floors and the musty smell of the 150-year-old building mingled together, slowly seeping into his senses. As his eyes adjusted to the light, Constance scanned the room, looking for alarms. He already knew where to find his file since the jailor fetched it out right in front of him. In only a few minutes he copied everything he needed into a pad he carried in a plastic sandwich bag. He placed the folder containing his arrest records and case file back into the cabinet, but gathered case records of other defendants and flung them across the room. He emptied the desk drawers on the floor and kicked the contents sending them flying.

The shoes Constance was wearing were stolen from Walmart and had never been worn. He knew that shoe prints were distinctive and could be traced just like a fingerprint. Yet he slogged around the room unconcerned. He intended to trash the shoes as soon as he was back on the ground. In only a few minutes, Constance was back on his nylon rope, en route to safety. He struggled, tugging and pulling as he ascended the wall. He returned to the rooftop of City Hall, back to the fire escape and on to the open street.

CHAPTER TWENTY-THREE

When Morgan reported for duty the next morning, City Hall was buzzing. Gladys was busy arranging parking meter tickets, but she looked up and smiled. Her face revealed a puckish astonishment, an expression that said "Something amusing is going on, but I'm not giving it up."

"What's happening, Gladdy?" Morgan asked. Gladys rolled her eyes, hummed through tightened lips, and shrugged. Morgan grimaced, thinking, *What the hell.*

Gladys knew everything about the activities at City Hall. Her ears were within proximity of every office in the place, but wrestling information out of her was like peeling bark off a tree. Morgan understood by her expression that it was pointless to ask again. He kicked the metal plate, the door bleeped, and he went inside. The chief's office door was open so Morgan could see Tony Morcelli sitting in a chair right in front of the chief's desk. It was a chair nobody wanted to occupy, commonly called "the hot seat." Two junior detectives were leaning on the doorway, and Ernie Linehurst was standing with his hands in his pockets beside Tony. To say it didn't look good would be an understatement. Sarge was leaning against the wall in the hallway, listening to the conversation. Even Roy was circling nervously near the coffeemaker.

"What the hell's going on?" Morgan asked. Sarge peeked over his glasses and nodded toward the chief's office. Morgan already suspected there was a serious conversation in progress, but Sarge's head nod confirmed it. Since Sarge was lingering within hearing distance, it implied that he didn't like what he was hearing.

Roy looked over his glasses and gave Morgan a head nod. So looking over their peepers and head nods had been the business of the day. Roy walked into the supply room and gave Morgan the "come here" head nod. Morgan snickered under his breath and followed Roy.

"Are we operating on sign language this morning?" he asked glibly.

"Somebody broke into the evidence room last night," Roy whispered.

"Was it Tony?" Morgan gasped.

"Hell no, but he was working when it happened. I think he's in deep shit," Roy said.

"Somebody walked right past the complaints window and went upstairs and broke into the evidence room?" Morgan asked, astonished at the possibility. He grimaced and waited for Roy to respond. Roy filled him in, telling him about the mess and the broken window. From everything he had been able to overhear, he thought someone came from the rooftop and broke in from the outside.

"It sounds like something you'd see in the movies," Roy said. Morgan was confused. How could that be Tony's fault? He was three stories from the evidence room.

Morgan went back to the hallway and joined Sarge. Smoke was circling his head, his pipe clenched between his teeth, his jaw set in contemplation. "I've had enough of this," Sarge said as he started down the hallway. He split the two detectives and pushed his way into the chief's office. "Sorry, Chief, but how about a little unsolicited input here," he snorted. His voice was low, like a big dog issuing a warning from way down in his throat. The office became as quiet as a graveyard. Tony looked up as though God had just sent a guardian angel.

"I'm embarrassed about this, same as you guys, but I don't see how any of this is Tony's fault! This is the most dilapidated police station in the downstate area. I'm surprised something like this hasn't happened before. Hell, we don't even have an alarm system in this place. Not even a panic alarm. It's harder to get into the squad room than it is to get in a window around here. How in hell do you expect him to know what's happening on the third floor?" His voice was still a low growl, but he had turned up the volume.

Roy had crept back into the hallway and was peeking over Morgan's shoulder. Morgan laughed softly from down in his chest. "Lackadaisical my ass," he said. Roy's eyes were the size of a goose egg.

The two junior detectives were shooed off and departed for their squad room. Ernie stuck his head out and smiled as he closed the door. It wasn't long before Tony was in the clear, the chief was patting Sarge on the back, Ernie was turning the cigar in his cheek, and the three veteran police officers were heading off to get on with their duties.

Having City Hall burglarized would make the police department look like keystone cops, but the truth was it would take a total overhaul to make the place secure. There was enough blame to go around, but none of it was Tony's. The chief was only reacting as any administrator would in that situation. The position he occupied was appointed but he had been a cop for twenty years before he was promoted. His departmental rank was lieutenant. One stroke of the mayor's pen would find him driving a desk through the ancient building instead of barking orders. He was in an unenviable position. "Mr. Mayor, someone broke into the police station and messed up the place..." It was human nature to be a little upset.

Ernie was back within a few minutes. He asked Roy to prepare a printed record from the teletype radio log for the last twelve months. Roy didn't like it but didn't protest. The teletype would be clattering for hours. The consensus was that it was a vandal who wanted the ultimate thrill of breaking into a police station. Ernie didn't agree. His fear was that there was a motive behind it. Something much more sinister, but he clearly didn't know what. It may have been someone seeking information from the police records. There would be a radio log entry of every person who had been transported to the police station, but the log would include every word that had been spoken. It would be a monumental task to go through it with a fine-tooth comb, but at least that was a place to start.

****

Dishes clattered and voices clamored inside the small café. Frances Constance hurriedly gathered yolk-covered plates, smilingly conversing with customers in the process. Roderick Constance sat on a stool at the dingy yellow counter. Smoke circled his head from a cigarette in an ashtray beside him. He picked it up, dropped it on the gray-speckled tile floor, and rubbed it out with his shoe. An old man next to him glared in disbelief. His nostrils flared. "I can't take that smoke," Constance said. The old man lit another and blew a puff of smoke sideways in Constance's direction. Constance moved to the next stool. "Get a newspaper, Frances," he snapped. Frances delivered eggs and sausage to a customer and picked up a newspaper on the return trip. Constance scanned the front page, and not seeing what he wanted he turned to page two. He smiled when he read the headline—*Willoughby Hills Police Department Burglarized*. He was proud of his handiwork.

Frances poured herself a cup of coffee. She sat down on the

stool next to Constance. "They ought to be watching the police station instead of bothering innocent people all the time," she said. Her voice was more nasal than usual. Constance didn't answer.

A red-faced man in coveralls folded his newspaper and placed a quarter on the countertop. "It makes me wonder what the world's coming to," he said. "If the police station ain't safe, what the hell is?"

The door jingled and Julie McBride came clumping through the door. She pulled at the bottom of her shirt trying vainly to cover her tubby belly. "Hello, Rod. I thought you were coming over last night," she said. Constance shrugged as he continued to read. After he had gone through the article twice, he and Julie left together, ignoring his ticket for the coffee and doughnut on the counter. Frances sighed as she rang up the cash register and dropped in the required eighty cents. For Constance there was a long day of planning ahead. Somebody was going to pay for the bullshit he was going through.

Chapter Twenty-Four

Irene Stokes and her husband Bob were an odd couple. Irene was outgoing, happy, and energetic. Bob was as dull as a made-for-public-TV movie. Irene worked for Best Homes Realty, and Bob owned and operated a small TV shop. They were both in their early sixties. Bob was a little quirky, and he looked like a troll with dark hair, bags beneath his eyes, and a nose as red as a baboon's butt. He might have been comical-looking except he wore a permanent scowl. In fact, he was a spooky little man to most people, but not to Irene. He was her grumpy, but sweet little goblin. Irene was a social animal with a wealth of friends. She worked out to stay trim and fit. They were as different as two people could be but it worked. She could see a smile on his face when the only hint was a slight twitch in the corner of his mouth, and he knew the difference between her genuine laugh and the chuckle she fabricated for her clients. Their differences had solidified their marriage because they were charmed by the distinctions. The dilemma was that Bob would soon find his life turned upside down, and their relationship would come under painful examination.

On March 27th, Irene and Bob sat on their porch swing watching the sun setting. Their conversation was as mundane as a stroll around the kitchen. Bob had sold two TVs and Irene had shown a house to an out-of-town couple. It had been warm and their lawn was beginning to turn green. They talked about spreading grass seed and putting down fertilizer.

It would be the last conversation they would ever have. That was how it always ends when someone disappears from your life—insignificant chatter. When they have vanished into the unknown or their bodies lowered into the earth, you would wade through fire to have them back for even a moment. Your heart turns blue, swollen with sorrow and regret. You'll wish you could tell them how much they meant to you and how good they were. You'll remember every little criticism you had, and you would move heaven and earth just to say "I'm sorry." On that last day you never look them in the eye and say "I love you." It's always routine chatter—just routine, mundane chatter.

At seven a.m., Bob pulled on his raincoat and glanced back into the bedroom to see Irene still sleeping. He would never see her again.

Roderick Constance marched through the brisk morning air heading along Richland Street from Willoughby Hills College. He checked his notes to be sure he was looking for the right address. He had once read that a woman went into surgery to have an eye removed, and when she awakened she was blind in both eyes. The doctor had erroneously plucked out her one good eye. Likewise, it would be a total injustice for him to go to the trouble of breaking into the police station to steal information only to go to the wrong address and murder the wrong woman. The thought somehow amused him.

When Bob Stokes drove onto Richland Street he saw the long-haired teenager with his hands shoved into his coat pockets. He was a scrawny, pale throwback to the Viet Nam war era. Being a little troll himself, Bob didn't judge people by their appearance. The fact that Constance was walking in his neighborhood early in the morning was nothing suspicious. Bob wouldn't remember him.

At 7:45 a.m., Irene yawned and glanced at the clock. She stretched and looked out the window. It had rained sometime during the night but now the sun was shining through the clouds. It looked like it would be a beautiful day. She went into the kitchen, poured orange juice, and popped a piece of bread into the toaster. She saw the coffee was already made. Bob had written a note. He would pick up grass seed and buy a new rake. She placed the note beside the toaster. It was then that strange sensations began to run through her. She could hear small noises, clicks, and creaky sounds. The house was getting older and noises were not uncommon, but there was something different going on. She glanced outside and the sunlight seemed far away, like in a dream. There was something different, something peculiar. If the essence of evil can be cast across time and space, it was pulsating throughout every particle in the room, finding Irene, tugging at her emotions.

There was no way of explaining the fear pounding in Irene's chest. She bore an eerie beckoning to advance down the hallway toward the garage. There was a voice inside warning her to turn around, but she kept going. Still, there was nothing rational about her fear. Small noises were nothing to cause alarm, but she felt defenseless and vulnerable. When she opened the garage door, it happened. She didn't hear the gunshot or feel the pain, but at the very instant before she vanished into eternal darkness, her eyes fixed on a murdering self-absorbed monster — Roderick Constance. Constance watched Irene fall and convulse and then become lifeless on the floor. He moved quickly to the window to scan the neighborhood. There was a man jogging on the sidewalk across the street. He didn't hesitate or glance around. It was clear that he didn't hear the gunshot. A boy riding a bicycle hurled a newspaper. It hit the house with a thud as he peddled down the street. Constance walked into the bedroom, put his hands into

148

his pockets, and looked around as casually as an invited guest. He went back into the kitchen and drank Irene's orange juice. Blood dripped from the bullet hole on Irene's forehead, pooling on the floor in the hallway. The bullet caught her right between the eyes. He was impressed with his work — proud. He grabbed a towel and tossed it across the room. It fluttered, falling silently onto Irene's face.

Constance grabbed Irene's feet and dragged her corpse down the hallway. Her car was in the garage with the trunk lid already open. Irene was small, so hoisting her body into the car was a simple task. Constance calmly went about cleaning the floors with bleach. When he was finished he drove Irene's car out of the garage, through the neighborhood, stopping for all stop signs and keeping it under the speed limit. He hit I-55 and headed north. He had a plan for Irene's body. A plan that would be a secret for more than thirty-five years.

CHAPTER TWENTY-FIVE

At five thirty, Bob walked through the front door of his home. He noticed a strange smell in the house. The prevailing odor was bleach, but there was also an unidentified pong lingering in the air. He sniffed and tossed his raincoat into the corner. He walked into the bedroom and saw the unmade bed. There was an empty juice glass in the kitchen sink. Irene was freaky about making the bed, and leaving a dirty glass in the sink was about as likely as finding a Sasquatch in the basement. Bob was immediately suspicious. He went to the garage and saw the magnetic Best Realty signs that had been attached to Irene's car doors were now lying on the floor. Bob rubbed the back of his neck. He was vexed but not yet spooked by the circumstances. It wasn't unusual for Irene to unexpectedly get a call to show a house. Bob turned on the TV and propped his feet on the ottoman.

At eight thirty, Bob was getting worried. He was rummaging through Irene's telephone log for numbers, when suddenly the phone rang. It was Delores Presley, Irene's manager at Best Realty. She thought maybe Irene was sick since she missed her appointments. Bob didn't hear anything Delores said from that point on.

"What the hell is she doing," he muttered under his breath.

At eleven thirty, Bob called the police department and

nervously reported Irene missing.

Ernie Linehurst met Bob on his doorstep at 7:45 the next morning. A night shift detective had talked to Bob and a statewide bulletin was released, but Ernie still wanted to do a follow-up interview. He inspected the house from one end to the other without detecting anything unusual, except for one detail. There was a lingering smell of bleach in the hallway. Ernie stood with his hands on his hips twirling the cigar in his cheek. He asked Bob if he could take up one of the tiles. Bob retrieved a hammer and putty knife. After a few sharp taps the tile popped loose. Beneath the tile there was a dark, damp substance. "Is that blood?" Bob asked. His face was already ashen but now turned completely pale. Ernie called for a crime scene crew to scour the house. The substance was in fact blood.

On April 2nd, Irene's car was found in a Holiday Inn parking lot fifteen miles north of Willoughby Hills. It was impounded and towed to the State Police crime lab in Pontiac, Illinois. In 1976, DNA research was underway but it was not yet a tool available to law enforcement. However, skin, blood, and hair analysis was commonplace. In those comparisons, technicians believed Irene's corpse was transported in the trunk of her car. That was the beginning of a haunting mystery that would be hashed over endlessly by Willoughby Hills policemen and citizens for many years to come.

In Willoughby Hills at every morning coffee klatch, Irene's disappearance was mulled over continually. When facts were few, gossip and speculation were plentiful. Bob had few friends, but suddenly everybody knew him. They were either vouching for him or criticizing everything he did. People were sipping coffee as gossip cascaded over countertops and dinner tables in a deluge. The budding consensus was that Bob Stokes was a little evil genius who murdered his wife. Bob Stokes was a broken man. Everything he cared about was centered in Irene.

Now when his head lay on his pillow at night, fear was his only companion. He didn't believe he could find sleep, but each night as his eyes adjusted to the darkness, the forms and shadows faded away allowing his eyes to close like the lid of a coffin. They sealed out the pain of loneliness, and sleep came furtively like dusk descending into night. That was now the sum total of his life.

CHAPTER TWENTY-SIX

In Willoughby Hills, murder was as rare as a Hale-Bopp burning through outer space. There were homicides in Willoughby Hills but they were usually done in a mad fracas or by someone in a jealous rage. People were never killed in premeditated machinations. Not in Willoughby Hills! Murder didn't go down well there. The natives were restless. They wanted someone brought to justice.

Ernie and the other detectives had followed every lead to a dead end. Even crank calls were painstakingly eliminated as possible leads. The state police had lent an investigator to Willoughby Hills, and the sheriff's office had a detective working alongside the three police department investigators. The first forty-eight hours are the most important, but they had come and gone without the slightest clue. When days turned into weeks, four of the five detectives working on the case had gone through every detail of the investigation and were left scratching their heads. They were ready to believe that a serial killer had come through town and killed Irene. Even in 1976, there were deranged murderers prowling the highways committing unimaginable crimes. Even so, there was a fly in the ointment. Serial murderers usually left their victims at the scene or dumped them in a ravine to rot. Irene Stokes had vanished.

In a callous world where murder and family squabbles ended in bloody massacres described on the nightly news in pedantic clatter without a grain of sympathy, it was odd to find a police detective who was bothered by someone being murdered, other than getting stuck with the overtime. Ernie Linehurst grieved through the daily grind. Irene's death weighed heavy on his mind. He had worked other murder cases, but there was evidence to follow, and in the end it was a matter of putting all the clues together. This was an extraordinary case. Clues were as scarce as calories in a cucumber. Ernie couldn't stop thinking about it. At night when he had done everything he could do, he would stew over the lack of evidence. He was stumped, but he wasn't ready to believe the serial murderer scenario.

Ernie didn't know there was a clue hiding in plain sight. It was there for anyone to see, but it was being tossed from one desk to another in trial preparations. It was a list of witnesses in the two Roderick Constance criminal cases. Tom Spencer had handled the burglary case when it was dismissed for lack of evidence, but Gary was taking the shoplifting case. If either of the crimes had been anything more than petty offenses, all three attorneys in the office would have been up to speed on the details. But since they were so routine, the trial prep in both cases was simply to talk to the witnesses, decide the order they would testify, and prepare a closing argument. The fact there was a missing witness in both cases was never cross-referenced.

One evening in April, Morgan was watching TV and Molly was going over deposition notes when Ernie Linehurst showed up at the front door. He looked as worn out as his dog-eared raincoat. His glasses were resting on the end of his nose, his cigar chocked into his jaw, and his fists were pinned against his hips.

Morgan was puzzled by the unexpected visit, but he invited Ernie in. He offered a beer, but Ernie turned it down. He took a seat on the couch, unbuttoned his raincoat, and slouched as though he didn't have an ounce of energy left in him. Morgan tried to start a conversation, but Ernie was too preoccupied to get on the same page with him. Molly watched from her desk, at times raising her eyebrows, bewildered by Ernie's demeanor. Finally, Morgan said, "Ernie, what the hell's going on?"

Ernie sighed, grimaced, and said, "Morgan, I need a favor. It's stupid, but I want you to go with me to do an interview—I mean if you don't have plans?"

It seemed like an odd request. There were six officers on duty (seven counting Joe), so why would Ernie need him to assist with an interview? Morgan suspected it was about the Irene Stokes investigation, but Morgan wasn't involved with the case. The entire department was astute to all communications coming down about Irene Stokes, but the duty guys were about the business of patrolling the streets, answering radio calls, and writing tickets. The last thing Morgan expected was to have the chief detective come to his home while he was off duty to ask for his help.

"Sure, Ern. Whatever you need, but..." Morgan stopped, shrugged, and waited for Ernie to explain.

Ernie's face seemed almost tormented as he began to stammer like a nervous teenager. "I don't really believe in this kind of stuff, but you know, I'm sort of out of ideas. I mean, I don't rely on this kind of thing," he said, totally making no sense.

Morgan was mystified. "Ernie, what the hell are you talking about?"

"I'm going to see a psychic," Ernie snorted. He turned his hands out and waited for Morgan to laugh in his face.

Morgan smiled. "Is that it? That's what has your underwear in a bunch?" He chuckled.

Ernie chuckled too. "Yes," he said. They both laughed again.

"Sure, whenever," Morgan said. Molly popped up from her chair. "I'm going too," she said and giggled.

"I was on my way there when I thought you might want to

go with me. But, ah, we have to keep this to ourselves," Ernie said. Morgan laughed again. Molly was getting her coat from the hall closet. They tried to mitigate how stupid it was with humor, but in just a few minutes they were on their way.

It was a quick drive to the subdivision north of Willoughby Hills, appropriately named Mystic Ridge. As they turned onto the interstate ramp, the Milky Way was strung across the universe like crystals glistening in the dark. The moon hung over the tree line, shimmering in an orange glow without a cloud in the sky. They were on the interstate for five minutes before they had to exit onto a tree-lined blacktop road a few miles from their destination. At that point everything changed.

The stars vanished as a thick fog surfaced, fulminating like a wind-driven cloud. Ernie slowed to a snail's pace and hunched forward peering over the steering wheel. Occasionally there were places where the fog lifted leaving wispy white ribbons of haze hovering over the road, deceiving them into thinking it was over only to find within the next hundred yards it was as thick as pea soup again. At one of those clearings Ernie was heading around a bend in the road when suddenly, like a phantom, a large coyote was standing in the middle of the road. His fur was silver, sparkling in the glow of the headlights. In the fog he resembled a ghost, waiting to fade into a miasma. He watched the car with yellow eyes sparkling in the light until it was upon him, and then he darted into the woods.

"Was that a wolf?" Molly cried.

"Coyote," Ernie said.

"It was eerie," Molly said. "I hope that wasn't a bad omen."

Both Ernie and Morgan laughed. Molly didn't.

They crossed a bridge, meeting another car coming from the opposite direction. They were so close and moving so slowly that Ernie could have shaken hands with the other driver. The fog was like a blanket, still thick and white as they went up a hill on the other side of the river. After they crested the hill, the air became crisp and frigid, and the stars were there again as bright as diamonds in the sky. There were no ghostly animals fading into the mist and no cloaked gentleman with blood on the corners of his mouth.

They found a mailbox with the name Gretchen Hamilton posted in front of a new, brick ranch-style home. Morgan expected to see a three-story house with cedar shingles and a round portico covered with vines and cobwebs. It was disappointing in a way.

****

At that same moment the fog was advancing into Willoughby Hills. Roderick Constance was walking to his mother's home. He had spent the last hour in the alley behind Jack Fink's house, pacing from one end to the other. In the middle of the block were two large German shepherds. At first they barked ferociously, but each time he passed, Constance tossed pieces of hamburger to each of them. After the first two or three passes, the barking was less intense. When the meat was gone Constance headed out to his mother's home. Morgan Cooper's apartment was on the route. He stopped on the sidewalk to study the residence and the surroundings. Occasionally a car traveling down 18th Street came out of the fog casting vague shadows, so Constance ducked between the trees to hide. He wasn't Jack the Ripper, he lacked the mystique, but he was just as dangerous. Constance was a murderer on the prowl.

****

Gretchen Hamilton had lived on the same plot of land her entire life. She replaced her old farm home with the new ranch-style house, but her lifestyle was pretty much the same as it had always been. She claimed that she was struck by ball lightning when she was eight years old, awakening something supernatural within her. She was unconscious for several days before she recovered. When she woke up she suffered unusual visions and dreamed about people and things she didn't know or understand. As she grew older she found she had insights into the future. Now she counseled people about everything from their love interest to financial affairs. She had several clients who were in the movie business who regularly flew in from California. She didn't charge a fee for her services, but all donations were welcomed. Movie people proved to be very generous.

As Ernie, Morgan, and Molly sat in the driveway snickering at themselves for visiting a clairvoyant, a teenage boy came out of the house and approached the car. "Mom says she's waiting for you," he said.

In just a few moments they were on the porch being greeted by a chubby woman with a broad smile. Ernie introduced himself, Morgan, and Molly. Gretchen said she knew their time was limited so she cut right to the chase. She directed them to her study. As they proceeded down the hallway, plush carpeting sank beneath their feet. Numerous autographed celebrity pictures were framed, lining the walls. Molly glanced into the master bath as they passed and noticed the antique claw-foot bathtub and the pedestal vanity with glistening antique brass fixtures. It was a beautiful house. Gretchen didn't charge for her services, but she was certainly getting some mileage from them.

When they entered the study the lights darkened automatically. "Special effects," Gretchen said. They all chuckled politely. A few minutes of small talk followed before Gretchen asked if Ernie had some of Irene's personal effects. Ernie produced a toothbrush. Gretchen giggled and covered her mouth. "That's a first for me," she said.

She was actually thinking about something like a nightgown or blouse. Ernie laughed at his own naivety as he dug into his bag and found Irene's nightgown. Gretchen touched the material. She rubbed it slowly between her forefinger and thumb. Molly's eyes were glued on her. Gretchen closed her eyes. She seemed very sincere. She was calmly looking beyond the room, past the material in her hand, onward to some location invisible to anyone but her. She appeared authentic, and if she wasn't, she had clearly mastered the ability to yank the chain of the nonbeliever.

"I feel fear. I'm confused. There's a darkness I've never experienced before but at the same time I sense fire—a deep infernal," Gretchen started slowly. "There's someone who needs me. Someone close to me," she said. She stopped and looked at Ernie. "Is there a Bob involved in this?" she asked.

"I can't give you any names," Ernie said. It was quiet for a moment. Molly's eyes opened wide, clearly revealing that the psychic was on to something. Gretchen closed her eyes again, laboring to get into a cabalistic barrio. "There is a dark shadow, but it's not Bob," she said. "I can't see," Gretchen said quietly. She closed her eyes tighter, breathing in a slow cadence, struggling fitfully to see into that dark hole between life and the hereafter. Finally, she opened her eyes. "That's it," she said.

Ernie frowned. That's it?"

"That's it," she repeated.

"That doesn't help me much," Ernie said.

"Do you want me to make up something," Gretchen asked facetiously.

"No, no, I don't. I'm just desperate. I know there's a killer out there. I don't want anybody else to die because I can't come up with a clue," Ernie said.

Gretchen looked at him sympathetically. "I can tell you one thing. This darkness—the shadow—the evil entity is youthful. If it's a male, he's not very old," she said.

The conversation went on, Ernie speculating without getting any closer to an answer. Occasionally the thought crossed his mind that the whole endeavor was ridiculous. People cannot communicate with the dead. It was absurd.

The entire session was over in forty-five minutes. As they

concluded, Ernie thanked Gretchen and shook her hand. Molly followed suit. Gretchen smiled. When Morgan touched her hand, Gretchen recoiled, releasing a gasp. She squeezed Morgan's fingers as she closed her eyes. "I can't tell you how I know this, or why, but young man, you're in grave danger," she said. Morgan smiled and shook it off. He wasn't just dubious, he thought the whole thing was stupid. He wasn't concerned about Gretchen's warning. He was a policeman, he was always in grave danger. Molly was worried enough for both of them.

CHAPTER TWENTY-SEVEN

In counties all across the country trials were being conducted on every manner of minor violations from jaywalking, burning trash without a burn permit, and a multitude of traffic offenses. The Roderick Constance Retail Theft trial fit into that category. It would probably evoke less than a paragraph in the local newspaper. Although Matt Corgliano would disagree, it just wasn't very important.

Morgan had been up late with Ernie forging through fog and facing grave danger (according to the fortune teller,) but still managed to make it through the night unscathed. Today he was scheduled to testify in a shoplifting case. He had to report for duty and then proceed to the courthouse. It was beyond irony that this case and their trip to see the psychic were all bundled into the same bale, but still a universe apart.

There were usually several cases called on the docket and most were over in short order. This case would be different because Dan Ingelman had asked for a trial by jury. Most lawyers would have stuffed their briefcases under their arms, gone to the state's attorney, and graciously accepted the plea agreement he offered, but Dan was predictably obstinate.

Jack Fink and Matt Corgliano were standing in the rotunda looking over the railing studying the numerous paintings of Abraham Lincoln in various stages of his life. There were paintings of young Abraham with an ax working alongside other early settlers, images of an older Abe riding a horse with a book in his hand, and finally President Lincoln in a pose as represented at the Lincoln Memorial in Washington, DC. Every courthouse in central Illinois had a myriad of Lincoln tales and memorabilia. Willoughby Hills was no different.

There were two courtrooms on the first floor, three on the second level, and a large one on the third story. The Roderick Constance trial was being held on the third level where there was little activity. It was as quiet as a train station at three o'clock in the morning.

Dan Ingelman was seated with Roderick Constance outside the courtroom reviewing the case file. Constance was wearing blue jeans and a denim shirt. His hair was in a ponytail. He was a strange looking little mouse, but there wasn't a person in that courthouse who would have guessed how far afield he had strayed from normality. He had already killed three people for starters, and he was still in business to kill a few more. Getting into his head wasn't possible—to understand how he could kill another human being for such trivial objectives wasn't fathomable.

The truth was that avoiding prosecution wasn't the total sum of his motives. Constance felt violated by the people he killed, as much as if he had been physically assaulted or humiliated by them. In his mind he was just getting even with them. There was a place somewhere inside his head that believed he had the right to do anything he wanted and nobody could stop him. He knew logically that there were laws against stealing, but emotionally they were for other people, not for him. It was a challenge and an insult for anyone to oppose him no matter how insignificant the issue. John Mason had done nothing more than occupy the same room, but Constance considered it his space. Any infringement caused his blood to boil. He silently stewed over the simplest things, envisioning ways to torture and kill people who had stepped on his toes. Now as he prepared for trial it was more of the same. The entire process produced a burning rage inside him. He hated everyone involved and wanted to brutalize and murder them all.

Inside the courtroom there were row upon row of empty seats. The court reporter was feeding paper into her shorthand machine while the bailiff was busy arranging the court docket. Jack Fink was in the rotunda patiently waiting to be called to testify. Matt Corgliano was pacing around grumbling about the judicial system being a circus act and a total insult to the victims who had to go through the process. He had testified in shoplifting cases before but it was still uncomfortable for him. He feared that phrases like "that little bastard" or words like "idiot" would pop out of his mouth. He stuttered and bumbled through his testimony because he had to use, in his words, less eloquent language.

When the judge entered the courtroom the Bailiff quietly said, "All rise." Chairs scooted as the participants stood up and waited for him to be seated. The preliminaries were short and the trial began in earnest. Gary called Jack Fink and led him through his observations, taking him back to the time when he first began to watch Constance. Dan interrupted several times, objecting on procedural matters and to almost every word Jack uttered. The jury was already irritated with Dan before Jack was dismissed. Still, Gary had maneuvered through the testimony to provide a clear picture of Constance stealing two pieces of meat.

Constance never looked at Jack the entire time. He leaned back in his chair and examined the Jury, watching every facial expression. He keyed in on a middle-aged woman who appeared oddly exclusive from the others. She resembled a 1950's suburban housewife. She had dark-rimmed glasses, a beehive hairdo, and she was wearing an aqua-colored shirtdress. But more than anything, she was wearing a sympathetic expression for the young defendant.

When Matt Corgliano was called to the stand, he marched across the courtroom staring at the jury from beneath his thick, dark, bushy unibrow. It looked as though he might want to lower his head and ram right into them. An agitated bull pawing in the dirt, snorting angrily would have been less menacing.

Matt's testimony was predictable. He believed it should have been obvious that Constance was guilty. He wanted to say that he was suspicious of him right from the start. He knew he had stolen from the store before but they just hadn't caught him until that evening. Wasn't it true that he went to the office to get Jack to watch him because he was suspicious, and in the end, didn't Constance steal two of his steaks? Wasn't that proof enough of his guilt? He wanted to say all that in his own words. That just wasn't how it turned out in the courtroom. Dan objected to Matt's conclusion that "Constance was suspicious." It was prejudicial. The judge agreed.

Matt tried to describe how he went to get Jack to watch Constance. That drew another objection because it was prejudicial. It was sustained. He tried to say it again with different words, but the judge stopped him. It seemed like a rude interruption to Matt. Sweat was beginning to tingle beneath his hairline.

Matt said Jack yelled that Constance had stolen two steaks and was headed out the door. Dan objected. The judge sustained. Matt could say that Jack called for his help, but he couldn't tell the jury that Constance had stolen steaks because it was hearsay. Only Jack Fink could testify to what he had seen.

By that time Matt was steaming and it was evident in his answers. If the fire in his eyes could have transcended distance, the judge, jury, and the whole damned courthouse would have been in flames. Gary Winstead was warned to have his witness confine his answers to yes or no unless he was testifying to something he had seen firsthand. He was talking to Gary as if Matt wasn't sitting right there in front of him.

What little restraint Matt had vanished. He turned in the witness chair and gawked at the judge with the innocence of a bewildered child. The filter between his brain and his vocal cords failed and the words rolled off his tongue with the eloquence of a lady mud-wrestler. "Judge, I don't know what the fuck you're talking about," he said.

If a pin had fallen to the floor at that moment, the sound would have rumbled like thunder. The judge sat upright, took in a deep breath, and promptly cleared the courtroom. The frustration had pealed Matt's self-control like an onion, leaving his true feelings hanging in the air with just as much potency. In all reality the judge was more than likely amused, but there was no way he could ignore Matt's insolence.

Matt was escorted into the judge's chamber where he was given a quick introduction to courtroom etiquette. He was fined $200 and then returned to the courtroom with a new appreciation for judicial procedure. When his testimony resumed he found it much easier to answer with yes or no replies. His disposition now was more like a tired old town dog than a mad bull. He found it much easier to respond to the questions without the seething anger percolating in his brain. The judge had put an end to all that.

When Gary asked him what his observations were when he was confronted by a woman in the parking lot, he was nervous about answering, fearing Dan would fly out of his chair shouting, "Objection!" He wasn't wrong. Dan's weedy little strands of hair fluttered in the air as if electrified. He sprang forward crying that the question called for speculation. Matt was astounded when the judge allowed him to answer.

He went on to say that the woman told the police officer she had seen Roderick Constance throw the steaks under her car.

Dan objected again. The judge overruled allowing him to answer, which totally confused Matt. What the hell? It didn't make sense. It came down to one little detail that until now he didn't know. He could say what he heard because the statement was made in the presence of the defendant.

Yes, sir, the whole damn process was straight from an insane asylum.

Constance was deflated and empty. It seemed at the moment that killing Irene Stokes had been for nothing. Even the police officer could testify to what she had seen because the entire conversation with her was right there in front of him. Being convicted seemed inevitable until he glanced at the 50's woman in the shirtdress. As Matt left the witness stand she was watching him through her catlike glasses as if he had stolen a pie from her windowsill.

Morgan was the last witness, and his testimony was short. He knew all the pitfalls and how to get his account into the record without Dan bouncing off the walls demanding that his testimony be stricken from the record. Naturally he left out the part where Matt jerked open the car door and threatened to break some of the defendant's bones. When he left the witness stand he was certain that Constance would be convicted. This case was nothing more than routine.

The jury should have been out for forty-five minutes, but ten hours later, the judge was called at home to report to the courthouse. When the jury returned they were still without a verdict. The judge asked them individually if they had reached a verdict. One by one they answered that they had not. He asked if further deliberation would help in reaching a decision. Their answer again was a disappointing, "No." The judge thanked them for their service and they were dismissed. As they filed out of the courtroom, the 50's woman glanced at Constance and smiled. The trial ended in a hung jury.

CHAPTER TWENTY-EIGHT

Morgan returned to the night shift. Molly was working in Zion, Illinois, a town just north of Chicago situated on Lake Michigan. Zion is a blue collar community, but there are miles of sandy beaches where the waves reach four feet high as they advance ashore, roaring with the same intensity as the surf pounds the sands on the California coastline. Although the city was within walking distance from the beach, there was a thick band of maple trees easing the traffic noise, leaving it as quiet as a midnight walk in a forest.

On Friday evening, Morgan drove from Willoughby Hills to Zion to spend his days off with Molly. When he drove into the parking lot she was waiting for him. The weather was beautiful. The stars were shining in a black moonless sky and a soft breeze was blowing in from the lake. The top was down on the Fiat and Morgan enjoyed the ride. He was in no hurry until he saw Molly, and then he wanted to fly out of the car before it stopped. She had been there all week and he missed her. It was his first real dose of separation anxiety. He watched her hurrying down the terraced steps as he guided the Fiat into the parking stall.

The smell of fresh water was in the air, and the sound of the waves was beating against the shore. The foam riding atop the sway was as white as snow effervescing in the dark water. Molly's soft curls bounced as she descended the stairs. She was wearing pleated tan slacks and a pastel, green halter top. Her skin was dark in the evening light. She moved with fluid, graceful strides. She was thin, beautiful, and radiated sophistication. Morgan felt very lucky at that moment.

"You finally made it," she said as she hugged him.

"Your tan's terrific," Morgan said.

"I love you," she said.

"I love you too, baby." The words came out pretty easily.

Morgan breathed the fresh air as they proceeded toward the hotel. "Did you miss me? Is everything all right at home?" Molly wrapped her arm around his waist and slipped her finger through his belt loop.

"Yep," Morgan said.

"Which one?"

"Both."

"How's the deposition going?" Morgan asked.

"Terrible. The second day we had testimony from a Canadian who spoke both French and English. He kept getting goofed up, changing from English to French. Finally, I just volunteered to translate for him and he just stayed with French. Now if it goes to court I'll have to provide transcripts in English and French," she said, blowing a strand of hair away from her face. She tried to conceal it but it was easy to see she was pleased with herself.

"Not many court reporters can do that, I'll bet," Morgan said, winking.

They stopped at the top of the terrace and looked out across the lake. There were lights flickering where small craft drifted along on the dark water. The breeze became noticeably cooler as they walked closer to the beach. Morgan gazed into the night, out over the water to that unknown location where all people go the first time they look into the endless horizon over the ocean, or in this case Lake Michigan.

His eyes were still fixed on the water vanishing into the darkness when he said, "You know, I haven't been anywhere like this."

Molly looked at him, mystified by his statement. "You've been to Chicago."

"This is the first time I've been to Lake Michigan. I saw it from Lake Shore Drive, but I've never been anywhere like this — or anywhere at all. I was a poor boy, remember?"

Molly frowned. She rested her arm on his waist, resisting the urge to hug him really hard.

"I've never seen the ocean. Hell, this looks like an ocean to me. I just feel naïve all of a sudden."

Molly hugged him. Her reaction was pride. She was proud to be with him. His experience as a police officer had made up for his lack of worldliness but he didn't try to mitigate one with the other. Even now, when he might have felt inadequate, he wouldn't try to pretend to be more than he was. If this were Acapulco or the Riviera, he might be in awe, but he would never feel elevated or diminished by his surroundings. He was a policeman from Willoughby Hills and never too far out of place. Because of that he was always sure of his part in the scheme of things.

The conversation changed to another subject as they continued into the inn. Molly was left with a warm glow. She felt very lucky to have a man with his feet planted so firmly on the ground. Morgan dropped the luggage in the room and changed into shorts and a T-shirt. They walked on the beach and talked about how the lake seemed so enormous. Morgan didn't want to highlight how overwhelmed he was, but his appreciation for the lake, the beach, and infinite stars overhead left him mesmerized.

Molly had a sweet little smile thinking, *Morgan, you really are a small-town boy*, but she kept that to herself. Not that he would be insulted, but that she was totally enjoying his respectful wonderment.

The hotel wasn't a four star, but it was very tastefully decorated. There was a large lobby with a fireplace and leather furniture. A few businessmen were scattered throughout the foyer with logbooks and ledgers in hand, scribbling and reading, preparing for who knows what as they took up their fair share of the acreage. Morgan mused to himself that it was the most sophisticated hotel he had ever stayed in.

When they were dressed for dinner, Morgan inspected himself in the full-length mirror. Although he was wearing an affordable blue suit from P.A. Bergner's, Molly believed he couldn't have looked any better in a tailor-fitted Armani. Molly wore a little knee-length black dress. It fit her perfectly revealing her thin but shapely figure.

When they walked into the bar, more than one head turned. Every man in the bar glanced at Molly, and Morgan got his share of glances from the gals. Morgan moved through the room confidently and self-assured. Molly was a little shy. She envied Morgan's composure. She believed his poise came from knowing who he was and never pretending to be something he wasn't. He was never surprised socially because he was always the same guy — Morgan Cooper — just in a different location.

They were seated at the bar as they waited for a table. Neither of them were regular drinkers but Morgan ordered a bottle of red wine. They sipped the wine until they were ushered to their table in the dining room where they could view the lake. When they finished dinner, Morgan ordered another bottle of red before they headed back into the bar. As they entered, two attorneys Molly had met earlier in the week spoke to her and nodded politely to Morgan. They were with the firm conducting the deposition Molly had been working on. As the evening progressed one of them kept turning and glancing at Molly. He was about twenty-seven, athletic, and noticeably good-looking. Morgan sensed a little envy navigating its way into his consciousness. *It must be nice to graduate from law school and work for a prestigious Chicago firm*, he thought. The other attorney was about the same age but he was pale, pudgy, and already balding. He belted down whiskey sours and eyeballed everybody in the bar.

After several minutes of gawking and glancing by the two attorneys, Morgan went to their table and introduced himself. He asked them if they wanted to join Molly and him at their table. He hoped they would decline, putting an end to the annoying stares, but they accepted. The pudgy guy gulped down what was left of his drink and ordered another before joining them. The other man chose a chair next to Molly directly across from Morgan. "So you're the policeman Molly's been talking about all week," he said. He adjusted his chair a little closer to Molly.

"Well, I'm a cop. She knows a lot of us. But yes, I suppose I'm the one," Morgan said. Molly moved her hand onto his knee in a reassuring way.

"Well, I'm Patrick, and this is James — right, James?"

The fat attorney looked through bloodshot eyes and said, "That's correct, my good man, and this is my little friend." He raised his glass in a toasting gesture. Molly forced a smile but Morgan watched James with insipid curiosity. The man was obviously drunk.

"I have to say this, Molly, the work you did on Thursday was superb," Patrick said, making eye contact with her.

"I agree," James said, raising his glass as he belted down another drink.

"That's the first time I've seen anything like it," Patrick added.

Molly thanked him in a reserved voice. It was a sure thing that Patrick was trying to impress her. He looked at the empty wine bottle. "Eating late?" he asked, nodding at the wine bottle.

"No," Morgan said. "We had wine for dinner. I don't know much about other drinks so we just stuck with what we had."

"Oh, there are many drinks for the ladies. There's Tom Collins, Black Russians, Daiquiris, Screwdrivers, Grasshoppers, and all kinds of drinks. Let me get one for you, Molly," Patrick said.

Molly squeezed Morgan's hand. "No, thanks, I like this wine," she said. She knew Patrick was trying to embarrass Morgan.

Patrick turned to the waitress and ordered another drink for himself and James, and another bottle of wine. The drunken James stared at Morgan through bloodshot eyes with heavy lids. "If you want to impress the ladies these days, you have to know what to order for them," he muttered incoherently. Morgan raised his eyebrows and watched the chubby man for an instant.

"I'd hate to rely on something so artificial," he said smiling, veiling a little irritation.

Patrick turned back to the table. "How do you like being a law dog, Morgan?" he asked with a ring of cheekiness in his voice. His words were a little more deliberate now, and his eyes were showing some redness.

"I love my job," Morgan said.

"I suppose you meet a certain type of individual doing what you do. You know, the "scrotes of the world," to quote Joseph Wambaugh."

"Sure. I'll bet you meet a few in the legal profession too, but probably better dressed," Morgan said.

"Do you intend to stay with it for the rest of your life?" Patrick asked. The question was obnoxious without extra topping, but Patrick's tone was completely condescending. Morgan's brow furrowed for an instant.

"I don't know. I haven't thought that far into the future."

Patrick smiled arrogantly, placing his finger inside his glass. "I worked at the state's attorney's office as an intern, and no offense to you, but some of those cops couldn't spell their own names. Their grammar was loathsome and to top everything off, they were the most obnoxious group of people I've ever met."

Molly squeezed Morgan's hand again. Morgan watched Patrick without revealing emotion. He ignored the insult. It made the young lawyer more determined to offend him.

"Did you go to college, Morgan?" he asked. Morgan didn't answer immediately. He was trying to decide if he should pretend this was anything less than psychological warfare. Giving courtesy another chance, he answered that he had graduated from Willoughby Hills College.

The balding, fat attorney choked on his drink trying to suppress a laugh. Patrick turned to his drunken friend and smiled as though they had uncovered a skeleton in Morgan's closet. Molly reached across the table and clutched Morgan's hand, making it clear she was taking sides. She hoped Patrick would get the message. He saw it as it was intended and instantly became offended.

"Well, if it isn't a couple of lovebirds," he spouted. His impetuous remark was so absurd that it struck Morgan as humorous. He rubbed his hand across his mouth to conceal a smile. Patrick glared at Morgan. He was obviously catching up with his friend on the inebriation front.

"You don't have to be such a snob. You're the one with the inferior education," he smirked.

Morgan couldn't refrain from chuckling. The conduct of the two men was so ridiculous it was becoming hilarious. "Listen, boys," he started, sounding much like someone talking to a couple of schoolchildren. "I invited you over here because neither of you had anyone intelligent to talk to, but now the only way I can tolerate you is by laughing at you and that's not polite, so we'll just say good night."

As they walked through the lobby, Molly congratulated him on his equanimity. It seemed she learned something new about him every day. Now she knew he could be charming and sarcastic at the same time. She didn't know if that was a good quality or not, but it was certainly amusing. She was proud of how he had handled the two men. They had started out to humiliate him and found themselves on the receiving end.

"I had my feelings hurt there a couple of times but I tried not to show it," Morgan said.

"I should have warned you about him. He's been asking me to dinner every day. I never encouraged him but he didn't need any. He's very pretentious." She placed her arm around his waist. "I'm sorry," she said.

"No apologies necessary. I knew right from the start what that guy was up to, but I knew it wouldn't work," Morgan said.

CHAPTER TWENTY-NINE

As the sun came up in Zion, Illinois, Morgan was already on the beach looking across the water. He was alone, the morning sky was overcast, and the lake was gray in the morning light. The water and sky were indistinguishable in the mist hovering over the horizon. A lone weeping willow was swaying in the breeze. It was so quiet that a raspy whispering sound carried along in the wind as the branches shifted and moved with each breath of air. Although Morgan had suppressed a yearning to see places exotic and far away, now there was an unseen power urging him to explore the world.

Molly walked down the beach. She was wearing tan Capri pants, a long-sleeved white cotton shirt with the sleeves rolled up, and her long brown hair was blowing in the wind. Morgan watched her, thinking, *It doesn't get better than this.* She put her arms around him and gazed across the lake. "I was just thinking about how happy you make me, how about you? I saw your pensive stare. What were you thinking about?"

"I don't know. Sometimes I'm embarrassed by how stupid my thoughts are. They're better left unsaid."

"You're selfish with your thoughts. You're not embarrassed. I tell you everything but you never tell me your private thoughts," she scolded. Morgan mulled it over for a moment. She was right, he was cautious about expressing his intimate notions and concepts. Sometimes his thinking was just crazy.

"Come on," Molly said, poking him in his ribs.

"It's stupid," Morgan said, "but all this water—the vastness of it. It overwhelms me. Just standing here looking out across it is like an incursion of emotions I can't explain. I can relate to those old tales about the 'calling of the sea' when some unknown force beckoned young men to sail the world's oceans. Does that sound silly to you?"

"No," she said.

He was a little embarrassed just as he thought he would be. "It seems silly to me," he said. Molly smiled and tugged at his arm, pulling him down the beach. She zigzagged as the waves rolled in playfully avoiding the cold water. Morgan facetiously suggested they go for a swim. The waves were pounding the beach and a cold mist permeated the air. Without pondering the suggestion for long, Molly declined. Morgan was happy she did.

When they returned to the room, Molly washed and dried her hair. Morgan lay on the bed watching TV. He flipped through the stations for a while, but most of the news was local. He wasn't interested so he turned the sound off. During a commercial he saw a picture of a young man. He was smiling, wearing a Chicago Cubs baseball cap. He looked familiar but Morgan didn't remember him. He didn't hear the message accompanying the photograph. It was a desperate father pleading for information about his son. There was a generous reward offered for information regarding his whereabouts. He had been missing since December 15th, 1975. His name was John Mason. Morgan didn't hear it. He didn't recognize that he was the young man who was popping his fist into the baseball glove in Kyle Brasky's room on the day he met Roderick Constance. The moment was lost. The clue hiding in plain sight was still elusive.

CHAPTER THIRTY

In Willoughby Hills, Ernie Linehurst was pounding the pavement in Irene Stokes' neighborhood. The sound of clattering lawn mowers and the smell of fresh-cut grass were declaring that summer had arrived. The desolation of winter was blown away by spring breezes. Magnolia blossoms and dogwood flowers had emblazoned the city with color for that brief transition between spring and summer, but now all that was gone, giving way to a cover of maple and oak leaves.

Ernie was like a hound dog circling frantically with his nose to the ground trying to find a scent that had grown cold. He was tired but he was convinced he would find one little clue and that small development would lead to another, and finally everything would come together. That was the way it always happened. Still, his persistence wasn't always appreciated. In the beginning people were eager to lend a hand or to volunteer information, but as time passed that initial eagerness to help had diminished. In fact, interest in finding a mysterious suspect was waning. Most people chose to think that Irene's husband had killed her. After all, he was a quirky-looking little fellow. Being off-looking was good enough to elicit a little speculation, wasn't it?

Ernie knew Bob was the most unlikely of all suspects, but gossip was cheap. Ernie had seen his face fraught with anxiety.

He'd seen his hands trembling as he watched Ernie collecting blood from beneath his kitchen tile on the day Irene disappeared. He had lost his wife—his lifelong friend—and now his fellow citizens believed he had murdered her. It was a cruel fate.

This had been the third time Ernie had canvassed the neighborhood. The greetings were often, "Hey, there's nothing new since the last time you guys were through here," or, "Listen, I'm too busy to go over this again." One irate resident threatened to call the chief if he came back again.

Ernie had parked across the street from Bob's home before he started his trek through the neighborhood. When he reentered his car the sun was dipping below the horizon. The fireflies were blinking just above the newly manicured lawns, and crickets clamored as dusk descended, stealing the last light of day. Bob's grass was the only yard without a new cut, looking ragged and unkempt. Ernie looked at the house noting that it was dark. It was a nice house, but it seemed bleak and empty. Ernie didn't want to think that Bob would kill himself, but the thought had crossed his mind. If that were to happen it would be tragedy heaped atop a tragedy. With pity and curiosity driving him, Ernie cut the engine and got out of his car. He pitched the stub of his cigar into the grass and lit another one. He saw the word "killer" spray-painted in red on Bob's mailbox. There was a sticky-note pasted to the storm door addressed to Bob's daughter stating that he was going to Kelly's Bar.

Ernie went back to his car and drove to Kelly's. He felt a little uneasy as he walked in. It had been several years since he had been in a bar. The place smacked of a distinctive odor he had almost forgotten. The ancient tactile sensations soared through time as he analyzed those old familiar aromas and sounds. The clicking of pool balls behind a partition and the mixture of voices droned through the smoke and the subdued colors of the neon signs. Old emotions were thick in the haze. He could almost smell the powerful odor of his father's stogie and hear his brothers giggling as his dad articulated forbidden tales to the other patrons. "Tell them the one about the elephant, Dutch," they would say, and the stories would tumble along in a rumbustious monologue. Ernie's mother had sent them to fetch their father, "And don't come back without him," she would say, but the lure of the tavern always dampened their resolve, and they just sat and listened.

The memories were bittersweet but Ernie pushed them aside and continued. He scanned the room until he saw Bob Stokes sitting at the far end of the bar looking sad and withdrawn. His hands were wrapped around his glass as he stared listlessly into it. Ernie slipped his leg over the stool next to him. "Mind if I sit here?" Ernie said. Bob turned and looked at him silently, nodded, and the smallest glimpse of redemption was there in his eyes.

Ernie pointed to Bob's drink and offered to buy a round. Bob looked at his nearly empty glass momentarily and then politely declined. "No, thank you. I've probably already had more than I need."

Ernie signaled the waitress, ordered himself rum and coke and another drink for Bob. "I hate to drink alone," he said. "If you don't want it, they can kill some bacteria in the drain with it," he added.

"Do you think it's a good idea to sit with me?" Bob asked, looking troubled.

"How's that?" Ernie said.

"Everybody thinks I killed Irene," Bob said choking out the words. Ernie looked at himwith sympathetic eyes, trying to convey support but hoping that pity wasn't revealed in his gaze.

"They say I killed her," he said again. His voice cracked as tears welled in his eyes. "Tonight someone wrote *Killer* on my mailbox."

"Some people are idiots," Ernie said softly.

A country song began playing on the jukebox. A woman

near them urged a man half her age to dance. "Come on, don't you like to dance?" she whined. The man's friends laughed and goaded him to do it, but he refused. She went to the next table and the process started all over again.

Ernie sipped his drink and waited for Bob to continue. He could hear a conversation in another part of the bar. There was a man talking about his tavern exploits. He declared that he was the "meanest son of a bitch in the place." There were broken noses and missing teeth all around Willoughby Hills (by his account) just to prove it. He had a dialect exclusive to barroom bullies and lowlife brawlers who were too stubborn to even try proper enunciation of the English language. They were proud to be ignorant and announced it to the world. So there he was proclaiming to be the toughest man in town and he was looking for someone to humiliate in order to expand his reputation.

In only a few minutes Ernie could feel him lurking behind him. His alcoholic breath assaulted his senses, and his body was brushing lightly against him. "Hey, I ain't seen you in here before," he said. Ernie glanced over his shoulder but didn't respond.

"What's your name?" he demanded.

"Frank Lloyd Wright," Ernie said.

"I think it's your turn to buy," he said. Ernie looked straight ahead trying to ignore him.

"Well, Frank, my name's Ralph Sampin. I'm the baddest son of a bitch in this town, and I think it's your turn to buy," he said as he placed his hand on Ernie's back. Ernie wasn't going to be intimidated by this fat lout. In twenty-five years he'd seen enough bullies like Sampin to fill McCormick Place in Chicago. Most of them were cowards trying to feed their own egos.

Just when Ernie was about to hand Sampin his ass, Sampin diverted his attention to Bob Stokes. "Hey, I know you, you're the guy who murdered his wife," he said.

Instantly rage burned through Ernie like lightning. He spun around on the bar stool, shoving his chest into Sampin with anger hot in his eyes. Ernie was like a bulldog with his face set in determination. All he needed at that moment to be as menacing was to have his lips curled back with teeth glaring and a low growl emanating from his throat.

Sampin was a man who bellowed about his prowess as if he were the grand potentate of Willoughby Hills. He wasn't afraid to pound a lesser man senseless or to demean and humiliate men who were smaller and weaker than himself, but he was a coward, just like most men of his ilk. Ernie understood that about him, and he could see deep down inside his eyes where his fear was billeted. Sampin saw the sneer on Ernie's lip and the ferocity in his stare. He tried to look back with an equally gritty glare, but his eyes drifted aside just as Ernie knew they would. He wore a dumbfounded expression, and inside his head he was trying to find a way to back down without exposing his fear. Ernie knew it, but he wasn't going to let Sampin off the hook. "Say it," Ernie growled.

Sampin looked away. "I wonder what he wants me to say," he said, looking around for support from his friends who were watching. He smiled trying to disguise his fright.

"I said, say it!" Ernie hissed through clinched teeth. Sampin looked back into Ernie's eyes. There wasn't an inch between their noses. Sampin's eyes were like saucers, pleading for a way out but he knew what Ernie wanted. He didn't want to give it to him, but fear was now dictating his actions.

"I'm sorry," he said softly. Ernie pushed him away. He saw Bob headed out the front door like an outcast with nowhere to go. At that moment Ernie wanted to find Irene's murderer more than anything he had ever wanted in his life.

Chapter Thirty-One

On July 4th, 1967, nearly a decade before John Mason met his ill fate, Frances Constance and her son Roderick were in Sanderville, Illinois, visiting her sister Theresa. Frances was two years older than Theresa, but she looked a haggard decade her senior. Theresa left Willoughby Hills when she was fifteen, leaving behind everything that plagued Frances — the things that would have plagued her too if she had stayed. She started a new life in northern Illinois where she met a boy who was working in an appliance repair shop. His name was Elysia Bell. He was smart and ahead of his time when it came to electronics. He married Theresa and started a business servicing two-way radios. He had a futuristic interest in cellular telephones, and people thought he was a dreamer when he talked about a time when ordinary people would be carrying cell phones around in their pockets. He often said, "Time will tell."

Elysia gave Theresa a good life. Although Theresa had nothing to do with how Frances had fared, sometimes she felt a little guilty. Theresa thought she may have sapped every bud of good luck the family tree had sprouted, leaving Frances with nothing but misfortune. Because of her misplaced angst, she tried to level things with Frances by inviting her to her home for an entire week during the first week of July each year. It was the closest thing Frances had to a vacation. They shopped in good stores, ate at nice restaurants, and lounged around Theresa's pool. On the Fourth of July, they spent the entire day picnicking in Sanderville Memorial Park. They always stayed through the fireworks finale under a star-filled summer sky.

The incidents in life that connect one person to another in small ways can go on forever and never amount to anything, but in some bizarre instances they find a way to span the gulf of time to change everything. In one unfortunate instance, a minor incident on July 4th 1967 would manifest itself in a senseless act of revenge nine years later. In a cascade of malicious deeds in Roderick Constance's life, this might have been the most egregious of them all.

It started in Sanderville Park where an occasional sizzle followed by a bang was proof that people were indifferent to the park's ban on fireworks on Independence Day. Volunteer uniformed security guards patrolled the park, armed with nothing more than civic pride and little wherewithal. Although even without official training or authority, they knew enough to recognize reckless conduct when they saw it. The two men who had the first shift were a young chubby "wannabe cop" by the name of Butch Scroggins and an old ex-Marine, Harlan Stancel. Harlan was hard to motivate, but Butch was stoked and ready for action.

Little Roderick Constance was ambling around throughout the day unsupervised with his pockets full of firecrackers. Only ten years old, he was already a minor version of the person he would become. Defiant and unwashed, he seldom combed his hair, and it hung in greasy strands in his eyes and mopped across his face. He might have gone unnoticed like most of the other children toting fireworks around the park, but Roderick liked to throw them near people just to watch them jump, and light up the always occupied portable toilets.

Before noon Butch Sroggins had his note tablet full of reports about a skinny little kid with dirty hair who was creating havoc. Harlan Stancil wasn't concerned, but Butch was on high alert. When they saw Constance, Butch honed in on him. Constance glanced at him nervously. Butch was like a bird dog on point, and the body language between them painted a picture of the hunter and his prey. It was predictable that Constance would run. When he bolted, Butch was slow out of the gate, but his teeth were set in determination. His prominent spare tire was pounding his authentic-looking police leather belt with such velocity that two buttons on his shirt were undone. Within a span of a hundred feet, Butch was already huffing for air. Constance could have easily left Butch in the dust, but he decided that hiding in a nearby Porta Potty was just the ticket. It would have left Butch scratching his head without a clue, but there were numerous people in the park who had watched Constance misbehaving throughout the day. At least a dozen citizens stood up to identify the receptacle sheltering Butch's fugitive.

The lock on the Porta Potty held little resistance as Butch gave the handle a mighty tug. The flimsy door was flung open revealing Roderick Constance squatting in the corner like a trapped little animal.

Butch clutched Constance's shirt collar and marched him off to the first aid station where he relieved him of his firecrackers and paged Frances over the loudspeaker system to fetch her son. Constance was released to his mother with a stern warning from Butch. He stood over Constance with a smile stretched across his round pink face. "Now you be a good boy and don't cause any more trouble," he said. The image of Butch's face was imprinted in Constance's memory for life.

In 1976, nine years later, Butch was given the Citizen of the Month award by the *Sanderville Gazette*. He coached little league baseball and proudly served as president of the Sanderville Youth

Football Association. As a Boy Scout leader and a volunteer Big Brother, Butch Scoggins was a "stand up" citizen in Sanderville, Illinois.

In other news Elysia Bell opened his second communications equipment store. He and his staff sold two-way radios, CB radios, cordless telephones, and an assortment of other gadgets that were coming into vogue. The *Sanderville Gazette* did an article on Elysia's innovating business model. Theresa sent a copy of the newspaper to Frances with the highlighted article about Elysia on the business page. Constance found the newspaper on his mother's coffee table. He didn't bother to read the highlighted article about Elysia Bell. He saw the picture pf Butch Scroggins standing in his front yard with the editor of the *Sanderville Gazette* presenting him with a Citizen of the Month plaque. He had a big cheesy smile prominent upon his plump pink face. The street sign in the background revealed that Butch Scroggins lived at the corner of Vanhuss and Maincross.

On June 11th, 1976, at the corner gas station, Constance bought a bag of Cheetos, a liter of Pepsi, and enough gas for a round trip to northern Illinois.

Butch Scroggins was grilling two hamburger patties on the burnt-out Smokey Joe on his patio. Three adolescent boys walking down the sidewalk shouted at him and threw a football across the yard. Butch lunged for it and knocked over the grill sending the Smokey Joe and the hamburgers flying onto the lawn. Butch clumsily made the catch and fired the football back.

"Good catch, Butch! Sorry about the grill."

"No problemo," he shouted back after a hefty laugh.

Butch gathered up the burgers and grill before going inside where he washed the meat and placed it into a frying pan. Butch usually ate at McDonald's, but occasionally he wanted a change in his diet (home-grilled burgers instead of Big Macs).

The little house where he lived was left to him in his mother's will. He was born there and never had another residence. He wasn't married and didn't have a girlfriend but he had many friends, women included. Butch was a good man and it was impossible to pry anything discouraging from his lips.

Early in the evening Butch turned down offers to go to the American Legion to have beers with his friends. He watched the Cubs lose to their arch rivals, the St. Louis Cardinals. They were fighting for the basement, but it was like the World Series for Cubs/Cards fans. Butch was a dyed-in-the-wool Cubby fan, and he never lost faith that next year would be a winner. He turned off the TV and muttered, "We'll get'm tomorrow."

After a few moments he cut the lights and headed out to sit on the front porch. It was a warm evening. The crickets were clamoring and the lightning bugs were blinking in the burnt umber glowing on the horizon. Roderick Constance parked his car in the alley behind a house with a realty sign planted in the front yard. He shoved the .22 Magnum revolver into his belt beneath his shirttail. He was careful to stay in the shadows as he walked north on Maincross Street. When he arrived at Vanhuss, he saw Butch seated in a well-worn La-Z-Boy rocker moving slowly back and forth as he gazed into the darkening sky. Butch didn't have a worry in the world.

Constance wasted little time crossing through the backyards to confront Butch. He glanced around making sure the streets were empty. There were long shadows stretching along the sidewalks and a gentle breeze was shifting the tree branches in a quiet rhythmic motion.

Constance approached Butch as casually as someone out for an evening stroll. He looked at Butch for a long time. Butch watched him with a placid but inquisitive expression.

"What are you doing, fat ass?" Constance said.

Butch chuckled, a little surprised, but not at all insulted or angered. He thought he probably knew Constance from

186

somewhere but couldn't remember. He assumed the remark was stated in good humor. Butch was used to people affectionately slandering him about his weight. He was the kind of guy people were so comfortable with that it was easy to tease him unmercifully. He expected it. Constance stared at Butch. The big pink face and broad smile hadn't changed.

Butch was puzzled. A skinny long-haired kid standing in his front yard staring like a lost soul. It seemed peculiar—spooky.

"I don't think I know you," Butch said, feeling a little uneasy. Constance was quietly staring from beneath a furrowed brow. His expression was unruffled, but Butch sensed a rage fulminating behind his eyes. Butch rose and turned to go into his home hoping to put an end to this unexpected intrusion.

Feeling invalidated and now insulted that Butch had dismissed him, Constance announced calmly, "You wouldn't remember me, but I remember you." He lifted the pistol and took aim. Butch turned to leave, shaking his head disgustedly, not really believing that it was more than a plastic gun and an evil prank. Constance was incensed when he realized he was losing eye contact with his victim. He cowardly and deliberately pulled the trigger more times than he could count. He watched Butch's back side jerk and convulse as he took his last step forward and then his last breath. A very fine and decent human being was nothing more than target practice for Roderick Constance, a kid without a soul. Butch Scroggins was the literal definition of a good man, and although it was little comfort, he would be remembered as such. The senseless and ugly act of a bad seed would be fodder for conversation until the event faded with time. It was something Constance was never asked about and something he would never mention to a living soul.

Butch didn't get the respect of having his murderer tried and convicted—not even a point in time or a place where his friends would be able to stand and condemn the punk who brought him down. His murderer would never be known and the case of Butch Scroggins would go down as a cold case, an unsolved crime.

CHAPTER THIRTY-TWO

On Monday night, Sarge's crew was about to begin their last night shift before moving onto the swing shift. After passing on information and assigning routine details to his men, Sarge quietly updated them on their old friend Ruben Jessip, the long-time janitor at City Hall. Ruben was eighty-six years old and in failing health. Until he became ill he was energetic, active, and still mopping floors and washing windows like a man half his age. He was small, quick, and light on his feet. By the way he moved around with little leprechaun-like alacrity, no one would have guessed his age. He had beady little blue eyes that sparkled like a mischievous child. He wore a fedora with a feather in the band and an "Eisenhower for President" button pinned to the rim. The policemen often tried to catch him off guard to remove it from his head, but he was as quick as a cat and they were seldom successful. Ruben was a very popular old gent around the police station.

Ruben never had a car. He called the radio operator each morning at five a.m. for a ride to work. It was against departmental policies for civilians to ride in the squad cars, but Ruben was the exception. The radio operator simply put out a call each morning that Lieutenant Jessip was ready. People with police radio scanners actually thought there was a Detective Jessip on

189

the roster. Giving the old boy a free ride was a pleasure to most of the duty guys.

Now Ruben was deteriorating and would soon vanish from his accepted role. He was another item the ancient building had outlived. Sarge told them that Ruben's cancer was advancing by the day and he wouldn't be around much longer. He gave them permission to visit him in the intensive care unit at the hospital as long as they maintained radio contact.

Morgan left the police station and went immediately to the hospital to see him. Visiting hours for policemen didn't exist so getting in to see Ruben at ten p.m. was as easy for Morgan as if it were three o'clock in the afternoon.

The long hallway was dimly lit, and the quiet was only broken by an occasional cough or heavy wheezing sound escaping the lungs of the soon-to-be departed occupying the rooms along the route. The distinctive hospital odor was strong on the fifth floor where patients were waiting in their final hours for eternal peace to come. As Morgan made his way to room 518, he tried not to mourn Ruben before he was gone, but he knew this was the end for him. This would be the last time he would ever see him.

Morgan stopped in the doorway to Ruben's room and looked in. Ruben seemed to be sleeping peacefully. Morgan turned to leave not wanting to disturb him. Ruben opened his eyes, somehow knowing Morgan was there. He called his name. Morgan went inside and tried a cheerful hello. He took a seat in a green vinyl chair beside the bed. "How're they treating you in here, Ruben?" he asked.

Ruben's lips turned up into a quirky little half smile. "Pretty good, Morgan, they got some good-looking nurses in here," he said.

Morgan watched him silently, trying not to show the pity that was percolating into his thoughts. Ruben looked straight ahead staring at the wall. Slowly, in a weak voice, he spoke. "I was dreaming about a time back in World War Two. My company was in training. They ran us for over five miles in heavy combat gear. You could drop out if you wanted to, they had a truck picking up the stragglers, but I didn't drop out, I stayed right in there. I was the smallest man in my platoon and the drill sergeant was worried about me. All the way he kept asking me, 'You gonna be all right, Ruben?'" The old man smiled. "Well, I was all right. There was only three of us left when that run was over. There was me, the drill sergeant, and some guy we all called Alabama."

Ruben closed his eyes for a moment. Morgan thought he might have dozed off again. Morgan watched him in the low light as his heart filled with sorrow. He had known Ruben for a long time and although they weren't friends in the same sense as he and Ed, or Sarge, he had a real affection for him. His heart was overflowing with sadness as the wanly old man talked about a time when he was the fittest man in a US Army battalion. His skin was sallow and seemed to be draped loosely over the bones in his face. Ruben had always been a waif of a man, and now he was a tiny little scarecrow.

Ruben's beady little eyes opened again. "That seems like it was only yesterday. Time goes too fast," he said.

Morgan nodded, not having anything to say, silently agreeing.

"Morgan, a lot of people say they wouldn't want to live their lives over again, but I would. I loved every minute of it." Ruben closed his eyes and drifted off to sleep.

Morgan stood there in the dark listening to Ruben's breath rising and falling. Everybody knows about old age and death from the earliest days of life, but feeling the pang of that knowledge often creeps up on you in unsuspecting ways. Time in its indiscriminate selection will take us all someday — that was a fact. For some people the realization comes when strength fades and fine-textured skin gives way to spots and creases, but for Morgan the brunt of it came at that very instant. It was in that fleeting moment when Ruben lie there in his bed, very old and very weak, talking about running faster and farther than all the others.

Morgan walked the long hallway with that melancholy uneasiness swirling around in his brain. That ancient fear that travels along the road of life was galvanized in reality. Old age and death are inevitable.

When Morgan stepped into the warm air, he looked into a clear limitless sky. He thought about how Ernie had talked that evening after he processed the crime scene when the old man was stabbed and bled to death in a drunken stupor. He may have felt just like Morgan was feeling at that moment. Seeing Ruben on the threshold of the unknown left him so strangely affected.

Near the hospital where Morgan had parked his squad car, there were several maple trees where it was dark and shadowy. Roderick Constance was standing in the shadows watching Morgan. "Keep looking at the stars," he whispered. He raised the .22 Magnum and took aim. It was the same gun he had used to kill four other people. He had been accurate so far and he couldn't miss from this range. He breathed deeply, cocked the hammer, aligned the sight, and pulled the trigger. That cop would never hear the rapport. The hammer fell forward, Constance flinched in anticipation, but there was no blast, only a click to break the silence.

Morgan heard something in the darkness. He was immediately on alert. He unsnapped the strap on his nine as he scanned the parking lot and tree line. He waited, and waited, and waited. There was nothing. He breathed deeply, the first air he had taken into his lungs since before the strange sound—the metal against metal sound that was very similar to the clicking of the .357 Magnum Bob Turner had threatened him with back in January.

Still feeling uneasy, Morgan slid into the squad car seat. He patrolled the alleys and side streets for several minutes before heading off on routine patrol. Roderick Constance had crawled beneath a small spruce tree where he hid until Morgan was gone. He checked the revolver chamber to find that the bullet had misfired. He cursed under his breath and headed back to the college.

CHAPTER THIRTY-THREE

It had been two months since Irene Stokes went into the deep, but she didn't go without a stir. The citizens of Willoughby Hills kept her memory alive in a daily rant. Everybody knew she was missing and most thought she had been murdered. The coffee shops and restaurants were full of customers who grumbled about the lack of progress in finding her. Most of them wanted Bob Stokes arrested.

Constance's first victim, John Mason, wasn't a concern for Willoughby Hills residents. There was no clamor to find him. He was dead, but the fact that he had not returned to Willoughby Hills College to finish school hadn't even raised an eyebrow. He was just another college kid who couldn't cut the mustard. Chicago was a long way from Willoughby Hills and John's status didn't matter to the Willoughby Hills gossip machine. There was a broken line, a gap separating Irene Stokes from John Mason. If the facts in the shoplifting case and the college dorm burglary had been made binding the two together, it would surely have drawn suspicion to Roderick Constance, but no one knew.

Morgan's crew rotated back onto swing shift. They worked two nights, three days, and two days off. Morgan and Ed were partnered up on routine patrol working the first of their two days. Ed was riding shotgun complaining about how boring it was working daylight hours. Both Morgan and Ed preferred breaking up bar fights, chasing down drunks, and patrolling for criminal activity. Day work consisted of investigating vehicle accidents, writing speeding tickets, and finding ordinance violations. It was important work, but just not for them.

They made their usual rounds through downtown and around the beltway before Morgan began to find his way into the residential areas. In the older neighborhoods in Willoughby Hills, the streets were paved with brick and bordered by ancient elm trees and manicured lawns. These homes were owned by lawyers, doctors, and businessmen. About the only calls coming from a neighborhood like this were to check out solicitors peddling magazines. Still, people liked to see a squad car occasionally cruising down the street.

Just as they were turning to head back to the business district, someone whistled and shouted, "I need the cops!"

Morgan hit the brakes and waited for whatever misadventure might be coming down. A tall, slender, athletic Bob Verderber ran from between two houses and smacked the hood of the squad car with his open hand. Both Morgan and Ed had known Bob for most of their lives so anything he did wouldn't surprise them. Bob was laughing, hoping he had startled his friends.

Ed rolled the window down as Bob propped his elbows on the door. "That always gets us, Bob. It just scares the shit out of us," he said sourly.

"Yea, I know. I saw you ducking into the floor," he said and laughed.

Bob was talkative and didn't consider that they actually had work to do. None of their high school friends took them seriously until they were subjected to the authority they had at hand. Bob wouldn't likely be grabbed by the long arm of the law but they had friends who had been. Most expected special treatment from them, and when it didn't happen relationships changed forever.

Most young cops find themselves in circumstances when they have to set aside ties with friends and step up to the plate, no longer bystanders but cops who are orbiters and enforcers. Some of their friends understood but others resented them, choosing to believe they were nothing but counterfeits all puffed up on self-importance.

Bob still saw Morgan and Ed as his buddies. His perception was that they were riding around in a squad car gassing away the day, looking at girls, and drinking free coffee at local restaurants. He thought their only involvement in law enforcement was to be privy to all the information the real cops were getting from the job.

"Hey, why don't you guys stop over at Mom's? She just brought out a jug of tea. Maybe you could take an honest break and have a glass of tea with an old gal who actually gives a shit about you," Bob said.

"I don't know how we could refuse such a gracious offer," Ed snorted.

Bob walked back to the sidewalk leading to his mother's front door. Morgan drove to the curb and parked. He left the car running, holstered his portable radio, and followed Bob into the backyard. They didn't bother to radio in that they were taking a break.

Mrs. Verderber was a perky mid-sixties woman with eight kids, all grown now. Morgan had spent many afternoons in her backyard shooting hoops and getting banged up in one-on-one with Bob, or being mauled in no-holds-barred pickup games. The Verderber boys were great athletes and weren't afraid to mix it up, but luckily they were good-natured and found little reason to quarrel about fouls or scores. Mrs. Verderber was always ready on the spot with a smile and a jug of iced tea.

Bob's brother John was slouching in a lawn chair and Mrs. Verderber was slicing a lemon for the tea. Her eyes lit up when she saw the two young cops. "You boys look good in your outfits," she said.

"Hi, Mrs. Verderber," they said in unison.

Mrs. Verderber went on to tell them she read about them sometimes in the newspaper. The "On The Record" section usually listed the names of the arresting officers on traffic offenses and misdemeanors. Sometimes there were brief descriptions of scuffles they were involved in. She went on to express that she worried about them. "I worry about your temper too, Eddie," she added.

Morgan grinned.

"I've got it under control, Mrs. B," Ed said.

Bob looked at his mother with a blank stare. He'd never thought about them getting hurt, or even that they had done anything at all dangerous. Bob was like most people. When he saw a squad car going down the street, he didn't make the connection that they were going somewhere to perform some function necessary for public safety. He wasn't there when they answered family dispute calls in the middle of the night facing down drunks who were stressed out, enraged, and sometimes armed. The number of violent calls they answered would have surprised him. They were just his buddies, all dressed up in police uniforms, riding around talking nonsense all day.

Whatever thoughts crossed his mind didn't stick because in just moments they were gassing away about high school days and comparing friends who had gained thirty or forty pounds in just a few years.

Mrs. Verderber interrupted the conversation when she asked about her friend, Irene Stokes. She suspected the worst, but she was holding out hope for a miracle. Morgan and Ed didn't provide any consolation. They were as in the dark about Irene as any other Willoughby Hills residents. Missing persons and murder investigations weren't their responsibility. They knew only that

Irene was still missing, and clues were few and far between. The conversation continued as they tried to recount the number of murders there had been in Willoughby Hills in recent years.

Ed was involved in one incident when a local barber walked into the police station and announced that he had murdered his wife. He slit her throat and buried her in a cornfield just outside town. Her body barely had time to turn cold before guilt overwhelmed him, tormenting him into an unsolicited confession. His court-appointed attorney tried to get him to withdraw his confession but being a staunch conservative, the barber argued that the county shouldn't burden taxpayers with the expense of trying a guilty man.

Morgan's closest brush with murder was the incident when the drunken old witch had accidentally stabbed her bony old boyfriend in the knee and he bled to death. It was a serious call, but it certainly wasn't a murder.

Mrs. Verderber surprised them when she stated that her father-in-law was shot by a man who intended to murder him. Bob knew the story and might have been able to quote it word for word, but he wanted to hear it again. He urged his mother to tell it. The fact that his buddies were cops made it more intriguing.

In 1925, Willoughby Hills had two coal mines in operation on the north end of Kickapoo Street. The area was now a new subdivision dominated by three-story brick homes. Nobody living there would believe they were living over a dirty hole of black grime or even that the city would permit something so filthy to exist within the city limits.

John Verderber was a supervisor in mine number two. He was a serious and dedicated mine employee and known to be a fair man. He was gunned down by a distraught employee whose life was in a downward spiral, so fogged by sad circumstances that his judgment was impaired. Verderber became his target because he was the only person left to blame.

His name was Pavel Miletich. He was an East European immigrant who had come to America as so many other Europeans had done, looking for a new life. His fiancé was still in Bosnia waiting for an opportunity to join him. Miletich worked like a dog and pinched every penny to be able to afford to have her join him in Willoughby Hills. He took a leave of absence and spent every dime he had to make a trip to Bosnia to bring the love of his life back to America. There were complications with her passport and Miletich came home alone and broke.

In those days miners were paid by the amount of coal they were able to dig out of the ground. It was measured by the ton. The underground vein of coal were called rooms. Some rooms were richer in coal than others and were assigned to the most valued employees, and those with greater seniority. Miletich didn't have enough seniority to be permanently assigned to any of the most productive rooms, but being a very diligent worker he was in line for one. When he returned from Bosnia, his job was waiting for him and he was immediately but temporarily assigned to one of the richest rooms in the operation by John Verderber. The employee who was entitled to that room was on leave of absence and would reclaim it upon his return. That point became the bone of contention leading to Verderber being shot.

Miletich was sullen and withdrawn but he showed up every day and worked like a dog. When the miner who was on leave returned, Miletich was reassigned to his previous position. He was enraged by the setback. He argued that he had dug and shoveled more coal than any other man in the mine and was entitled to stay where he was. He angrily confronted Verderber, to no avail. Verderber had given his word to the other man, and his word was as good as gold.

The next morning Miletich took the train from Willoughby Hills to Springfield where he bought two .32 caliber handguns. That evening when the parade of men with blackened faces surfaced from the earth, Miletich was waiting. He caught up with Verderber and another supervisor on the railroad tracks north of the train station. There was a third man with them but Miletich shooed him off waving one of the .32s in his face, telling him he had no quarrel with him.

Miletich opened up with both guns blazing. Verderber was hit in the neck. The other pit boss was nailed in the leg as he tried to flee. Miletich emptied both guns but only those two bullets hit their mark. Miletich was swarmed by miners and other pedestrians as he fled. He was chased north on the railroad tracks where he was tackled by a policeman and another citizen. A passing motorist was stopped and Verderber was loaded into a car and transported to Dr. Bradburn's office on Ottawa Street. Dr. Bradburn stopped the bleeding and bandaged the wound. The same motorist waited and then transported Verderber to St. Clara's Hospital.

The bullet that hit Verderber went in through his neck, traveled down his spine, and lodged in his sixth vertebra. St. Clara's Hospital didn't have a surgeon who felt confident in digging out the bullet so he was released and sent home. After two weeks Verderber and his uncle took the train to the Mayo Clinic in Minnesota where the bullet was extracted.

Miletich was tried for attempted murder, found guilty, and sentenced to fourteen years in prison. However, after serving two years, Verderber wrote a letter to the parole board on behalf of Miletich, and he was released. Both young men, Verderber and Miletich, lived up into their nineties without ever seeing each other again.

There was no doubt that Miletich tried to murder Verderber. He did it in broad daylight with a good portion of Willoughby Hills watching. He wasn't hiding his rage or his anger, there was nothing sneaky about it. It was atrocious and misguided but a genuine human emotion that people could understand.

Morgan and Ed were fascinated by the story and like most people who knew the tale, they understood the motive and had some sympathy for Miletich.

There was another tale unfolding at that moment that was beyond understanding. Roderick Constance was planning to strike again. Unlike the story of Pavel Miletich, his motives and actions were void of anything that might elicit sympathy or understanding. When Miletich shot Verderber, he was burning with emotion, but Constance was as cold-blooded as a serpent in the Garden of Evil.

CHAPTER THIRTY-FOUR

On June 29th, Jack Fink and his beautiful, pregnant wife, Theresa, had dinner at Kelly's Bar. Jack had a few more beers than usual, but Theresa was sipping Diet Coke. It was eleven p.m., the jukebox had stopped playing, and the voices were clamoring with less intensity as the evening was winding down. Jack's two brothers were still poking fun at him for being a "sissy boy," working in a grocery store pushing paper while they were doing real "man type" work building the Fink Brothers Construction Company. Even at that moment they were both still wearing Sheetrock dust and splotches of wallboard compound. They weren't embarrassed or even uncomfortable with their appearance. The beer went down just as well in working clothes as it did in a sports coat and tie.

When the laughs and teasing were over, Jack stumbled to the car. To say he had his nose wet would have been an understatement. Theresa did the driving as they were headed home.

Earlier in the evening, Roderick Constance walked from Willoughby Hills College to 527 Sangamon Street, staying as much in the shadows as possible. It was dark, a mist hung in the air, and a halo encircled the streetlight at the end of the alley between Keokuk and Sangamon Street. Traffic was sparse.

The visibility was so diminished by the heavy air that seeing a pedestrian walking in a darkened alley was almost impossible.

Constance was wearing dark clothing and his hair bobbed in the wind. His arms were swinging mechanically as he took long, deliberate strides. When he arrived behind Jack Fink's home, two huge German shepherds barked and dashed to the end of their chains with their ears pinned back, a foreboding deterrent to anyone who would dare to trespass. Constance pitched two round balls of hamburger that barely hit the ground before they were gobbled up. He rubbed and petted the dogs as they licked at his face. The shepherds knew him. He was the man who came out of the darkness late at night with fresh meat in hand. They trusted him.

Five-twenty-seven Sangamon Street was in an old neighborhood. It was a small two-bedroom house, with black shutters and white aluminum siding. It sat close to the street in line with all the other small houses on the block. The alley behind the homes was lined with garbage cans and utility sheds. Jack Fink had a utility shed. There was a pile of old lumber and a rolled-up carpet remnant that had been there for several weeks stacked against the back side of the shed.

Constance petted the dogs again for good measure and then proceeded to the pile of junk. He unrolled the wet carpet and fetched out the twelve gauge Winchester pump shotgun he had placed there earlier in the evening.

Wasting little time, Constance headed for the house. One of the shepherds growled with fur bristling on his back. "Good boy," Constance said quietly. The dog stopped and watched him cross the yard. There was a side door into the residence where there was a shared entrance into the basement and kitchen. Constance knew the door would be unlocked. He also knew Fink wasn't there. He had stalked Jack and knew most of his habits and activities. In fact, he had already been in the house twice before just to check it out. Jack would come through the same door Constance came through. He always parked his car at the curb in front of the house, walked down the narrow sidewalk between his home and the neighbor's house, and entered that door without using a key. He would turn on the kitchen light and then go into the living room to turn on the TV. It didn't make a difference whether it was night or day, or a weekend. It was always the same.

Constance never believed he would be caught or punished, but still he was cautious. He had checked out several criminology books and studied crime scene investigations from the college library. That in itself was proof he was no genius. Even a police cadet knows that you research a murder suspect's reading material. Still, in his mind he was as wily as a fox.

He learned that shell casings and rounds fired from a gun can be traced to the weapon they were fired from. Shotgun shell casing can be compared to firing pin impressions, but the buckshot can't be accurately matched. That was the reason he was using the Winchester. He also knew that shoe prints are comparable. He already utilized that bit of information when he burglarized City Hall. He wore new shoes and discarded them after he had finished the job. By studying the criminology books, he knew experts would be able to guess his weight by foot impressions in mud or soft dirt, and by measuring the trajectory of the bullet they would know how tall he was.

Before he began to execute his plan, Constance used the Coke machine key he had stolen from Joe's van. He emptied several pop machines in the area because he needed ready cash to finance his getaway. Since the coins were handy, he packed his pockets with change to alter his weight by several pounds. Now as he was waiting for Jack Fink to come home, he prepared the crime scene. He placed a kitchen stool in the living room where he would stand pointing downward on his target, changing the trajectory of the shotgun blast.

Jack and Theresa arrived at home at 11:45 p.m. The ground was still damp, but the mist had ended, the clouds separated, and a full, brilliant white moon was shining in a clear, star-filled sky. Constance could hear them talking as they walked along the narrow sidewalk. He knew they would be coming through the side door. Jack would flip on the kitchen light and then proceed into the living room to turn on the TV. He would look up to see Constance standing on the stool. It would be the last thing he would see. Theresa would scream and run back outside. Constance would let her go. She meant nothing to him.

The door creaked open and then a thud. Jack fell into the doorway and lay on the steps laughing. Theresa giggled and stepped over him. She hit the kitchen light and then headed for the living room. Jack got off his knees and followed her. Theresa stepped into the living room. Roderick Constance was standing over her with the twelve gauge pointing directly at her. She screamed and threw up her hands. The roar of the shotgun blast was deafening as buckshot ripped through her chest, killing her and her unborn child instantly. Jack turned to run but a second blast hit him in his left side and sent him reeling across the floor. Jack gasped and reached out for Theresa as he pushed himself toward her, dragging his intestines across the carpet. Constance calmly stood over him, watching him for a moment. "Do you remember me?" he sneered. He pumped another round into the chamber and pulled the trigger. Jack's skull was blown into the next room and his brain splattered against the wall.

The dogs were raising hell in the backyard as Constance stepped out onto the stoop. He stopped as if stifled, frozen in thought. He turned and hurried back into the house. He had forgotten to gather the shotgun shell casings. He quickly located the casings and fled. This time as he ran for the alley the dogs were gnashing fiercely, charging at him as if to tear him apart. He ran with adrenalin gushing through his veins. The change in his pockets banged against his leg, flying from his pockets, jingling as it danced on the asphalt. His breath was rapid and his chest was tight. When he crossed Keokuk Street into the darkened alley two blocks away, he slowed to a jog. He giggled as though he had just won the lottery.

As fate would have it, Constance was left short of committing the perfect crime. As he stood on the stoop in the bright moonlight, he was as still as a deer caught in headlights. Sandy Winghert, the next-door neighbor, was looking out the window in horror. Constance's face shining in the light, his pale blue eyes were as washed out as a photograph negative, and his skin as white as snow. His tangled stringy hair was pulled away from his face, revealing every detail of his features. That face was as blanched as an apparition materializing in a 1930's horror film. The optic was permanently etched into Sandy Winghert's memory.

CHAPTER THIRTY-FIVE

Before the police arrived, Constance was northbound for Joliet where Julie McBride was waiting for him at the Holiday Inn. She didn't know what Constance had done but she knew something was going down, and she was there to provide an alibi for him. The old Chevy wasn't a race car but it had plenty of steam. The speedometer was bouncing off ninety-five miles per hour. The bag of change from the Coke machines was lying next to him in the seat. He would have to use it to buy gas but not while in Willoughby Hills. The murders he had just committed didn't faze him. He was a man without a conscience, but still he didn't want to be caught.

In legal terms that was the difference between the sane and the insane. The absence of guilty feelings didn't matter, only that the offender realizes the consequences of his actions. Most people would believe someone who would kill another without feeling anything would be insane. Any action to cover up or evade being caught is an admission that you know the consequences. Constance didn't feel anything, but he didn't want to be caught. He wasn't insane.

Police cars arrived at 527 Sangamon Avenue with sirens wailing and emergency lights flashing. People were standing in their front yards with their minds churning, fearful and curious about the sudden attention the neighborhood was getting.

Within moments police officers were swarming the area, on foot and in squad cars. A yellow police tape encircled the entire yard, and barricades were erected on both ends of the block and the alleys behind the Fink residence. An ambulance was parked in front of the residence with emergency lights flashing. David Sager, the night shift sergeant, was standing on the front porch next door with Sandy Winghert. Her face was buried in folded arms as she wept softly. When Ernie arrived he keyed the mike to advise the radio operator to send a crime scene crew. He talked briefly with Sager and instructed him to transport Mrs. Winghert to the police department to go through the department mug shots while her memory was fresh.

The smell of gunpowder was lingering over the dead bodies when Ernie walked in. He didn't have to examine the wounds to know the weapon was a shotgun. He retrieved a camera from his pocket and circled the room clockwise taking pictures. He was careful not to disturb the crime scene before the technicians arrived but he wanted to have a good look anyway.

He studied the young woman lying on her back with her arms raised and eyes wide open. She saw something in the dark and the expression of surprise was still there on her face. She died so suddenly and violently that she was still wearing the look of fear in her eyes.

Jack's face was gone. Whatever expression he wore was lost when the gun blast tore off most of his face and skull. Ernie saw where he was hit in his left rib cage. He assumed that was the first shot. He had probably seen his wife blown into eternity. He sat back on the couch and stared at the grotesque scene in front of him. "What kind of animal would do something like this," he muttered. Outside he could see the red and blue flashing lights. People were rubbernecking, trying to catch a glimpse of the action.

The quiet morning air carried a tune from a radio through the window. A young ambulance attendant was holding a transistor radio in his hand, tapping his toe in rhythm with the song. Ernie was suddenly consumed by a rush of anger. The Ernie Linehurst that everybody loved for his patience and humility was becoming very exasperated. He walked to the front door and then stomped his way to the attendant, his anger growing with each step. The pressure of the Irene Stokes investigation and now this ugly scene had pushed him over the line. He stopped just short of arm's-length, knowing that if he were any closer things would go downhill in a hurry. The attendant flinched in surprise.

Ernie couldn't control his anger as he lashed out. "Hey, you gum-chewing idiot! Turn off that fucking radio before I stick it up your ass!" he growled. The young attendant backed up with a start.

I'm sorry, I didn't know you were..."

"I know you didn't know, but from now on when I'm the officer in charge, you show some respect for the dead. I don't know if you have enough brains to know when it's appropriate to play your goddamned teeny-bopper music, so you stand there in one spot until I tell you to move. Don't say anything or ask questions. Do you understand that?" he shouted.

"Sir, I understand," the ambulance attendant said.

Ernie turned with a snap, teeth still clenched as he returned to the house. Before he reached the doorway, he was already sorry he had blown up. He wasn't God, and it wasn't his responsibility to control another person's morality. He wanted to go back to apologize, but instead he sat back down on the couch. At that moment the crime scene crew arrived. A familiar crime scene tech stuck his head inside the door. "Oh, fuck, what happened here?" he asked.

"Come on in, Sam," Ernie said. "That's what we're here to find out."

The evidence handler looked at Ernie momentarily then said, "This isn't getting to you, is it, Ern?" He pointed to the bloody bodies on the floor.

"I think I'm coming apart at the seams, Sam," Ernie said.

"Why did you come? We've got other detectives, you know. Not as good as you, but they can handle it."

Ernie rubbed his face as though he were very tired. "The chief called. He told me to take the initial report. He knows I'm working the Stokes case but he wanted me down here anyway."

"That's cause he knows you work the shit out of a crime scene, Ernie," Sam added.

Ernie thought about what Sam said, then moved slowly to rise. "Well, I guess we better get to it then," he said.

****

Roderick Constance was speeding north on I-55. He stopped and filled his car and paid for the gas with change. Traffic was light so Constance was motoring along at ninety-seven miles per hour, hoping to be in Joliet in less than an hour. Julie McBride was there waiting for him. Constance called her from the pay phone in Hovey Hall after he had killed Jack and Theresa Fink. Julie faithfully made cash purchases in Joliet and kept the receipts knowing that Constance wanted them. He would study them, set it to memory, and use them for his alibi if it ever became necessary.

State Trooper James Dyer was running radar at mile marker 208 just south of Pontiac, Illinois. He was about to wrap it up and head into headquarters to grab a cup of coffee when he saw headlights in the distance closing in on him fast. Even without the new hand-held radar, he knew this one was balling the jack. He pointed the gun and clicked in ninety-seven on the digital screen. Dyer was the only trooper working the road and knew he would have to get into position to make the stop in advance of the speeding vehicle. He took the inside lane and gunned it. When Constance passed him he had slowed down but still hitting eighty-five, he realized too late that the state policeman had a lead on him. His heart was pounding when he saw the red lights activate as the squad car swung in behind him. The .22 Magnum was wrapped in a towel beneath the seat under his feet. He squirmed as he tried to reach it. The glaring light in his mirror was blinding as it filled the interior of his car. The bag of change slid off the front seat and thumped onto the floor.

Constance stopped, his heart still pounding, still blinded by the spotlight and the bright headlights from the squad car. It was impossible to know if there was more than one trooper in the car — another gun-toting police officer just outside the light, waiting for him to make a false move. He kicked the .22 with the heel of his shoe shoving it farther up under the seat.

Trooper Dyer approached the car cautiously. Constance rolled the window down and turned to watch Dyer walking up alongside the car. His right hand was resting on his nine millimeter with the strap undone. Constance could see Dyer but he was nearly obliterated by the glare behind him.

"Put your hands on the steering wheel," Dyer ordered. Constance was slow to do as he was asked, still trying to decide whether to grab for the handgun. He decided it was best to let things play out. Dyer took a position alongside the car with the doorpost between himself and Constance. Dyer was a good trooper. He never took anything for granted, especially at one o'clock in the morning. Behind the doorpost he was partially shielded, and it required the driver to turn sideways in an awkward position to respond to questioning.

Speeding isn't a criminal offense, but twenty-one miles over the speed limit in 1976 required a court appearance. At ninety-five miles per hour, Constance would have to appear in front of a judge. The bond was routinely thirty-five dollars, but at that speed it was raised to fifty. Trooper Dyer was cautious with

Constance, but there was no reason to believe he was dangerous or represented any more of a threat than any of the other speeders he had stopped that day.

Constance was quiet and cooperative. Trooper Dyer wrote the ticket for ninety in a seventy mile per hour zone, giving Constance a break on the bond as well as the mandatory court appearance. When Constance presented thirty-five dollars in quarters for bond, Dyer became suspicious. After the ticket was written and bond posted, Constance was sent on his way. Dyer made an entry into his activity log about receiving all the coins for bond. It was odd for someone to have access to so much change, and it usually indicated some kind of criminal activity.

CHAPTER THIRTY-SIX

At three a.m., Constance was lying in bed at the Holiday Inn in Joliet with Julie McBride at his side. Constance had little interest in Julie romantically, but he needed her. Constance wasn't stupid, and he knew it was dangerous for Julie to know so much about him. He realized he would have to kill her when the time was right.

At seven a.m., Dan Ingelman was sitting at his kitchen table with his face resting in his hands. He heard the radio reports of the double homicide just like almost every other Willoughby Hills resident, but he was more troubled than any of them by what he had learned. He knew the name Jack Fink. Jack was a witness against one of his clients. He had testified against Roderick Constance in a recent shoplifting trial. It ended in a hung jury and the case was set for a retrial, and now Jack was dead. He wasn't the only witness in the case who wouldn't be testifying in the second round. Irene Stokes was also a witness but she was missing and believed to be dead — murdered. If that wasn't troubling enough, John Mason was the single witness against Constance in a separate offense and he had disappeared before the case went to trial. It didn't take much of a leap to wonder where Constance was when the crimes were committed. Dan didn't know Constance well, but he knew he was a strange little

213

freak without an ounce of respect for the law or anything else. It wasn't too far-fetched to believe this young defendant would murder witnesses to avoid a conviction.

For any citizen who cared about law and order, it was an easy call—you informed the police department of the circumstances and let them get at the little bastard. The problem was that Dan was his attorney. Did attorney-client privilege apply? If he decided to violate the client-attorney privilege, would the information he revealed be suppressed? Any evidence obtained from the poison tree would be permanently banned from being used in court. Dan couldn't think of a court precedence regarding anything like this. The Fink murders were so disturbing that Dan wasn't thinking clearly. In a fit of anxiety, he decided to call Ian Rogers. They were adversaries, but Dan respected Ian, and although Ian would have to prosecute the case he was convinced he would be fair with him under the circumstances.

Dan called and Ian arranged to meet him at the courthouse before it opened to the public. Ian was dumbfounded as Dan laid out the facts. He muttered "unbelievable" each time Dan presented another incriminating detail. When Dan finished, he asked, "So, is this privileged information?"

Ian looked at Dan in disbelief. "Are you all jammed up about this? I know you've had a hundred cases where you've argued attorney-client privilege, Dan," he said.

"I am jammed up. I think I know the answer but I need your opinion. This is serious. This is murder, Ian."

"He didn't tell you any of this. It's not privileged information," Ian said. Dan smiled.

"Of course you're right. I knew that," he said, embarrassed that his legs had gone mushy on him.

"We need to get Detective Linehurst down here now," Ian said. He waited for Dan to comment, but he was quiet. "You're welcome to sit in, Dan." A vague smile appeared on his lips. Dan nodded that he would. He had already passed the point where he would be precluded from defending Constance. Technically he was now part of the prosecution.

Tom Spencer and Gary Winstead were called in to assist as things unfolded. The courthouse doors were still locked so Tom was waiting at the door when Ernie arrived. The huge empty building was different now as they walked across the rotunda toward the elevator. The sound of their heels clicking across the marble floors echoed off the walls with a hollow, vacant sound.

Ian had given Ernie a few details on the phone but preferred to keep the bulk of the evidence for a face-to-face with the chief detective. Ernie's mind was churning and likewise so were his questions to Tom. Ian instructed Tom not to discuss the case with Ernie until they were sitting in his office, but Tom couldn't control himself. They stood in front of the elevator in the dimly lit rotunda discussing the case in quiet tones as if they were Bob Woodward and Deep Throat hiding in the shadows passing secret government information. Tom was apologetic because he hadn't discovered the connection between the missing witnesses before it had escalated into more deaths. Ernie consoled him in an unconvincing smattering of broken utterances. Both were left feeling uneasy as the elevator took them to the third floor.

Ian Rogers was sitting at his desk with the Roderick Constance case files stretched out in front of him. Dan was on the couch with his bony legs crossed like a skinny old birdman. His hair was mussed and his face swaddled in gray stubble. He looked like he had just gotten out of bed.

"We've got some real convincing circumstantial evidence here, Ernie," Ian said.

Ernie took a seat as Ian read through the files, frequently deferring to Dan to add to the commentary. Ernie was quiet. Even a child could have connected the dots once all the information was laid out in front of him. It was clear that Roderick Constance had murdered John Mason, Irene Stokes, and the Finks. Ernie wanted to find him and put a collar on him, but he knew there was still evidence to be collected. The crime scene was still being processed even as they were talking.

"We need to contact Matt Corgliano, and also brief Morgan Cooper about this. At this point I don't have any idea where Roderick Constance is. Maybe he's decided to go on a killing spree — you know — revenge. Maybe he's not even trying to stay cool about it. You know, just do everybody in and go down in a blaze of glory," Ernie said.

Ian stared blankly at Ernie. It was evident the thought had never crossed his mind. "Of course you're right. We should do that right now." He handed the file to Tom and instructed him to contact Corgliano.

Ernie called for a departmental meeting. He needed all hands on board. He requested help from the state police and the sheriff's office. They needed to locate Constance and put a tail on him. The circumstantial evidence was pretty hefty, but it was clear the case wasn't ready to go to trial. Now that Constance had been identified, physical evidence would roll in on a wave, but they needed time.

The chief of police wanted Constance arrested and jailed immediately, but the state's attorney and the chief detective were adamant about putting a case together first. There wasn't one piece of physical evidence to connect Constance to any of the murders at that point other than the fact the victims were all witnesses against him. Dan knew Constance best and he was certain that Constance would never confess to anything even with a mountain of evidence staring him in the face. He agreed it was best to uncover additional information before bringing him in.

When the departmental meeting was over, Ernie asked Morgan to stay and talk with the state's attorney and him. Ernie thought it would be best for Morgan to take a few days off and get out of town. Morgan refused, but agreed to coop with Ed until Constance was taken into custody, but he wasn't going anywhere. Molly would have to stay with her mother in Decatur.

There were three witnesses against Constance who were either dead or missing. Thirteen dollars in change was found strung out in the alley behind the Fink residence. A record search found that Illinois State Police Officer James Dyer took thirty-five dollars in change from Constance near Pontiac less than two hours after the murders. Constance filled his gas tank in Minonk, Illinois, and the attendant remembered him using quarters to pay for it. There were ten Coca-Cola machines emptied sometime during the week in the Willoughby Hills area prior to the murders. Telephone records were checked from the pay phones in Hovey Hall, and a call was made to the Holiday Inn in Joliet, Illinois, where a friend of Constance was registered. Finally, Sandra Winghert narrowed a photograph of Constance down to one of the three possible suspect's photos she had viewed as the man she had seen exiting the murder scene. In other words, Constance's goose was cooked.

His vehicle was located in the Holiday Inn parking lot and the state police were tailing him. It was only a matter of putting together the charges and filing the arrest warrant.

****

Constance drove back to Willoughby Hills from Joliet with one eye on the rearview mirror. He kept seeing a black 1974 Chevy with a spotlight and whip antenna. He knew it was a police car.

There were many places in the USA where covert police techniques were being used that enable police investigators to be invisible in plain sight, but Illinois apparently wasn't one of them. Authorities handling the surveillance might as well have hung a sign in the window of the car stating "Surveillance Vehicle in Use." The two troopers tailing Constance were taken right off the road and swapped out their Smokey Bear uniforms for blue blazers, tan pants, and round-toed black shoes. They stuck them into a black unmarked radar car and said, "Go get'em, boys." A yellow banner blowing in the wind would have been less conspicuous.

When Constance and Julie arrived in Willoughby Hills they went directly to Julie's apartment. Julie unloaded her luggage as Constance hurried inside. He watched out the window as the squad car parked two blocks away. He never believed he would ever be caught, but now the weight of the possibility was coming down like a wet blanket. Julie wasn't concerned. The fat, rich girl who looked more like a sloppy, rotund alley-hopper never thought much beyond her next meal. The truth was she had caught a break. If Constance had been able to pull this off, she would have found herself taking a long dirt nap.

A more reasonable-thinking person would have run at that point, but that mulish side of his reasoning was maneuvering into focus. Constance rationalized that they had no case on him. If they did, he would already be under arrest. As bizarre as it was, Constance had convinced himself that he could beat a murder charge as well as the pending shoplifting case. Now his plan was to lose the state police, locate and murder Morgan Cooper and Matt Corgliano.

Insanity? Could he appreciate the consequences of his actions? Yes—still sane.

CHAPTER THIRTY-SEVEN

Every policeman on the department was nervous about Roderick Constance being on the loose, but they all knew the system. Once Constance was arrested everything changed where his rights were concerned, especially if he "lawyered up." So now they were waiting it out. Still, there was police work to be done — traffic accidents to be investigated, family dispute calls to answer, and routine patrol to be conducted.

There was also something else going on. There were TV reporters from Peoria, Springfield, and Chicago milling around outside the dilapidated City Hall asking questions. The Fink murders were still a fresh news story, but they were asking questions about Irene Stokes. It was obvious there was a leak. Ernie Linehurst was buried in crime scene photographs and lab reports as he put together the case against Constance. Still, occasionally he walked to the window and scanned the traffic, noting the TV vans parked across from the courthouse. He looked into passing cars hoping to see the face of Roderick Constance. He was anxious and agitated because he had been notified that the state police surveillance vehicle had lost Constance. They described him as a slippery little eel who was as cunning as a coyote, but the truth was they were just too inept to do the job. The Illinois State Police were the best in the country for controlling traffic, accident reconstruction, and apprehending fugitives, but routine criminal work and surveillance wasn't in their repertoire. Ernie blamed himself, but the Willoughby Hills Police Department didn't have the manpower to keep track of Constance when he was meandering all over the state of Illinois. State Police Command had assured Ernie they would find Constance and stick with him like "white on rice."

Ernie wanted to explode, but instead he bit down on his cigar and stared blankly out of those angry little black eyes. He hung up the phone without making a comment but he was steaming. He only hoped that if they didn't find Constance he would be foolish enough to show up for his shoplifting trial just four days away.

Ernie wanted Morgan Cooper taken off the road but Morgan stubbornly resisted. He was a cop, and it was his job to arrest criminals, not run and hide from them. Sarge agreed, and his word was final. Still, Sarge was worried. It was Friday and they were starting their first night shift duty on swings. The police department swing shift at first glance was designed by a madman, but Willoughby Hills was like many agencies with less than fifty officers — they had to make concessions. The hours were split between two days, one morning, and two nights. Each crew worked one month of straight days, one month of nights, and a month working the dreaded swing shift. The fluctuation was difficult to adjust to. The first two days of swing shift left some of them just going through the motions.

No rational-thinking person would have believed how illogical Roderick Constance was behaving, but what was now known about him had everyone on high alert. Still, nobody really thought death was waiting around the corner for them, not even Morgan Cooper.

Ed was with Morgan as they reported in for the weekend night shift. He was talking so loud that Ron closed the door to the radio room to keep him from bleeding his opinions over the microphone as calls were being dispatched.

"If I see that little son of a bitch, I'm pinching his ass. I don't care what the Dicks say!" Ed boasted.

Sarge stepped around the corner and pushed his glasses down on his nose. "Ed, cut the shit now. If you see Constance, back off, log his position, and let the State tail him," he said.

Roderick Constance who had been little more than a nuisance was now elevated to public enemy number one. Taking him into custody was on the mind of every Willoughby Hills cop. Ed was just verbalizing the sentiments of the entire department.

"Sarge, we all know he's a murdering little bastard. He needs to be right here in that holding cell in the back!" Ed barked.

Sarge put his fist on his hips and stared at Ed. His scowl turned into a glare.

Ed pulled his neck in and his legs were bent in a fake buckling as he tiptoed past Sarge saying, "Meow, meow, meow."

Sarge laughed, took off his hat and smacked Ed with it. "I mean it, damn it!"

"I got it," Ed said.

The shift meeting was nothing more than six guys describing what they were going to do to Roderick Constance. Most of it was nothing more than bluster but some of it wasn't.

Before they grabbed their clipboards and headed off on patrol, there were a few jabs at Ed, insinuating that he might be going off to dreamland because it was their first night of the swing shift. Sarge was waiting at the door to the parking garage when Morgan and Ed were walking down the hallway. He cleared his throat and plucked his pipe from his mouth. Ed tried to look straight ahead as he walked by, but his eyes were cocked sideways, focusing on Old Sarge.

"Ed," — a long pause followed — "I know the guys were only half kidding about you dozing off. I don't approve of sleeping on duty anytime, but tonight especially. Partner up with Morgan, keep your eyes open, and stay alert."

"Sarge, I know. I got it," Ed said. The truth was that Ed did get it. He was as good as any cop on the department, maybe one of the best. He was as keyed-in as he had ever been. Morgan Cooper was his best friend, and he knew Jack Fink. He had put a collar on the dirty little bastard who murdered Jack and he was let go for lack of evidence. It was the burglary case at Willoughby Hills College. John Mason was the boy who reported him and then went missing. Ed got it all right. It was personal to him.

****

Roderick Constance had ditched the surveillance vehicle and was holed up in a dingy motel on the north side of Springfield, Illinois. He had talked to his mother on the phone and learned that the police had been to the restaurant asking questions about him. There was also a police car sitting a block away watching her house.

After talking to his mother, Constance sat on the bed staring at the dirty carpeting. The urine odor from the broken toilet stool permeated the room. Cheap pictures of cowboys chasing buffalo were hung crookedly on the walls where the wallpaper was peeling and faded. He was there alone. The room was as gloomy as a crypt. Julie McBride accompanied Constance to Springfield, but she was trolling the area afoot looking for something to eat.

In the bathroom the faulty toilet was hissing as the water passed continually through the valve. The blinking light outside shone through the window washing Constance's pale skin in an amber glow. His long, stringy black hair hung across his face as he leaned forward, looking tormented and defeated. The hissing sound from the toilet seemed louder and more irritating, becoming an unbearable ringing inside his brain. He was holding the .22 Magnum, twirling the chamber and cocking the hammer. An uncontrollable flash of anger raged through him as he jumped to his feet and pointed the Magnum at the broken stool. Just as he started to pull the trigger, Julie opened the door and stepped into the room. She had a fried chicken leg in her fist and an open bucket of Kentucky Fried Chicken under her arm.

"What are you doing?" she asked.

Constance gritted his teeth and gasped in disgust. The fury of hatred and anger were flashing in his eyes. "Shut up, you fat bitch!" he bellowed.

Julie's eyes were like saucers, and the dumbest expression ever to dawn upon a human being washed across her face. She was totally shocked and dumbfounded. With her mouth still open she raised the chicken bucket and meekly said, "D'you want some chicken, Rod?"

Constance turned the gun and stuck the barrel against Julie's head. "You stupid fucking whore, I'll kill you right now if you eat another bite," he shouted. Julie spit out a half-chewed piece of chicken into her hand. Constance ran his hand through his hair, shoved the gun into his belt, and fell backward onto the bed.

An hour later Julie was sitting quietly at the end of the bed with the chicken bucket still under her arm. Her oblique muscles were so tight that her breathing was labored and her ribs were aching from the strain. For the first time since she became involved with Constance, the weight of what he had done was coming down on her like bricks. She was dumb, but having a gun shoved against her head had sharpened her thought processes. Now there was a fresh but somewhat desiccated recurring thought that she might be murdered before this was all over.

Constance hadn't moved for an hour, but finally he sat up and rubbed his eyes. He stood up, approached the window, and peeked out. There were cars moving slowly up and down the street, none of them resembling a squad car. He twirled the chamber in the .22, opened the door, and walked out. Julie exhaled, placed her face in her hands, and bawled.

****

Police work is hours of boredom and moments of terror, but more often than not, just hours of boredom. The taverns and restaurants were still serving alcohol at one a.m., but it had been quiet and boring. Morgan was driving and Ed was riding shotgun. The parking spaces on Chicago Street and Broadway were emptying, and patrons moseyed to their cars.

"Half these bastards are drunk," Ed said.

"Yes, but we can't arrest them for drunk driving before they get into their cars," Morgan said.

"Oh, you mean we have to watch them, see if they weave over the line, pull over to the curb, and puke, piss their pants—stuff like that," Ed said.

Morgan smiled. "Yep, probable cause."

"Sure thing," Ed said.

****

Roderick Constance turned into the Chicago Street Amtrak parking lot. He watched the squad car turn into the alley. The alley lights came on as the police car slowly stopped. Two cops got out and walked along the alley shining their flashlights into different directions until they had covered the entire length of it. One of them was Morgan Cooper. They went back to the car. It slowly turned onto Broadway Street and headed east.

Constance had seen this routine several times over the last few months. He knew they were checking doors and windows for broken locks or anything suspicious. Police officers were taught to vary their patrol activities, but most of the time it was routine. If they saw something fishy, their concentration was honed in. Constance knew their workday nuances. He was certain they wouldn't be so casual if something sprang up on them in the dark.

Morgan guided the squad car into the alley behind the Yellow Dog Inn. He shined the spotlight across the pavement and into a corner where there were several large boxes piled against the side of the building. As Morgan started to back out of the alley, the boxes began to move and fall. Both officers bailed out of the car and approached the boxes, staying in the darkness outside the scope of the spotlight. Morgan kept his nightstick ready, waiting for more movement. The boxes shifted again as a smattering of mumbling and coughing filtered from beneath the pile.

"Come out of there!" Ed shouted as he unholstered his nine-millimeter.

The cardboard separated as a tubby old man wobbled to his feet with one arm across his eyes blocking the glare from the spotlight. He held a bottle behind his leg in the other. "What do you want?" he demanded.

Ed recognized him immediately. "Well, you old son of a bitch," he snorted.

"Who is it, Ed?" Morgan asked.

"You should know, the old bastard tried to kill you a few months ago," Ed said.

"Bob Turner?"

"Yep."

"Shit."

"I haven't seen you since they shipped you off to get dried out," Ed said disgustedly.

"They sent me to Danville and I was okay for a while, but I can't go the rest of my life without a drink, boys," he whined.

Morgan had learned a long time ago that you couldn't rehabilitate an alcoholic at a chance meeting in an alley. He wasn't going to waste his time on dialogue with Bob Turner. "Get in the car, we'll take you home," he said.

Ed snorted and shook his head. "We oughta throw his old ass in the drunk tank. The drunken son of a bitch might go home and get his gun."

Morgan chuckled.

225

"You're a forgiving fucker, that's all I got to say. Maybe next time he'll kill you—maybe that'll satisfy you," Ed said.

"Don't take me in, boys. I'll go straight to bed if you take me home," Turner pleaded. His eyes were bloodshot slits. Ed glared at him as he waddled down the alley to let himself into the backseat of the squad car.

Ed rolled his eyes as Morgan taxied Bob Turner to his home and helped him to the front door. When he returned to the car Ed said, "You know if he kills his wife tonight, it's all your fault." Morgan quickly glanced at Ed, but he didn't laugh.

"Let's go get a doughnut," he said.

Roderick Constance followed the squad car from a distance in a rental car from Hertz. He was getting skillful at stalking his victims. He knew everything about Jack Fink and now Morgan Cooper. He could prowl around without being detected as well as keeping one eye on the rearview mirror for cops who might be following him.

When the squad car pulled into the Melocream doughnut shop parking lot, Constance continued on for another two blocks. The Bell Telephone office was kitty-corner from the doughnut shop enabling Constance to keep an eye on the two cops. It was handy that a pay phone was there too because he would need it.

The urban legend that all cops love doughnuts wasn't exactly a cliché, especially in Willoughby Hills. Carl Meyer owned, operated, and baked the doughnuts, worked all night getting them ready to distribute, and waited on customers during the morning rush. He had one employee who had been with him for many years, and the two of them made every glazed cake and cream-filled doughnut on the property. He loved policemen and welcomed them into the kitchen to eat their fill and down as much coffee as they could get down their pieholes. The shop was closed to the public from eight in the evening until five a.m. Every policeman on night duty stopped at least once a night.

Joe Bernard was there more than he was on patrol. No common citizen ever had such a fantastic treat as a fresh, hot, Melocream doughnut. They were steaming when they came off the wire and the aroma was irresistible. The commoners had to wait until five a.m. when the doughnuts were at room temperature.

Carl was waiting for Morgan and Ed with several hot-glazed beauties on a paper plate. "Eat these, they're rejects," he said handing them to Morgan. Morgan looked at them. They appeared perfect to him. "What's wrong with them?" he asked.

"They got some raisins in 'em. Goddamn raisins are the cockroach of the pastry industry. Damn things get into everything," Carl said.

"I like raisins," Ed said, grabbing one of the glazed.

****

Roderick Constance dropped a dime into the coin slot and dialed the police department. He told the radio operator that he was the night janitor at Lucky's Bar on Broadway Street. He said there was a prowler in the alley behind the tavern, a large guy just walking around.

Morgan had taken the portable radio with him so they weren't on an official break. When they got the dispatch they stuffed the doughnuts into their mouths and headed for the squad car. They were only a few blocks away from the call so they were there within a few minutes. It was 2:20 a.m. The streets were empty and all the taverns were closed. Ed grabbed the shotgun as they exited the car. Morgan took his nightstick and unsnapped the strap on his holster.

Prowler calls were a dime a dozen. Most of the time it was a drunk who had slipped out the back door of one of the taverns, trying to sober up before driving home, or a shop owner making a late night of it. Occasionally it was actually someone up to no good.

Lucky's Bar was in the center of the block. There were

apartments upstairs over the bar. It had a fire escape and a service ladder to the roof. It was the only building on the block that wasn't attached to all the others, leaving a narrow passageway from the alley back to the main street. Roderick Constance was there waiting.

Morgan glanced at Ed as he carried the shotgun in a ten and four position, ready to shoulder, point and shoot, just as he was taught in the academy. Morgan chuckled. "Are you serious?" he asked.

Ed grinned. "Hey, when the old man chews my ass twice within a half hour about staying alert, I'm playing the game," he said.

"Okay," Morgan said as he unholstered his nine. "We'll probably scare the shit out of some drunk back there."

Constance had packed his shotgun. It was cradled in his arm. His breathing was heavy and his heart was pounding. When he killed John Mason his reason included his hatred for him, but the bulk of it was to avoid prosecution. It was the same for the Finks. Butch Scroggins was killed just for the fun of it, and Hightower was killed for money.

Now things were different. Constance didn't want to go to jail, but there was something much heavier weighing on him. He didn't particularly hate Morgan Cooper, but he hated everything he stood for. Every human being living in that cloud they called normality was his enemy. He despised their accents, their clothes, and the way they laughed. He hated them because they thought they could go about their lives without realizing how insignificant they were. Their rules were nothing more than nuisances thrown up to impress others about how thoughtful and concerned they were about society. It made them feel important, and they saw themselves as good people walking a straight line to heaven. He hated them and he wanted to kill as many of them as he could. Those who had authority were even more despicable. They were the people he wanted to kill the most. He couldn't wait to blow Morgan Cooper's brains out in that alley.

Morgan and Ed were silhouettes slowly easing through the shadows. Constance looked down the barrel of the shotgun and pumped a shell into the chamber. Morgan stopped in his tracks. His eyes opened wide, his expression frozen on his face. "Shotgun!" he shouted.

The sound was deafening as the blast roared down the alley. The flash lit up the night like a bolt of lightning.

Morgan dove for shelter behind a metal dumpster. It seemed like he was moving in slow motion. His shoes were filled with lead weights, and he was toting a hundred pound bag of grain on his back. As he went down, his head banged against the dumpster. A gray cloud formed in his eyes and he was left momentarily blinded. Ed was flat on his belly in the middle of the alley. "Are you hit?" he bellowed.

Morgan was disoriented, but he knew it wasn't a bullet wound. "I'm okay, I think."

"Are you hit?"

"No, no, I'm okay. Blood trickled down his nose and dropped onto the pavement. Ed scrambled on his stomach to the dumpster ahead of two more blasts. The smell of gunpowder was strong and a blue haze hung like a cloud. "He's on top of Lucky's," he said, gasping for air.

"I'll put a couple of rounds up there!" Morgan said. He jumped to his feet and stretched out over the top of the dumpster. He flipped the safety on the nine and started firing. He sent fourteen rounds in the direction of Lucky's Bar before the gun clicked empty. He hit the release, dropped the empty clip onto the ground, and slid another into the gun. His hands were shaking.

Constance could hear bullets hitting the brick chimney behind him, and the steel guttering rang like a bell as hot lead was raining down on him.

Ed popped up and pumped three blasts onto Lucky's rooftop. The guttering was torn loose as it screeched down the brick facade taking out a window as it went. The bricks on the chimney scattered violently across the rooftop as the buckshot tore into them.

Constance whimpered as he ran for the fire escape. He drug the shotgun, banging the iron steps with it as he went. He cut into the opening between the buildings and headed for his car. Sirens were wailing as red and blue lights flashed from every direction.

The alley behind Lucky's was suddenly lit up like a Christmas tree with white light from spotlights and the flashing red and blue emergency lights. Sarge came running up the alley in a hunched position with his shotgun in hand. "Details, now!" he demanded.

"Ambushed! Top of Lucky's," Ed said, pointing down the alley.

"Joe, bring the lights down the south end of the alley and light up Lucky's Bar," Sarge barked into the portable radio. "Get a car in position in front, and two cars to triangulate the block from Broadway."

Ron had already dispatched an ISPERN alert for backup. Two state cars and two county cars were on their way to assist. Joe brought the van up the alley with enough brilliance to raise the dead. In just moments there were eight police vehicles surrounding the area with enough light to make it seem like a bright, sunny afternoon. In only a few more moments, Sarge, Morgan, and Ed were standing on top of Lucky's looking at the damage the buckshot and the nine millimeter had done, but there were no dead or wounded. Constance was in his car on County Road 1500 taking the back roads to Springfield.

At least ten off-duty police officers hurried to the police station when they heard chatter on their police scanners. They picked up portable radios and hit the streets in their personal cars, stopping everything that moved. Ed and Morgan were at the police station writing their reports and answering questions from the detectives. Ed talked excitedly as though he had just won the Super Bowl, not at all troubled by what had happened. Morgan was more somber. Roderick Constance was never mentioned but he was on everyone's mind. The first night of the swing shift ended without any evidence indicating who ambushed Morgan and Ed, but they all knew it was Constance. They were given three days off with a caution from Ernie to stay alert. Roderick Constance's misdemeanor trial was set for Monday morning at nine a.m. If he wasn't found and grabbed by then he would be arrested at the courthouse, providing he showed up.

Constance made it back to Springfield. Julie was gone. She caught the Amtrak and headed for Chicago. Constance was in his bedraggled motel room alone. The amber blinking light flashed through the plastic window coverings casting eerie shadows into the room. He was still shaken from his gun battle with the cops. He had never felt a single emotion other than satisfaction when he killed his defenseless victims, but when the Grim Reaper's shadow had come so close to descending upon him he was jolted into the new reality that *he* might die in this undertaking. Now, as he was retracing everything in his mind, he was washed in anxiety. He calculated that he would be arrested if he showed up for his trial on Monday morning, but he knew if he ran it would look like he was guilty of murder. Still, in his warped reasoning he thought he had a chance to beat a murder rap. He had no idea of the mountain of evidence they had against him. If he had known, he surely would have run.

Morgan and Ed would not be on duty until Monday on the afternoon shift. Constance was scheduled for trial at nine o'clock Monday morning. Everyone thought he would be caught and in the slammer by then, but if not he would be arrested at the courthouse when he reported for his hearing. Ernie wanted Sandra Winghert to get a good look at Constance without putting him in a lineup. She had narrowed his photograph down to one of three possibilities in the photo lineup at the police station on the night of the Fink murders. Ian Rogers didn't want to take a chance on her identifying the wrong man, therefore, if she had an opportunity to see him outside the police station it might enhance her chances of identifying him. Making an identification in a lineup is risky business. There would be several other men with similar builds and hair color for a witness to choose from, but the courts held that it was the only fair way of identifying suspects. If the police apprehend someone and parade them in front of a witness and ask, "Is this the guy?" it would be suggestive and prejudicial and the identification would not be allowed. The courts allow an identification on a situation where the suspect is apprehended within a reasonable proximity of the crime, and that is called a "show-up." The key is that it must be within a reasonable time and proximity.

If Constance were to be apprehended outside the courthouse and taken into custody, he would have a right to be viewed in a lineup situation. If Sandra Winghert witnessed the apprehension and she identified him at the point of arrest, it would also be prejudicial since it wouldn't be within a reasonable time and proximity of the crime.

Ian Rogers thought it would be best to allow Constance to enter the courthouse unmolested, report to the bailiff, and be seated outside the courtroom just as he would at any other trial. Sandra Winghert would be allowed to walk around in the waiting area looking at the people who were there without any instructions. If she identified Constance as the man who murdered Jack and Theresa Fink, it would be incontrovertible. Dan Ingelman said if he were representing Constance, he would argue that it was prejudicial, but he also thought he would lose.

So that was the plan. Naturally Constance would be arrested at the moment he was located prior to Monday morning at nine a.m., but if he wasn't in custody by then they were going to let him walk right into the courthouse. Sandra Winghert would be placed in a location where she could see him and hopefully identify him as a murderer. If she failed to put the finger on him he would be arrested anyway. The circumstantial evidence on him was plentiful. Now it was just a matter of time.

CHAPTER THIRTY-EIGHT

Time doesn't stand still, but sometimes it moves very slowly. Languidly it passed, and Monday morning finally arrived. With it came an infinitely blue sky with only a few transparent white clouds skirting along the horizon. A soft breeze rustled the trees and the supple green grass shifted silently in waves. Morgan was in the cemetery alone, quietly evaluating the last year. He stopped for a moment when a red-winged blackbird hovered over an approaching cat. She beat her wings and screeched violently to chase away the curios feline. When the intruder was gone and her nest was safe, it was quiet again.

Morgan walked among the granite markers and read the names and eulogies printed on them. Some people had died more than a hundred years ago, others only recently. Their ages ranged from the high nineties to those who had lived only a few hours. Some were born dead.

The gravestones were diverse. Some were large and elaborate with fancy stonework and intricate designs. Others were mere rocks with simply a name to identify the dead. Ancient grotesque trees with knotty limbs were poised as though they guarded the graves from trespass.

Although time had reduced the inhabitants to an equal status, it was apparent here as in life that existence is not fair. For some there is long life happily filled with "dear loved one," while others live and die alone and in the interim struggle to survive. For those who have been honored with elegant monuments and their resting places carefully maintained, life was more comfortable for than those whose graves were less endowed and abandoned. But now the common characteristic was that they were void of pain and hardship. Just as they were without accomplishment and happiness.

It was sad to be alone in a cemetery, left to contemplate fate and destiny. Even those things beyond the iron railing seemed soundless and devoid of life. Cars and trucks were passing by and children were playing but the clangor was subdued—so close but too distant to feel real.

Morgan wondered what it would be like to be dead. Would someone someday stand over his grave and ponder over his existence? What was his life like? Did he have a legacy? A hundred years in the future would anyone experience a single emotion because of his life on earth?

Jack and Theresa Fink lay beneath the ground. Their common marker stated only the dates they were born and the date they died. They were laid to rest on the same day, but would anyone ever ask how or why? Would their dying represent anything? Would time erase their memory from life's records and not a single person feel emotion at their passing? The memory of John Mason and Irene Stokes would have to serve their loved ones because their remains will have turned to dust in some unknown location. When everyone who loved them are gone, then so will their existence be erased from the earth.

Everything good in life comes from interaction with others. Accomplishments equal nothing when they're not appreciated by at least one other person. If a man possesses the world but can't share it with others, it's worthless. The most important thing in life is people. Roderick Constance chose to reduce human life to something without dignity, even to the point he could destroy it. He wanted to elevate himself, but in the end he gained nothing and in the process contaminated his own existence.

Morgan turned from the cemetery and walked away. Roderick Constance was toast. He was going to jail and would be tried for murder. Maybe he would get the chair, but still Morgan wanted there to be more. He wanted Constance to be sorry for what he had done. He wanted him to appreciate how horrendous his acts were and to regret them. Still, he knew Constance wouldn't have remorse for what he had done. He was a sociopath, and there wasn't a grain of humanity in him.

CHAPTER THIRTY-NINE

On Monday morning Morgan received a call from Ernie Linehurst. He wanted Morgan to meet him at the courthouse at eight thirty a.m. Ernie thought it would be poetic justice if Morgan were the one to serve the arrest warrant on Constance. When Morgan arrived there were TV crews from every city within forty miles of Lincoln County. They huddled outside the courtroom and milled about the rotunda with cameras and video ready to pounce. One young attorney from another district stopped and asked the bailiff what was going on. He had never seen TV crews and video in misdemeanor court.

When Morgan opened the frosted double doors and entered the courthouse, several cameramen trained their equipment on him. He was rushed by newsmen who stuck microphones in his face as flashbulbs exploded in unison.

"Officer Cooper, are you the policeman who arrested Roderick Constance on the shoplifting charge he's here for this morning?"

"No comment," Morgan said, taken by surprise.

"Is it true that Constance is suspected of firing the shots that nearly took your life on Friday night?"

"No comment," Morgan said again pushing his way past the crowd.

237

Ernie walked halfway down the stairs between the first and second floors to meet him. "Well, it looks like you've become an overnight celebrity," he said.

Morgan wanted to say something contemptuous of Constance to show that all the attention wasn't going to mitigate how he felt about him, but he couldn't think of anything. He hated what Constance had done, and no amount of attention was going to change that.

Ernie put his hand on Morgan's shoulder as they continued up the stairs. At some point prior to Morgan's arrival, Constance and a newly court-appointed attorney had taken the elevator and now sat on the long oak bench outside misdemeanor court. Jack Fink's brothers were across the rotunda sitting quietly with their wives. Two deputies were closely watching them. There was no reason for them to be there other than to see the man who murdered their brother. It seemed that everyone in Willoughby Hills knew what was going down. There were at least ten police officers on the second floor of the courthouse waiting for the go-ahead to put the arm on Constance.

The state's star witness, Sandra Winghert, was with Tom Spencer in the witness waiting room. Ian wanted her isolated from everything happening in the courthouse. When Ernie and Morgan arrived, Ian joined them. He asked Sandra if she knew why she was there.

"You asked me to come down here to take a look around. To see if I might see something suspicious," she said.

"Is that all?"

"Yes," she said.

The conversation seemed strange, but it was necessary. Ian didn't want there to be even the least impropriety in their meeting—no suggestions or influence from law enforcement.

As they walked out into the rotunda, a news crew saw her and made a move to follow but were intercepted by a deputy. Ian was at one elbow and Tom was at the other. Slowly they walked around the railing on the second floor. Sandra Winghert scanned the lobby studying the faces. Ernie and Morgan walked across the room to take a position closer to Constance. Ernie didn't worry that he would run but he wanted to be near just to get it over with.

"When Ian signals, we'll just go over there and grab him," Ernie said.

Morgan nodded.

When Sandra saw Constance, she stopped. Constance was sitting with his hands dangling between his knees staring at the floor. When he looked up their eyes met. Sandra's stomach turned as she remembered seeing her friend Theresa Fink lying blood-soaked on her living room floor.

"That guy makes me sick," she said, pointing at Constance.

"What are you saying?" Ian asked.

"That guy murdered my friend," Sandra said.

Tom Spencer didn't wait for Ian to signal Ernie. He spun around and pointed at Constance. Ian smiled. Ernie took the warrant from his pocket and handed it to Morgan. They took the walk across the rotunda as several uniformed officers followed them. Constance leaned back on the bench and crossed his arms. Morgan stepped in front of him. "Roderick Constance, you're under arrest for the murders of Jack Fink and Theresa Fink."

The court-appointed attorney stood up and examined the warrant. He nodded his head and handed the document to Constance.

"You have a right to remain silent. You have a right to an attorney. If you cannot afford an attorney, one will be appointed to you at no cost. If you make a statement, anything you say can and will be used against you in court."

Constance stood up, turned his back to them, and crossed his arms behind him. Morgan patted him down for weapons. Two deputies stepped forward and handcuffed him. Policemen came from every direction to secure the young murderer. As he was led away he glanced over his shoulder, made eye contact with Morgan, and smirked.

CHAPTER FORTY

The months passed quickly. The grand jury, the suppression hearing, the trial, a guilty verdict, and finally the sentencing, and it was all over. The death penalty was temporarily suspended in Illinois so his life was spared, but Roderick Constance would never see the light of day again.

CHAPTER FORTY-ONE

The bodies of John Mason and Irene Stokes were never found. Morgan remembered how he felt when he arrested Constance — the look on his face and the way he smirked as they took him away. Many times Morgan had thought about that moment and what might have been going through his mind. The recurring thought was that the arrogant smirk was because he knew he was leaving behind a mystery for them to contemplate and never solve. Was Constance that perceptive to know Morgan would always wonder where he had left his victims? Did he know he would still think about it thirty-five years later, not daunted by it but still curious? Was that too egotistical to believe Constance would be concerned about what he thought?

CHAPTER FORTY-TWO

Jennifer Lopez was showered with applause as the colorful lights faded to black. They cut to a commercial where a man in a gray business suit deposited a blue recycling bag into his sidewalk bin, and then got into his 2012 mint green Prius. A rich low voice said, "Going green, it's the right thing to do. Buy Toyota." A lot of things had changed in the last thirty-five years. Nobody was worried about an Ice Age on the horizon. Now the world was in a spasm about global warming instead. General Motors was bankrupt, Wriggly Field had lights, the Soviet Union was on the ash heap of history, China was a world economic superpower, and the United States had elected a black president.

Although Morgan was only slightly heavier than he was when he was twenty-six, his hair and mustache had turned gray. His business had produced more money than he thought possible, and his books had provided a generous sense of accomplishment. He and Molly were bored, but they were happy.

Ernie Linehurst was dead, Sarge was in a nursing home, and Ed Woodson was the chief of police. That was proof positive that longevity had benefits. Nobody could believe it when Ed was appointed, and once he was, everybody and his dog tried to get him out. He was sixty-six and pledged that he was staying until he was seventy, no matter how hard people tried to get him removed.

So far Morgan's life had been good. But still, that will-o'-the-wisp mawkishness that settles upon men his age had not passed him over. He was sitting there in his underwear watching TV, an activity he hated, thinking about writing a book about something that happened a lifetime ago.

What the hell! Why not? He would do it. He made the decision to write that story. But still, he had to know how the book would end. There were at least two people whose story needed to be told. His mind was set. He was going to Chester, Illinois to visit Constance and vie for an interview. The next morning, he contacted the Department of Corrections and obtained Constance's permission to visit.

CHAPTER FORTY-THREE

Time wasn't a discriminating element in Morgan's emotional attachment to Roderick Constance. It was the same in 2012 as it was in 1976. He wanted to hate Constance, but he didn't. He couldn't have grieved more for the victims than he had because of his personal involvement in the case, but just as he had struggled to understand in the beginning, it was curiosity that demanded action.

Morgan wasn't obsessed with the lingering mystery, but the nagging question was how could Constance have justified such an unspeakable act? He had killed two people, their unborn child, and was suspected of murdering at least two others merely because they were going to testify against him in a misdemeanor trial. He terminated their lives and sentenced their families to mourn them for eternity for little more than inconvenience. It was incomprehensible. Morgan couldn't get his mind wrapped around it. Little did he know that Constance had laid two other souls in their graves. Now as he drove south on Illinois Route 3 in 2012, with those memories from 1976 swirling around in his head, he wanted more than ever to get answers.

The two-lane highway meandered along through the hills and valleys, sometimes skirting the bluffs above the Mississippi River. At times the view was breathtaking, distracting Morgan from the task at hand. It was early May. The dogwoods, royal empress, and crab apple trees mingled among the fresh green leaves of the maple and oak trees, inundating the hills with brilliant color. Morgan had always appreciated beautiful scenery, and he was mesmerized by the view, but still there was a gnawing sensation in the pit of his stomach. It seemed surreal to be headed down the highway, surrounded by an awesome view, to interview a man who had stalked him, towing a blueprint for homicide. Morgan had a budding alien feeling, much like Norman Dale symbolized in *Hoosiers*, as he drove the narrow highways in southern Indiana with the dry leaves flying away in the wake of his 1952 Chevrolet—a face etched in growing anticipation, advancing into the unknown.

The casual will-o'-the-wisp ambiance drained when he topped the hill into the parking lot of Menard Correctional Institute. The brown concrete stone structure hulking over the Mississippi looked more like an ancient Russian municipal building than a correctional facility for hardened criminal minds. The administration building was three stories with two tiers of Greek ion columns. In the 1930's, it had probably served as the reception center for visitors, but now that portion of the prison was empty and surrounded by a twelve foot fence capped with barbed wire. The only entrance was at the gatehouse manned by several uniformed correctional officers. There was a stainless steel speaker embedded in bulletproof glass where you awkwardly leaned forward casting your voice into it, much like shouting into a tin can. Preliminaries were conducted at that location. The first set of routine questions were asked by a guard and answered by the visitors. If all visitor information checked out, they were allowed into a narrow room with a heavy metal door at each end. Visitors were locked in and searched for weapons and contraband. If they were found to be safe and contraband-free, they were allowed to leave at the other end of the narrow room where they were greeted by two uniformed guards. At that point the guards escorted them to the visiting room where they waited to be called.

It was a mundane, lackluster process. It would have been more fitting for daunting music to have been playing, intensifying as Morgan advanced through the progress, culminating in a face-to-face encounter with a menacing adversary. But it was none of that. It was uncomplicated and routine.

Morgan was left in the visiting room to wait. In only a few minutes he heard a steel door open and a man entered being followed by a guard. The guard closed and locked the door behind him. Initially Morgan didn't recognize him, but after studying him for a few seconds, there he was—Roderick Constance. Morgan was struck by how outwardly normal he appeared. He remembered him with sunken cheeks, ashen skin, and hair as greasy as a shop rag. Back then he fit the description of a maniacal serial killer. Thirty-five years had turned him into a man who might have just delivered your new appliances. Now he was wearing the standard prison-blue work shirt and dungarees. He had gained weight. His cheeks were full, his skin had a healthy glow, and his hair was short and graying around the temples. His eyes were the same—a faint, almost colorless blue. He focused on Morgan with an analytical glare. Morgan was already sitting. Constance slid into his chair across from Morgan. Heavy steel mesh was the only thing separating them. Morgan expected a glass window and a telephone like he had seen on TV and in the movies. This seemed more cordial. It made him uncomfortable. The last thing he wanted was congeniality with a cold-hearted murderer.

"We can get a private room if we need to," Constance said.

There was a shelf extending from one end of the room to the other on Morgan's side of the wall with chairs lined up for visitors, but Morgan and Constance were alone. It was quiet and empty.

"Why do we need a private room?" Morgan asked.

"You cops need privacy, don't you?" Constance said.

"I'm not a cop," Morgan said. There was a long uncomfortable silence that followed. Morgan waited for Constance to speak, but he didn't. He just continued to study Morgan with those pallid blue, empty eyes. Morgan thought that questioning a criminal when you had jurisdiction to do it was easy. Having authority to grill someone, to be duty-bound to get answers, was easy. Finding a way to descend into the mind-vault of a convicted murderer without a modicum of leverage was more challenging.

"I'm a writer," Morgan said, feeling a bit pretentious. He had published two novels and both had sold just over two thousand copies, not exactly a resounding endorsement of his writing skills.

"I've read your books. They weren't very good," Constance said.

The remark stung a little. It was meant to, Morgan realized that, but Constance was the first person who had ever said that to his face. There were about twenty reader reviews on Barnes and Noble's book site and none were disparaging. Most were flattering. Morgan smiled at his naivety. How could he be offended by a cold-blooded murderer?

"Why would you even read my books?" Morgan asked.

Constance looked at him for a long time. The wheels were turning behind his eyes. Finally, he said, "Why would you come here to visit me?

"I was the one who arrested you on the shoplifting charge, the thing that started all of this," Morgan said.

"That's the reason I read your books, we've got history."

"So..." Morgan said, not knowing where to go from there.

Constance leaned back in his chair and crossed his arms. It was a defensive position that Morgan recognized from his years in law enforcement. He leaned back to retreat and crossed his arms to lock himself down. Getting the truth out of a person when they were shielding themselves in that manner was difficult at best.

They looked at each other. Finally, Morgan said, "I was never a detective when I was a policeman. I was an investigator for the state's attorney's office, but that's more trial prep than anything else — not real detective work."

From that point in the conversation, it was a cat and mouse enterprise. Morgan was accustomed to walking the invisible line drawn by the court's governing interrogations. He had reverted back to his years in law enforcement where such games were necessary. A police officer can't engage in interviews where there is a quid pro quo, a tit for tat. A promise or a deal is fruit from the poison tree. An out-and-out accusation might garner a lawsuit or result in a complaint of official misconduct. It was a fine line to walk, and Morgan was welded to the restrictions he had absorbed in his twenty-three years on the job. But as a writer, a private citizen, or just an old guy trying to satisfy his curiosity, he wasn't bound to those limitations. He could ask anything he wanted to ask. Still, old habits die hard and he was stuck with them. He wanted to make Constance feel comfortable with him, to put him at ease, then to pick his brain. Compliments were always the best way to get there, but in reality he just wanted to blurt out, *Did you kill Irene Stokes? Did you kill John Mason? Where are they? Tell me, you sick bastard!* Behind his eyes there was a burning sensation, like acid on raw skin. It wasn't hate. He had already rolled that over in his mind until he was exhausted. It was desire — a psychological stinging inside his mind. He knew Constance had stalked him and would have killed him if he could have, but that didn't explain the depth of his interest. It was beyond any rational explanation.

"You look different," Morgan said. Small talk, the first step in the process.

"So do you, you look old," Constance said. He clearly didn't care if Morgan was offended.

"Being old isn't all that bad," Morgan said, thinking if Constance had his way, he would have been a good-looking corpse back in 1976.

It was quiet again. Constance leaned forward in his chair and laid his arms across the ledge. He clasped one hand over the other. His body language had suddenly changed. Now he was ready to play ball. "I hope my trip down here wasn't an exercise in futility," Morgan said.

Constance smiled vaguely. The expression on his face was the same look you get after you've pulled the Old Maid from someone's hand. The ends of Constance's mouth shifted and the slight smile was now a straight line. He looked demon-like just for a split second, which validated even more Morgan's feelings of utter contempt at not only being in his presence but having the nagging curiosity that brought him there. How could Constance be so arrogant about his malevolent silence? Morgan had thought about Constance for thirty-five years and now that he was there, he suddenly felt deficient. It was insane but it was almost as though Constance occupied an exalted position over him. He was an incompetent loser and had done nothing more than murder some innocent people, but strangely it had elevated him.

"Why did you kill those people?" Morgan asked.

Constance leaned back in his chair and crossed his arms again, raised his eyebrows, and said, "They were going to testify against me. I had to kill Jack Fink but his wife was just in the wrong place at the wrong time." Morgan was shocked at Constance's matter-of-fact reply. He might have been talking about the weather or the flavor of ice cream he liked. Was it really that easy?

"Don't you ever feel guilty? Do you ever find it hard to sleep at night, I mean, thinking about murdering someone like that?"

"I never thought much about it. I mean, I was young and full of hate. I still am. I hate most of the people in here. I'd probably kill some of them if I could. I've killed people you don't even know about," Constance said.

"Did you kill John Mason and Irene Stokes?"

"That's something you'll have to figure out for yourself," Constance said, looking directly into Morgan's eyes.

"You know the death penalty has been rescinded, don't you?" Morgan asked.

"Sure, but that doesn't scare me anyway. Hell, it takes ten years to get to the chair. You know that, don't you?"

"Why don't you just give up the info on Mason and Irene Stokes?" Morgan said flatly.

Constance looked at Morgan for a long time before he spoke again. There was something in his gaze that was different now. He didn't look like a monster or a hideous serial killer. He was just a man in a blue work shirt and jeans. He could have been a carpenter or the guy who worked at the corner garage.

"I'm keeping that for myself. It's the only thing I've got. It's the only thing about my life that I have any fucking control over," he said.

"That sounds like an admission to me," Morgan said.

"Yea, try to get the state's attorney to go to trial on that," Constance said.

"Then I suppose the families will never have closure, never be able to bury their dead," Morgan said.

"I don't care about their families," Constance said and smirked. "Do you know how many times they've come here to question me about that? Detective Linehurst was here every year until he fell over dead — the state's attorney's investigators too." Morgan already knew that. After all he was one of the state's attorney's investigators, but he had never been assigned to make the trip.

"What makes you tick?" Morgan asked quietly.

"I liked the game. The entire thing was a game—the shoplifting seemed exciting, but the killings were something else, man. When I killed that grocery clerk, I felt so much satisfaction you wouldn't believe it. That fucker caused me so much trouble. It made me feel better, that's what made me tick," he said.

In a world where the Soviet Union had crumbled right on TV in real time, the invention of home video, VHS, CD players, cellular telephones, smart bombs, GPS positioning, and cars equipped with technology beyond belief, Constance was stuck in a world where killing and stealing were exciting to him. How pathetic.

"I was hoping there would be more to it," Morgan said. "I was hoping there would be some deep-seated trauma that had set you off. Some unyielding urge, or voices inside your head that controlled your thoughts, or something evil possessing your mind. I was hoping it was something like that. I didn't want it to be just some punk who liked the way it felt to kill another human being," Morgan said.

Constance was quiet. Morgan's rebuke didn't affect him.

Now he wanted to provoke Morgan, to poke at him. "Do you want to know what I did with the bodies?" he asked bluntly. "I mean, we could play this game. You guess and I'll tell you if you get it right."

Morgan's eyes narrowed. We'd sent unmanned space vehicles to Mars. There were 134 space shuttle missions. Heart transplants were as common as a tonsillectomy. The medical advancements in the world were unfathomable. But Roderick Constance hadn't changed. He looked better, but his mind was a shit-hole of adolescent litter. He was no different than he had been in 1976. Still, Morgan needed to play along.

"Okay, I'll bite. I know you're not about to make a confession, but go ahead, give me a hint."

Constance slid his chair away from the bench and shouted,

"Hey, guard." If he was about to disclose where he had put Irene Stokes and John Mason, it had to be quick. It was obvious he was headed "stage right."

"Where are they?" Morgan asked. He tried to sound reticent, but he couldn't disguise his impatience.

"I'll give you a hint," Constance said.

Morgan frowned. This wasn't what he expected. But hell, what did he expect? Did he really think a sociopath like Constance would open up and confess to a couple of murders he had committed thirty-five years ago? Had he kept his mouth shut waiting for good old Morgan Cooper to skate in to grab the glory?"

"It's an easy riddle, just one question. If you get it right, I'll tell you," Constance said.

"What?"

"That's it. What would you do with a dead body?" Constance said displaying an evil grin.

"That's it? That's your hint!" Morgan snorted. "You're fucking crazy!"

Constance watched Morgan's face, pleased that he was irritated. "Just one thing, don't over analyze it. Just answer the question. What would you do with a dead body?"

The guard escorted Constance from the room. Morgan was left sitting there thinking, *What the hell! What a waste of time.* He might as well have been sitting in the living room in his boxer shorts watching TV. "What would I do with a dead body? What kind of a question is that!"

****

When Morgan left the prison, he was empty. It was a feeling you got after being all hyped up over a football game, and it ended in a tie. It was an exhausting waste of time. He thought about the stupid question Constance had posed as he drove through the small town of Chester. It was a town on one of those high bluffs above the Mississippi River. He was taking a different route than he had used coming in. Morgan had decided to cross the river on Route 51 where an ancient two-lane bridge led into Missouri. He would catch I-55 at Perryville and go north to St. Louis before crossing the Poplar Street Bridge back into Illinois.

When he reached the tollbooth, the attendant was standing outside holding traffic as a funeral procession turned off the service drive and crept onto the bridge. As the hearse cut in front of his car, Morgan thought, *That's what I would do with a dead body – I'd take it to a funeral home and have it embalmed.* He chuckled at the thought. But then he remembered Constance's caution not to overanalyze the question. Constance asked what he would do with a dead body. He didn't ask him what he'd do with a murder victim. If he didn't overanalyze the question, that's exactly what he would do. He would take it to a mortician. He paused for a long moment, then chuckled again. "I must be nuts," he murmured, discarding the thought completely.

CHAPTER FORTY-FOUR

Morgan returned to Willoughby Hills and continued to wind down his life toward retirement. In 2013, he turned sixty-five and was eligible to draw his Social Security. He had withdrawn his retirement from the police department and rolled it over into a civilian retirement plan. His 401K plan had reached maturity at the same time. Now he would have to begin making withdrawals on both of them or he would be penalized. He didn't like the thought of retirement, but the forces of old age were closing in on him. Molly was already retired and had been hinting that she would like to go to Greece and Italy. She knew it was a dream Morgan had coveted for years too, but refused to acknowledge. She thought now was the time to do it.

Morgan nevertheless wanted to write another novel. Constance was clearly the subject he wanted to write about, but even now, a year and a half since he talked to Constance, he was left with a bad taste in his mouth. The moronic question Constance asked him wasn't even a factor, but just being around him had been discouraging. Not only was Morgan civil to a psychopath who had tried to kill him, but being civil seemed to diminish the gravity of his crimes. In addition to that, Morgan was left with the same old nagging questions he had before he made the trip. Where did he bury the bodies of John Mason and Irene Stokes?

Morgan didn't realize that even at that moment a situation was developing that would drag him back in.

On March 15th, Morgan drove to the police station to pick up Ed for their morning coffee. A new mayor had been elected and rumors were hovering about that Ed was heading for mandatory retirement. Ed was a more reserved Ed Woodson than he had been back in the seventies when he and Morgan patrolled the streets. He was certainly more politically correct and careful about his language, but still hardheaded and unafraid of a fight.

"I'm not leaving until I'm seventy!" Ed snorted as he opened the car door and slipped into the passenger seat. Morgan looked at him apathetically. He knew Ed was up for the battle, but he also knew he would lose. Ed had retired when he was fifty-five and worked as a firearms instructor for the state police before being brought back as chief. His notable career included the firefight he and Morgan survived with Constance (although it was never proven that Constance was the shooter) in addition to surviving being shot in the line of duty twice, once in an attempted bank robbery and another in a domestic violence call. He was a hero in Willoughby Hills, and firing him would certainly be unpopular. Still, at his age, it was a certainty. Morgan didn't want to talk about it. His opinion on the matter was better left unsaid.

"My wife wants me to retire," Morgan said.

"You're already retired, butthole," Ed said flippantly. He had a professional demeanor in public, but with Morgan he was the same old Ed. "Sending these young cop wannabees of yours out serving papers ain't exactly backbreaking labor," he continued. Ed was never happy with Morgan's decision to acquire a private detective license. He thought Morgan should have stayed in law enforcement just as he had.

Morgan smiled. He'd heard it all before.

"And all those books you've been writing, hell, you don't have time to work," Ed said.

"*The Long Winter's Night* was seven years ago, Ed. My last royalty check was for two dollars and eighteen cents. Not exactly a burgeoning enterprise," Morgan said and laughed.

"I thought you were gonna write that book about Roderick Constance. You could make a shit-pot full of money around here on that book," Ed said.

Morgan glanced at Ed, grimaced, and sighed. "Too much crap under the bridge. Too many years ago to remember everything we did. Too many questions left unanswered. Hell, Constance would probably sue me for the rights," he said.

"Still, that would be a good book. And besides that, I wanted to tell you about what's happening with him," Ed said.

"He can't be up for parole," Morgan said.

"No, the Department of Corrections called me to tell me he wanted to fess up on the whereabouts of Irene Stokes and John Mason. He said he buried them under I-55 while it was under construction. He said he put 'em in the dirt where they were pouring concrete, and they were paved over."

Morgan eyed Ed suspiciously. "Really?"

"Yep, one of my guys, the state's attorney's investigator, and a state police detective, are going down to Chester to pick him up. They're gonna drive him around and try to locate the place where he put 'em."

"Why would he do that?" Morgan asked almost angrily.

"He's got cancer. He's dying. The devil will be coming for his soul pretty soon."

So that was it. Constance was giving up the ghost, and he wanted to cleanse his soul before heading into the blankness of death. If Morgan still wanted to write the story of Constance and his prey, he would have to settle for a mundane, predictable conclusion. The story of an evil young man who shamelessly murdered innocent people, but in the end decided that his chances in the afterlife would be better if his sins were discharged before entry. He was no different than every other murderer who got religion before passing into the mist. *My conscience is unburdened, oh, Lord, I'm coming home!*

It made Morgan steam beneath his collar to think about Constance burnishing his iniquities in the eleventh hour, but that wasn't what was going down. Constance had one last thorn to jab in Morgan's side before leaving the world.

A week after Ed notified Morgan of Constance's plea, Ed called him on his cell phone. It was an urgent matter. Morgan already knew that Constance was in town under the custody of the Illinois State Police. They had been driving up and down I-55 trying to locate the two separate places where Constance had deposited Irene Stokes' and John Mason's remains. He was lodged in the Willoughby Hills holding cell on the first night but had collapsed on the second day and was transported to Willoughby Hills Medical Center. He wasn't yet in Satan's grasp, but he was receiving fluids intravenously and was being fed through a tube in his nose. Ed called to tell Morgan that Constance wanted to talk to him.

After some consideration, Morgan agreed to visit Constance, but inside his mind guilt was percolating to the surface. He wanted to know about the two victims who left the world without an epitaph, and he needed Constance for that reason. But to comply with Constance's request was like cooperating with someone who had been elevated by the very atrocities he had committed.

Nevertheless, he met Ed at the police station and Ed drove to the hospital. Constance wanted to talk with Morgan alone. The state police investigator argued against it. He wanted to be in the room with them, but Constance refused to talk to anyone besides Morgan. Constance had used all the influence he had just to get out of Menard under the pretense that he could find where he had buried Irene Stokes and John Mason. After a long day and a half of examining different locations along I-55, the detectives assigned to the detail suspected he had been blowing smoke the entire time. They were perturbed and wanted to extract the truth from Constance, but he was already a convicted murderer who was dying of cancer. He was immune to threats. Ed made the final decision that Morgan would do the interview alone before calling Morgan to relay Constance's request.

When they arrived at the hospital they entered through the emergency room doors. Morgan saw his reflection in the glass. He was gray and frumpy-looking. He wasn't that young police officer who was strong and athletic, so high-minded that he wanted to be the example of what a policeman should be. He recalled the "off the record" discussion with Leonard Wilson and how it had affected him. Now he knew there were a lot of lines in life that a person would cross, and then cross back over again. He was there at the behest of a lowlife murderer, and he wondered if it was for Irene Stokes and John Mason or just his own selfish curiosity?

If there was a line to be crossed, he wasn't being dragged, he was there voluntarily. He was there with his aged friend, standing in the doorway to their past, trying to put a period on a tragic time in the history of their little town. In those days and times so long ago, Roderick Constance's transgressions were horrendous and worthy of outrage, and should still have been in 2013, but drive-by shootings were a daily occurrence in the news. Children were being gunned down in places where their safety should have been assured. Still, every life counts. That was what society had forgotten. Irene Stokes and John Mason weren't merely statistics to him. They were people who were deprived of their lives by someone evil. Morgan wanted to bring it to an end.

It was only fitting that the hospital was in its final days before being put to rest. Willoughby Hills had a new medical center just recently completed, and only a few patients were being treated in the old complex. As Morgan and Ed proceeded down the hallway there were empty beds lining the walls, left there for final disposal. They took the elevator to the fifth floor where two Willoughby Hills police officers were standing guard at the door. Morgan glanced at them and said to Ed, "They look like high school kids on dress-up day."

Ed smiled. "They look like you did when you came to the complaints window at the old police station on your first day of duty."

Morgan laughed.

Ed stopped to talk to his junior officers, simply to acknowledge them. He asked a few questions pertinent to Constance, but he knew already that even though Constance was a convicted murderer, security wasn't a concern. They were there for pretense only. Morgan waited at the door, not at all anxious about the meeting. He thought it would be no more worthwhile than his rendezvous had been in 2011. Ed opened the door and motioned for Morgan to enter.

As Morgan walked into the room, he was stunned. The man he had seen in Menard had deteriorated into a diminutive scarecrow. His hair was scant and completely gray. His face was ashen, his cheeks sunken, his eyes were distended and yellow. Amazingly, his appearance was more similar to the maniacal killer now than he had been when Morgan talked to him in Menard. Despite his death-warmed-over appearance, his condition didn't educe Morgan's sympathy. He had already lived thirty-eight years longer than he deserved.

"Come in," Constance said weakly. Morgan approached the bed, but he didn't speak. He waited for Constance to make the first move. "I guess you probably suspect by now that I didn't really bury John Mason and the old lady under the highway," he said as he went into a coughing fit. He spit into a tissue, releasing a painful moan.

"It doesn't surprise me," Morgan said.

"Did you ever think about the clues I gave you?" Constance asked.

"Do you mean the idiotic question that everybody asked themselves every time the issue comes up? What did he do with the bodies?" Morgan said sarcastically.

Constance cleared his throat, closed his eyes, seemingly collecting himself to continue. After a few moments he said, "That's not what I asked. I wanted to know what *you* would do with a body," he said.

"I know that," Morgan snorted, hating himself for descending into a dialogue with Constance. He was trying not to forget in the midst of unearthing information that the person he was talking to was an evil demon incarnated in a human body.

"I know your answer, but you're too stubborn to say it," Constance said.

"I'd take a body to a mortician, just like any other normal person would do, but then again, I'm not a cold-blooded murderer," Morgan snapped.

Constance coughed again so pathetically that Morgan thought he might die right on the spot. Yet to Morgan's astonishment, Constance recuperated and began his narrative. He told the story of December 15th, 1975, driving in a blinding snowstorm to Riverside, Illinois, where he arranged a meeting with John Mason beneath the Kankakee River Bridge. John was manipulated into a deadly trap by extortion and deceit. Constance recounted in his frail voice how he shot John while he begged for his life. He stopped to remind Morgan that he happened upon him that same morning as Morgan was heading out to work. He gave him the phony story about running his car into a snowbank. Morgan remembered but didn't comment.

Constance had never uttered a word about killing John Mason until that moment. He had informed the Department of Corrections that he would assist law enforcement in recovering his body, but he had never confessed directly that he had killed Mason. It was likewise with Irene Stokes. Nothing he said was motivated by a yearning to cleanse his soul, but instead inspired by his deviant nature, even on his deathbed. That point would become clear as the conversation progressed.

"I drug Mason's corpse through the snow for a hundred yards uphill and stuck him in my car trunk. He was about bled out before I got him there, but I had some plastic cleaning bags laid out to keep blood out of my car anyway," Constance said, as though Morgan might be concerned about the condition of his car. He went on to explain that he was exhausted when he finished. Morgan listened intently, but there was a nagging question impeding his thoughts. Why was Constance unburdening his secrets to him? Of course Morgan was the officer who arrested him, but that was nothing more than handling a routine call. How did he become a component in the issue? It was true that Constance tried to kill him, but Morgan had never interrogated him or had any major part in the investigation. Morgan was just an old guy now, thirty-eight years later, who survived Constance's death list.

"Where is he? Where did you put him?" Morgan asked.

"I put him in the same place you would put a dead body," Constance said quietly.

"What?" Morgan asked crossly. His eyes narrowed. Was this going to be a repeat of their Menard meeting? In just moments he would know that this time everything would be different.

"I took him to a mortuary, just like you would do," Constance said. He then went on to tell the story of a sick, drug-addicted, poor soul by the name of Calvin Washington. Constance was introduced to him by Tyrone Hightower, a fellow student at Willoughby Hills College. Calvin was so drug-dependent that he would do anything for a fix. Washington owned a mortuary and cemetery, and operated it alone. The place was shabby and rundown, but according to Hightower it was a money-making machine. Constance recounted how the three of them were gathered in the dingy basement crematory with the stench from the damp earth seeping through the mortar, and mold was climbing up the walls. As the flickering from the flames danced on the walls shining through the cracks in the ancient furnace, Constance hatched the plan for killing John Mason. He killed Hightower that same night and dumped his body in the street near the Robert Taylor Homes—a detail he related in a mundane exposition with as much emotion as discussing killing a fly.

Constance was terrified of Leroy Barber, the local drug lord, but it was a lucrative opportunity to provide Calvin Washington with drugs, so he did. He never got to know Washington, but he became acquainted with his habit and his needs. On December 15th, 1975, he delivered heroin in a bag and a body in the trunk of his car. Calvin helped him carry the body into the funeral home where they shoved it into the cremation furnace. John Mason's body was consumed by the flames while Calvin shot up on heroin. Calvin didn't bother to ask Constance where the body had come from. He did the same thing with Irene Stokes.

Morgan never took his eyes off Constance. He had expended every ounce of energy his frail pathetic mass could muster. Now he lay with his eyes closed breathing in short, shallow gasps. Constance was standing in the doorway to the hereafter, or hell, or at best an infinite void. Morgan watched anticipating that it would be sooner than later. He had endured Constance describing without even a measure of compunction, how he killed John Mason and Irene Stokes, and then burned their bodies. Now as Morgan stared at him—the man who tried to kill him—he was fighting off the urge to feel sorry for him.

"Why am I involved in this deathbed confession?" Morgan asked.

Constance opened his eyes and turned his head in order to

face Morgan. "You wrote two books. You came to Menard to interview me so you could write about what I did. I wanted to be sure you got it right. I want you to write a book about me," Constance said weakly before heading into another coughing fit.

Rage instantly gushed through Morgan, smacking him violently in his gut, burning its way through to settle and burn on his face. "You son of a bitch," Morgan whispered. Any sympathy he had for Constance vanished in a blink.

"You're offended," Constance rasped, followed by a mocking grin.

"I won't do it," Morgan snapped.

Constance turned his head away and looked at the ceiling. He was silent for a long moment. Finally, he said between those short weak gasps, "Yes, you will. People like you want others to know what you're feeling. Every white guy in the joint who can put two sentences together is writing a book. They're just like you. They want people to see the world through their eyes."

That was it! Constance was the epitome of selfishness even as he was dying. He wasn't concerned about his soul burning in everlasting hellfire even as he lay in death's throes, but he was willing to give up his ghastly lifelong secret to a novice author just to have his name in print. Morgan wasn't going to indulge his stupidity a minute longer. "I'm leaving. If you want to give a statement to the police, there's a couple of cops right outside," he said. He turned and walked out the door.

Constance died thirteen days later.

CHAPTER FORTY-FIVE

The new Willoughby Hills mayor called Ed Woodson into his office. He had decided that Ed would retire. Ed's initial reaction was to release a string of obscenities which might be bouncing around in space even today. He swore that he would fight the mayor until he drew his last breath. In the end, he went quietly. The Department threw him a grand soiree and the mayor presented him with a plaque that would be hung in the hallway of the new police department, honoring his service to the department and to the city. Ed made an elegant farewell speech and thanked his old friend Morgan Cooper, an honorary attendee who was situated way in the back of the hall.

Later, when drinks were served, Morgan and Ed found a dark corner where they reminisced about the good old days as they put away a couple of beers. It was impossible to tell war stories without rehashing being ambushed in the alley behind Lucky's Bar. Ed had been shot twice in the line of duty, but both times it happened so quickly that he didn't have time to be afraid. Fortunately, he was equipped with a bulletproof vest and survived. When he and Morgan were blindsided in the alley with bullets raining down on them, it was different. Time stood still. His heart was in his throat, and fear got deep into his mind. He had always said it was the scariest thing that ever happened in all of his career. Morgan agreed.

They never revisited those days without talking about Roderick Constance. Ed already knew every detail of the confession Constance made to Morgan on his deathbed, but they agreed to keep it between the two of them. There was no way of proving anything he said. Ed thought it would make a good story to tell to strangers at a tiki bar on the beach.

As the janitors were picking up paper cups off the floor and cleaning off the tables, Morgan and Ed were alone. A few last dogs were lingering around the bar, but out of earshot. Ed tipped the last of his beer and slammed the glass on the table. "What about that book you were gonna write, Morgan, old boy?" he asked.

"I've thought about it a lot, but the last thing Constance said to me was that he knew I would write it even though I said I wouldn't. He said people like me want the whole world to know how we feel. He said guys like me want people to see the world through our eyes," Morgan said.

"It's true, butthole," Ed said.

Morgan laughed.

"You could write the whole thing and call it fiction. You don't have to use his name if that's what's bothering you," Ed said.

"I might. I might just do that," Morgan said.

The End

Before You Go...

HELP AN AUTHOR

write a review

THANK YOU!

Share your voice and help guide other readers to these wonderful books. Even if it's only a line or two your reviews help readers discover the author's books so they can continue creating stories that you'll love. Login to your favorite retailer and leave a review. Thank you.

About the Author

Tom Brewster was born and raised in mid America at its best, the State of Missouri, to a third generation of loggers and parents of ten children. He could be considered the middle child if you count by five. He learned life lessons on the boot heels of Pop who spoke little, and Mom, a woman far wiser than her education and background, and big brother Glen with more than a fair amount of humor. He left home when it dawned on him that we were the family that charitable organizations would deliver Christmas boxes to only to be thrown off the porch with a mixture of pride and frustrated anger. Some of his early homes included an abandoned houseboat, a deserted dance hall, and for a few days a tree house so that he wouldn't miss work at the sawmill just up the road. Finally, Uncle Sam firmly invited him to become a soldier. He courted his wife on foot, in worn combat boots before deciding to get a real job when she agreed to marry him. He attended local and community colleges and found a home at the Lincoln, Illinois Police Department. He developed a kinship to the brilliantly quirky State's Attorney and worked as his investigator after leaving the police force. Always preferring to be his own boss, he finally found his niche as a state-licensed private investigator. His biggest accomplishments, however, remain his children, Alison and Ryan, and their children and hopefully generations to come who will enjoy this read, The Hung Jury.